PRAISE FOR THOMAS KING

"At once plainspoken and poetic, King is equally at home with his vivid, often comic characters and with the vibrant natural world in which their dramas are played out."
—*People*

"Thomas King is beyond being a great writer and storyteller, a lauded academic and educator. He is a towering intellectual." —*The Globe and Mail*

"He's a master of the lethal one-liner. . . . King wants to make his readers smile." —*Calgary Herald*

"Thomas King has become Canada's most wide-ranging and best-known writer of novels, stories, children's books, essays, films and TV programs that recreate, with wry and wise compassion, the dilemmas that have bedeviled the current and historical lives, myths and realities of aboriginal people in North America. And therefore of all of us."
—*Winnipeg Free Press*

"Thomas King is funny. And ironic, sarcastic, clever and witty. His writing style is direct, offbeat and accessible."
—*Edmonton Journal*

THE RED
POWER MURDERS

THE RED POWER MURDERS

A DreadfulWater Mystery

THOMAS KING

HARPER PERENNIAL

Published by Harper Perennial, an imprint of HarperCollins Publishers Ltd

First published by HarperCollins Publishers Ltd
in an original trade paperback edition: 2006
First HarperCollins ePub edition: 2015
This Harper Perennial trade paperback edition: 2017

HarperCollins books may be purchased for educational, business, or sales
promotional use through our Special Markets Department.

HarperCollins Publishers Ltd
2 Bloor Street East, 20th Floor
Toronto, Ontario, Canada
M4W 1A8

www.harpercollins.ca

Library and Archives Canada Cataloguing in Publication
information is available upon request.

ISBN 978-1-44345-538-1

Printed and bound in the United States

HB 06.27.2023

For my good buddy Carol Millerfeather,
'cause there ain't no pleasure but meanness

ONE

The motel room had all the ambience of a laundry hamper, but as Mitchell Street lay back on the bed, he realized that he was feeling as good as he had for the past twenty-five years. And if things worked out, he was going to feel even better. He unclipped the holster from his belt. Not that he was going to need it. But the gun reminded him that he could change his mind at any moment, drive into town, and just shoot the sonofabitch. That possibility alone made him smile. Something he hadn't done in a very long time.

Nebraska had been a carton of chuckles, a flat, dry, dusty slab of land stuck between South Dakota and Kansas, whose main attractions were genetically modified corn, mercurial weather, and football.

And Cabela's.

Cabela's was a quarter-section amusement park of guns, clothes, and dead animals stuffed together under one roof and cleverly disguised as an outdoor outfitting store. There was an indoor pond with neurotic trout swimming in nervous circles and an outdoor archery range where you could test the latest in bow-and-arrow technology on paper targets tacked to bales of hay. Once, because he was curious about the store and because he was bored, he had driven the four-hundred-odd miles from Omaha to Sidney, a nothing town in the southwest corner of the state, and he never did it again.

Omaha.

It was bigger than Sidney. But that was about all that could be said for it. Street didn't know what people saw in the West. Big skies and empty spaces. Nothing to do and nowhere to eat.

Living in New York had been difficult, but it had

also been exciting, and when he was sent west to take over the office in Salt Lake City, he was sure he had arrived at the edge of the known world. He had been wrong, of course. In those early halcyon days in the kingdom of Brigham Young, he hadn't known about Omaha.

Omaha.

After the fiasco in Salt Lake, he had had to endure eighteen long years in Omaha before early retirement had saved him. The next few days wouldn't make up for the suffering, but a little payback, late though it might be in coming, was going to be sweet. Someone famous had said that living well was the best revenge.

Bullshit. The best revenge was that moment when your enemies wished they had never been born.

He looked at the clock radio by the bed. Still time for a quick shower. Maybe a drink at the bar. He closed the folder and put it on the desk. Amazing how the past could catch up with you.

The knock on the door startled him. The meet wasn't for another hour. At the truck stop south of town. Not here at the motel. Then again, maybe it was the maid come to turn down the bed and leave a chocolate on his pillow. He had stayed at places where they did that. Before he had been shipped off to the so-called Great Plains to rot. Before his career had blown up in his face.

Tomorrow was going to be different, he told himself as he went to the door. Tomorrow was going to be like the song. The first day of the rest of his life.

TWO

Thumps DreadfulWater was slumped on his favourite stool, waiting for Al to rescue him with a cup of coffee, when Archimedes Kousoulas came through the front door of the café, waving a mailing tube at him.

"Aha!" said Archie, his voice filling the room and rattling the windows. "There you are."

The cold air that slipped in the door behind Archie was sparkling and sharp. Thumps could stop kidding himself. Summer was gone. Fall was gone.

"I've been trying to find you." Archie climbed onto the stool beside him. "Two weeks I've been trying to find you."

"I've been out of town."

Actually, he had been out of the country. Canada, to be exact. Calgary, to be specific. Benton Wolfchild, an old friend from university, had called to tell Thumps that he was getting married. Benton hadn't asked him to come to the ceremony. And Benton hadn't asked him to take pictures of the wedding. But good friendships carried responsibilities, and Benton was a good friend.

"So, you haven't heard the news."

Now that Thumps thought about it, he hadn't heard any news. A week of hanging out with Benton before the wedding and another week of photographing the Rockies between Banff and Jasper after the wedding hadn't left much time for newspapers and television.

"You know," said Archie, "you don't look so good."

"I was up late."

The last day in the mountains it had begun to snow, and the drive back had taken thirteen hours, most of which were spent in a gas station in Sweet Grass, eating microwaved burritos and watching the blizzard close highways and annoy motorists.

"You look worse than that."

Thumps laid his head on the counter. "I haven't had any coffee."

"American coffee," said Archie, with a grimace. He was a short, compact man with silver hair and a dark well-trimmed moustache that covered his upper lip. "Did you know the Greeks invented coffee?"

Alvera Couteau strolled out of the backroom with a pot of black coffee as though she had all the time in the world. "You look chipper."

"Coffee. Black."

Al put the pot on the counter and waited.

"Please."

Thumps closed his eyes and listened to the coffee flow out of the pot into his cup. Little waves of heat washed over his face. This is nice, he thought to himself.

"You want a straw?" asked Al.

There were other places to get breakfast in Chinook. Faster places. Cleaner places. Places where you didn't have to put up with marginal manners and latent sarcasm. But there was no place that served better hash browns. Or better coffee. Thumps dragged the cup closer to his face.

"Just breakfast."

"The usual?"

"Alvera," said Archie, who could see he had lost Thumps, "did you hear the news?"

"This about that writer guy?"

"See," said Archie, poking Thumps on his shoulder. "Alvera knows about the news."

Thumps held up one finger. "Extra salsa, please."

Al set a cup in front of Archie and waggled the pot.

"Sure," said Archie.

"His cat die?" asked Al.

"No," said Archie. "He thinks he's tired, but I think he's depressed."

"If he got a job," said Al, "he wouldn't be depressed."

"I have a job," said Thumps, trying to ignore both of them.

Al wiped her hands on her apron. "Maybe that Ridge guy coming to town will cheer him up."

"Depression's a funny thing," said Archie. "Anything's possible."

Thumps pulled his head off the counter and opened his eyes. "Ridge?"

"Aha," said Archie. "Now you're not so depressed."

"Not . . . Noah Ridge?"

"Good news will always cure a depression."

"Noah Ridge isn't a writer."

Al reached under the counter and came up with a copy of the *Chinook Tribune*. "He is now." She strolled up to the front of the café and tossed a handful of potatoes on the grill.

"He's on tour," said Archie.

The picture was of Ridge, all right. Thumps knew that face as well as his own. A lot older, but the same crooked grin. The same cold, sparkling eyes.

"Not every day we get a big-time revolutionary like this in Chinook."

Thumps went looking for his coffee cup. "Ridge isn't a revolutionary."

"*Time* magazine once called him the Che Guevara of North America." Archie pulled a poster out of the tube, unrolled it, and pinned the edges with the salt and pepper shakers. "So, what do you think?"

"Don't you have a bookstore to run?" Thumps rubbed his face and discovered he hadn't shaved. Had he brushed his teeth?

"A little culture never hurt anyone," said Archie.

"Ridge isn't culture."

"And we want to hire you."

Al poured a puddle of eggs on the grill and flipped the potatoes. Thumps watched as a warm cloud of steam rose up to the ceiling.

"We?"

"The library committee," said Archie. "I'm the president."

"The library committee wants to hire me?"

"Just don't charge us too much."

"For what?"

"To take pictures, of course." Archie took a sip of his coffee and made a face. "This is going to be an historic moment."

"You already have the photograph for the poster."

"Sure," said Archie. "But we want to document Mr. Ridge's visit to Chinook. You know, portraits, action stuff, candids. Maybe something with the new library in the background."

Al brought the plate over and set it down in front of Thumps. Scrambled eggs, sausage, hash browns, whole-wheat toast, extra salsa. "You think you can manage a regular fork?"

"He's not as bad as he looks," said Archie.

"'Cause I got a nice lightweight plastic fork I can let you borrow."

"Say," said Archie, "you get your cheque yet?"

Al made a face and twisted her head to one side. "I called. She said it was in the mail. You believe that?"

"Al's waiting for a cheque from her cousin in San Francisco."

"Family," said Al, "you can't say no."

"That's the way Greeks are too." Archie squirted a pool of ketchup on Thumps's plate and cut off a piece of sausage.

"Those are mine."

"Native people are supposed to share."

"It's a cliché."

"I plan to share the treasure with you when I find it."

The treasure, Thumps did not have to be reminded, was the mythical cache of gold that had supposedly been brought north by soldiers from Cortes's army and left somewhere in the mountains around Chinook. Whenever Archie wasn't minding his bookstore, he was nosing around in canyons and caves and large crevices, all those handy places where sixteenth-century Spanish soldiers might stash bullion. And Archie was determined to find it. Thumps had to admire the research the man had done on the subject, though Thumps was sure you would have more luck finding a flying saucer stashed in the mountains around Chinook than you would Aztec gold.

"Don't forget Elvis and the Beatles." Archie rubbed the sausage in the ketchup.

"Beatles?" Somehow, Thumps realized, the conversation had got away from him.

"Famous photographs," said Archie. "The photographers who took them are probably rich."

Thumps could feel his eyes drooping. The only people he knew of who would want a good photograph of Noah Ridge were in law enforcement. And there was no money to be made there.

"When's he coming to town?"

"He's here," said Archie. "Arrived last night."

"Okay." Thumps sighed. "Tell me where and when."

"The reading's tomorrow night." Archie licked his fingers and slid off the stool. "Wear something nice."

Thumps sat on the stool and looked at his empty plate. What the hell was someone like Noah Ridge doing in Chinook?

"Almost forgot." Archie stood in the doorway and let the cold air rush in around him. "The sheriff wants to see you."

"About what?"

"Noah Ridge, of course." Archie rolled the poster up into a tight tube and tapped it against his hand. "Seems as though someone wants to kill him."

THREE

When Thumps had left the house that morning, the air had been brisk. He had debated driving to Al's, but after sitting hunched behind a steering wheel for most of the night, he needed a good walk to perk him up. Besides, his Volvo had little appreciation for cold weather. Anything close to freezing and the car would begin to sputter and stagger. It wasn't a problem with engineering. The Swedes knew how to build a car that could handle frigid weather. Thumps was certain it was temperament. His particular Volvo simply preferred to be warm. And if it wasn't warm, it preferred not to start.

Walking to Al's had been pleasant enough, but sometime during breakfast, a wind had snuck up, knifing in out of the north. Thumps zipped his windbreaker over his chin, jammed his hands in his pockets, and headed for the sheriff's office. When he had left the house, there had been only three things on his list for the day.

Go to Al's.

Go to the Salvation Army thrift shop.

Go to bed.

He had no interest in seeing the sheriff, but Hockney's office was the closest warm place on his new and improved list, and right now that was reason enough.

So, Noah Ridge was in town. Maybe things did travel in circles. How many years had it been? Fifteen? Twenty? Thumps did the math. Closer to twenty-five. It seemed impossible. He had been a student in those days. In Salt Lake City. At the University of Utah, a sprawling urban campus huddled in the shadows of the Wasatch Mountains. Mormon country. Home to one of the few home-grown North American religions. Joseph Smith. Brigham Young. Polygamy. A remarkably businesslike religion. A natural extension of covenant theology. Humans and God agreeing that success in business was an economic indicator of spiritual grace. And salvation.

At first, Thumps had had a hard time separating the people from the religion, for Mormon theology had a decidedly racist angle to it. Blacks were the sons of Ham and cursed. Indians and Mexicans and South Pacific Islanders were Lamanites, who would, in the fullness of time, turn "white and delightsome." Thumps had liked that phrase. White and delightsome. As if it were a reward. As if it were something to look forward to.

Some of that changed when the head of the church, Spencer W. Kimball, had a revelation concerning Blacks. God, it seemed, had changed his mind, and now the Mormon faithful could welcome the sons of Ham into the fold. The progressive element of the church rejoiced at this good news, in much the same way that stockbrokers welcome a bull market. The conservative element threatened to secede, though in the end, the threat was more noise than substance. And, predictably, with the burden of segregation lifted, the church expanded its proselytizing activities into Africa.

The cynic in Thumps knew that the religion wasn't the individual. Some of his best friends had been Mormons. But he also knew that a few enlightened parishioners weren't the measure of the religion.

Salt Lake City was an unlikely place for Noah Ridge to land. But one day, there he was. Already a national figure, every bit as charismatic as Dennis Banks or Russell Means. The head of the Red Power Movement, or RPM as the press had decided to call the organization, partly because of the enormous energy of Ridge himself and partly because the name played well in print. Thumps had never quite figured out if RPM was a companion to the better known American Indian Movement or a splinter group. So far as he had been able to tell, it was both.

SHERIFF DUKE HOCKNEY was sitting behind his desk, working his way through a stack of paper. Police work, Thumps remembered from his days as a cop on the north coast of California, was ten percent catching crooks and ninety percent filling out forms.

"Close the door."

Thumps pulled his hands out of his pockets and rubbed them together. He should have grabbed his gloves when he left the house. He should have bought a heavier jacket. He should have stayed in bed.

"Archie said you wanted to see me."

"You want coffee?"

"I want it to be spring."

"I want to be rich," said Hockney, without cracking a smile. The sheriff did not have a particularly well-developed sense of humour. The only time Duke ever made a try at a joke was when he was grumpy or annoyed. "What are you doing for the next couple of days?"

"Trying to stay warm."

Hockney pushed his cup to the edge of the desk. "Pour me some while you're at it."

Hockney did not believe in drip coffee. The old metal percolator sat on a small table against the far wall. Thumps tested the weight. If he hadn't known better, he would have thought Duke was melting lead for bullets.

"You know," said Thumps, "there are people in the world who make a fresh pot of coffee every day."

"Don't forget the cream."

Not that Hockney had any cream. Just a big brown jar of white powder. Thumps dropped a teaspoonful into the cup. It lay on the surface for a moment, bubbling, like a snowball on a lava flow, before sinking to the bottom without a trace.

Thumps and Hockney had never really become friends. And maybe that's the way it was with cops and ex-cops. Shortly after Thumps arrived in Chinook, the sheriff had come by to say hello and to talk about cops they both knew. And that had been that. No barbecues. No card games. No beers at the local bar.

Someone who didn't know any better might have thought that the sheriff was standoffish, but Thumps knew that wasn't the reason. Most of the good cops he had known in his life were loners, men who kept to themselves and their families. Maybe it was the job. Maybe it was temperament. Maybe it was the depression that came from knowing what one human being could do to another.

What Thumps did know was that Hockney was a good cop. A good cop who didn't know the difference between hot coffee and hot tar.

"I wouldn't drink that if I were you."

"You're not me," said Hockney. "What about it?"

"What about what?"

"The next few days." Hockney wrapped his hands around the cup.

Thumps wondered if hot tar held heat longer than hot water. "I'm busy."

"Doing what?"

"Taking pictures."

"Of Noah Ridge?"

Thumps felt as though he was about to step into a hole. "Archie hired me to capture the moment."

"Perfect," said Hockney. "You get paid twice for doing one job."

Thumps sighed. He could see where this was going. And he didn't like it.

"I need a deputy."

Hockney had two full-time deputies, Lance Packard and Andy Hooper. Lance was young and green, a good-natured kid who gave out speeding tickets with a reluctance that made people feel sorry for him.

"What about Lance?"

"He's at a conference in Denver."

Andy Hooper was a harder piece of work, a man who understood law enforcement as a personal punishment visited on the wicked and the undeserving. Andy had an Old Testament mentality that allowed him to divide the world into good and evil, black and white, rich and poor. Lance liked to believe the best about people. Andy went looking for the worst.

"Andy?"

"He's busy."

So, Andy was back in Hockney's doghouse. "So am I."

Hockney snorted and swirled the coffee around in the cup.

Thumps tried the offensive. "Weren't you going to fire Andy?"

"I changed my mind."

"What about one of the guys over in Missoula?"

Hockney leaned back in the chair. "You were in Salt Lake same time as Ridge, weren't you?"

"You asking me to play bodyguard?"

"Nope," said Hockney. "He's got himself his very own FBI agent. Nice young man. Stopped by this morning and introduced himself. All official-like."

Ridge had drawn that kind of attention in Salt Lake too. FBI. State police. City police. Even the security services of the Mormon Church. The joke that went around was that there were more people watching Ridge than there were members in RPM.

"Evidently, he's written a book." Hockney wrinkled his nose. "One of those tell-all exposés."

"You read it?"

"Parts," said the sheriff. "Has an interesting chapter on that woman. The one who disappeared."

Lucy Kettle. Thumps had met her at the University of Utah. She was there on a scholarship, working at the American West Center. Cheyenne, if he remembered right. Lucy was smart, good-looking, serious, and opinionated. Not a combination that sat easy with everyone.

Men, for instance.

Noah Ridge, on the other hand, was a beer commercial. All action and motion. Feathers and leathers. Headbands and dark glasses. Thumps was never sure how much of the warrior-macho was for the cause and how much was for the cameras. Thumps suspected Ridge didn't know either.

Lucy had a hard analytic side that liked to under-stand the problem before she went to war. Ridge didn't need a reason. The two of them had little in common, but by the time the Red Power Movement opened its storefront on Main Street, Lucy had quit her job at the American West Center and moved in as the organization's communications director.

Then one fall evening, she headed home and was never seen again.

"How about it?" said Hockney. "What do you think happened?"

No one worried when Lucy didn't show up the next day. But after a week, when she didn't return to work or to her house, the police rolled into RPM headquar-ters and arrested Noah with little more than a fervent hope that they could hang a murder charge on him. And to further their cause, they slipped rumours dis-guised as fact to an eager press that fought over every tidbit like magpies on road kill. One story cast Lucy and Noah as lovers in a romance gone bad. Another saw them as opponents in an RPM power struggle. There was even talk that Ridge had discovered that Lucy was a mole working for the FBI.

They were all nice theories, but when the dust cleared, Ridge was still standing and the police were left holding air.

"There was a postcard waiting for Mr. Ridge at the hotel," said Hockney.

Thumps waited to see if the sheriff was going to tell him about the postcard or if he was going to make him ask.

"'Happy trails, kemo-sabe.'" Hockney leaned back in the chair. "'Today is a good day to die.'"

Thumps felt his body tense.

"The Gene Autry/Lone Ranger bit is cute, don't you think?"

"Roy Rogers/Lone Ranger."

"Whatever." Duke leaned forward. "But the best part was the card itself."

"Salt Lake City?"

"Damn, DreadfulWater," said Hockney, unable to keep the smile off his face, "you still have all the moves. So, exactly what happened down south?"

"Don't remember."

"Sure you do," said the sheriff, who was enjoying this more than Thumps would have expected.

"Police and the FBI turned that case inside out and upside down. Came up empty."

"That's the way I hear it too." Hockney wrote something on a piece of paper and slid it across the desk.

Thumps looked at the figure. "For one day?"

The sheriff snorted. "Two days. Maybe three."

"Playing deputy pays pretty well."

"Better than playing photographer," said Hockney.

"You think this is serious?"

"Don't know. And don't much care." Hockney looked at the bottom of his coffee cup. "But if someone is going to kill Mr. Ridge, they're sure as hell not going to do it in my town."

THE WIND WAS stronger now. And colder. As Thumps walked to the Sally Ann, he realized he hadn't said no to Hockney. He pulled his neck down into his jacket. Maybe it was time to take that trip he had been promising himself. A trip to someplace exotic. Someplace photographic. Someplace south. Where he could go for a working vacation and take it off his income tax. Like the big photographers. Adams, Sexton, Mann,

Sturges, Leibovitz, Salgado, Mark, Bond. Not that he brought in enough income to write it off. Or even to show up on the tax radar.

Someplace quiet. Someplace where he wouldn't see Anna and Callie every time he closed his eyes. Maybe a trip to such a place would help put those ghosts to rest. If nothing else, a trip would buy him space and time.

Hockney didn't need a photographer, and he didn't need another deputy. What he needed was a babysitter. Someone who would make sure that Ridge didn't become an embarrassment. Hockney had correctly deduced that Thumps knew the man from his days in Salt Lake. What the sheriff couldn't know was how well the two men knew each other. Or how they might feel about finding themselves together in the same room.

FOUR

red and Della Blueford took turns running the
Salvation Army thrift store. As Thumps opened
the door, he hoped that it was Fred's day.

"Well, hello, stranger."

Thumps liked Della well enough, and he probably
would have liked her even more if she hadn't been so
enthusiastic and optimistic all the time. Not that she
had all that much to be optimistic about. She had lost
a breast to cancer three years ago, Fred had suffered
through a series of minor heart attacks, and the twin
girls they had adopted had both been diagnosed with

fetal alcohol spectrum disorder. Thumps knew people who had collapsed from much less weight. But Della always seemed to have a smile and a good word, as though it were her job to cheer up the world.

"Snow's going to be here any time," she said. "Bet you can't wait."

"I need a coat," said Thumps, trying to sound upbeat. "Something warm."

"Oh, yeah," said Della. "That windbreaker's not going to do the job. That's for sure."

"Maybe something with a hood."

Della shook her head. "I had just the thing."

"But . . . ?"

"Sold it last week. You in a hurry? People don't tend to be as giving when the weather turns."

Thumps looked out the window. A storm was forming in the mountains. He could see it edging over the peaks. "Like to get one soon."

"Don't have anything just now, but who knows what'll come in tomorrow."

Thumps stood by the door, gathering up the last bit of warmth before he headed home. "Everybody okay?"

"Couldn't be better," said Della with a big smile. "Couldn't be better."

THE NORTHERN CALIFORNIA coast had been damp and foggy, but the temperature rarely dropped below fifty degrees. As long as you could manage long stretches without ever seeing the sun—and Thumps could—you were fine. Chinook didn't have a temperature it didn't like. Summers could send the mercury well above one hundred, while winter could find it huddled at thirty below.

Freeway was asleep on the kitchen table when Thumps opened the front door and filled the house with cold air.

"Get off the table."

The cat fluffed her fur, pulled her feet under her body, and glared at him. The two weeks Thumps had been gone had not sat well with Freeway.

"Don't give me that. Rose came by every day."

Rose Twinings was his neighbour four doors down. She had two dogs and was not particularly fond of cats, but whenever Thumps had to be away, Rose would come by and feed and water Freeway and change her litter. She would even sit with the cat and tell her stories. Most of them were about the great deeds that dogs had done, and Thumps was not sure whether Freeway appreciated this.

"Did she tell you about the dog of Flanders?"

This was Rose's favourite story. Every time Thumps went to Rose's to ask her to babysit Freeway, he would have to listen to this story. He had no idea how many times the cat had had to suffer through it.

"Hungry?"

Freeway did not answer rhetorical questions. As a matter of fact, she didn't do much of anything. Thumps admired that quality in the cat. Not a bad life if you looked at it from the correct perspective.

Thumps got the canned cat food from the refrigerator and breathed through his mouth as he peeled back the plastic lid. Freeway slid off the table like warm syrup on hotcakes.

"Don't gobble."

Again, a waste of breath. Freeway always gobbled. And then she would stroll over to the rug and throw up. Not all the time. Not enough to be predictable. Just enough to be annoying.

Thumps put the kettle on and sat down at the table. Maybe he should take the sheriff's offer. The money would help pay for that fantasy photography trip. What could happen to Noah in a couple of days? Especially with the kind of protection he was amassing. An FBI agent. Sheriff Duke Hockney. And Thumps DreadfulWater, armed to the teeth with a Canham 4x5 field camera, a Pentax spot meter, and a Ries tripod.

The kettle began to whistle. Thumps fished a tea bag out of the drawer and dropped it into the hot water. Then he went looking for the phone. Noah wouldn't have come to Chinook for free. Half the man might be activist, but the other half was entrepreneur.

Thumps dialed Claire's direct number, hoping he could slip by Roxanne Heavy Runner, the band's office secretary. Roxanne was nice if you liked abrupt and martial. Today it was just too cold to manage Roxanne's manner or her advice. Sometimes Thumps was lucky.

"Band office."

Sometimes he wasn't.

"Hi, Roxanne. It's me, Thumps."

The noise on the phone sounded vaguely like planes with propellers strafing ammunition dumps.

"You got that picture done yet?"

Thumps had promised Roxanne a print of the Snake River with the Tetons in the background. He hadn't said when, and Roxanne was not much for delayed gratification.

"It's almost done."

"You said that two months ago."

"Is Claire in?"

"Business or romance?"

"Business."

"'Cause she hasn't got time for romance."

Thumps was sure Roxanne didn't intend it, but whenever he heard her voice, his first reaction was to duck. "I need to ask her something."

The grinding sound on the phone was either a bad connection or a tank driving over bones.

"She's up at Buffalo Mountain."

There was no pretense to Roxanne, and she wasn't much of a joker. What you saw was what was there. Thumps leaned against the side of the refrigerator and sighed. Loudly enough so Roxanne could hear.

"You want me to tell her you called?"

"Sure."

Thumps put the phone on the table and ran through the possibilities. Noah could have come to Chinook as part of a book tour. From time to time, writers did show up in town for a reading, poets for the most part, along with a trickle of self-help, diet, gardening, and regional-history sorts. There had been a Native guy come through with a novel that had the word *water* in the title. Thumps had gone to the reading and had barely been able to stay awake.

But Thumps couldn't imagine that any publishing company would deliberately send someone like Noah Ridge to a place like Chinook. And he couldn't imagine Ridge coming. Not on his own. When Ridge was in Salt Lake and at the top of his game, he had done speaking engagements all over North America and Europe. His standard fee then was five thousand dollars, seven thousand if he could get it.

Then again, maybe Thumps was just being hard on the man. Noah, like Dennis Banks and Russell Means, had brought national attention to the problems Native people faced. He had taken on government indifference and corporate colonialism. He had helped organize young people on reservations and in cities. For all that, he had also been an unrepentant egotist. At least when Thumps knew him. Maybe he had changed. Maybe he had mellowed.

Maybe he had found God.

Thumps knew all about "maybes." It was the first thing cops learned. It was the last thing cops forgot.

Thumps picked up the phone, dialed the sheriff's number, and got the answering machine. Thumps had a list of things he disliked. It included answering machines, cellphones, and those little computers you carried around in your shirt pocket.

The sheriff, on the other hand, was fond of those kinds of gadgets. Thumps tried Duke's cellphone number.

"Make it good."

"It's me, Thumps."

"I know who it is."

"I was thinking . . ."

"Good," said the sheriff, cutting Thumps off. "Meet me at the Holiday—"

Thumps was in the middle of thinking of a good way to tell the sheriff that he'd help out with Noah, without making it seem as though he wanted to, when he realized that the line was dead.

FIVE

The Holiday Inn sat just off the interstate. Thumps could remember when all roads in the West ran through towns rather than by them. And while he understood the efficiency of highways, he also felt that you lost a great deal of the romance of travel if all you did was barrel along at speeds that numbed the mind and blurred the landscape. Slowing through towns forced you to see something of where you were going. On the highway, the only sights of any interest were the large green signs that called out the mileage.

Thumps took the back way. He had just made the turn onto the frontage road when he realized that the sheriff had not told him where they were to meet. Thumps's guess was the coffee shop. He wondered about the rest of the world, wondered whether people in Greece or India or New Zealand met in coffee shops when they wanted to talk with friends or business associates or lovers, wondered if coffee shops were just a North American phenomenon.

Beth Mooney's Chrysler station wagon was backed up to the front door. Not a good sign. While Beth had a family practice, she also doubled as the county coroner. So far as Thumps knew, Beth and the sheriff didn't meet socially, and when you saw the two of them together, it usually meant a body.

Thumps wasn't sure if he was intrigued or annoyed at Hockney's invitation to a crime scene, but as he eased his Volvo into the parking lot, he could feel the old tensions from his days on the Northern California coast. From his days of playing cop. It was an unpleasant feeling, akin to having the wind knocked out of him. But it was also invigorating, like coming down a steep hill on skis.

Thumps didn't hear the knocking right away. For one thing, it was faint, more a distant tapping. For another, he was too busy looking for a parking space.

"You can't park here." The man standing by Thumps's window was probably in his late thirties, with thin hair and a long face that made him look as if he were in pain.

Thumps watched the man as he tapped his knuckles against the window of the car.

"You can't park here."

Thumps rolled his window down just enough to hear what the man was trying to say, but not enough to let the warm air escape en masse.

"What?"

"You can't park here." The man hooked his fingers over the top of the window the way salesmen in movies wedged their feet into doorways.

"I'm supposed to meet the sheriff."

The man let go of the window, stepped back, and looked at Thumps's car. "You undercover?"

"I'm a photographer."

"Okay," said the man.

"What happened?"

"Just don't park in the handicapped zone."

Thumps found a spot, jogged into the lobby as quickly as he could, and headed straight for the fireplace, where a happy gas flame was calling to him from a stack of bright ceramic logs. Neither the sheriff nor Beth was in the lobby. Thumps had assumed that the action would be someplace else. He just hoped that getting there did not involve going back outside.

The heat from the fireplace was disappointing, but Thumps persevered, moving his backside as close to the glass doors as he could. From here he could see the front of the motel and much of the parking lot outside. And from what he could see, Hockney's SUV was nowhere in sight. Maybe the sheriff hadn't arrived yet, which meant Thumps could go on standing in front of the fireplace until hell froze over. Which, as he recalled his brisk walk from the car to the motel, it was preparing to do.

"Are you Mr. Dreadful . . . ?" The young woman was smiling and waiting for Thumps to fill in the missing piece.

"Water. DreadfulWater."

"What a great name." The woman had a bronze-coloured tag that read "Jill." Thumps tried to think of all the jobs that required you to wear name tags. Most of them were in service industries where making your name available was supposed to be a gesture of friendship and goodwill. "The sheriff called and said he'd be a little late. He said to send you down when you got here."

Now that he thought about it, Thumps remembered that police officers wore name tags too.

"Down?"

"Room 110," said Jill. "He said to say he'd join you shortly."

"I'll wait for him here."

Jill didn't look happy with this response. "Room 110 is at the end of the corridor. On your left," she said, recovering her good cheer. "You're supposed to have a camera."

Thumps settled back against the fireplace and closed his eyes. He could hear Jill standing in front of him, waiting, but he could also feel the heat spreading up his back and down his thighs. Being warm was like being rich, Thumps decided, easy to get used to, hard to give up. Never enough of either.

* * *

39

By the time Hockney limped into the lobby, the rivets and the zipper on Thumps's jeans were beginning to melt.

"This as far as you got?" Hockney tried to smile with little success.

"I was cold."

"Where's your camera?"

"In the car."

Hockney looked down the hallway and then back at Thumps. "When I say, 'Where's your camera?' you're supposed to rush out and get it."

"How about you buy me a cup of coffee?"

"You had coffee at the office."

Just the thought of the ingots smelting in Hockney's coffee pot made Thumps's stomach clench. "No, I didn't."

Hockney looked down the hallway once more. "Ah, what the hell," he said. "Andy can use the practice."

The coffee shop at the Holiday Inn looked nothing like Al's. It wasn't hazy or dark or damp. It was bright. Brass fixtures and plastic ferns, green walls, and marbled linoleum. Everything polished and sterile. It reminded Thumps of an upscale furniture store that had leased space in a hospital.

"So," said the sheriff, snuggling into a booth with maroon tuck-and-roll upholstery, "what about it?"

"What about what?"

"Noah Ridge."

It was warm in the coffee shop, and Thumps found himself in no great hurry to do anything. Talking with the sheriff wasn't the worst way to spend the rest of the day.

"Saw Beth's station wagon outside."

"I saw it too," said Hockney.

"Trouble?"

"One of the guests died."

"You're letting Andy handle a case with a body?"

"He's a cop."

"No, he's not," said Thumps. "He's just renting the uniform."

Hockney grunted and picked at a spot on the place-mat. "No profit in going there."

"Aren't you curious?"

"Nice thing about dead people," said Hockney, dropping his hat on the seat beside him. "They don't wander off."

From the back of the coffee shop, Thumps saw a

young man hurrying to the table with menus. He was probably nineteen, maybe twenty, and he had a name tag just like Jill. His read, improbably, "Jack."

"Good morning, gentlemen," said the young man. "I'm Jack, and I'll be your server today." Jack held out the menus, but neither the sheriff nor Thumps made any effort to take one. Jack didn't miss a beat.

"So, do we know what we want?"

Thumps found himself trying to think of ways to get Jack and Jill together.

"You got cheeseburgers here?" said the sheriff.

"Yes, we do," said Jack, who either had good genes or a great orthodontist.

"And fries?" said Hockney. "They give you a lot of fries at this place?"

"Cheeseburger and fries," said Jack, turning to Thumps. "And for you?"

Thumps glanced at the menu and settled for a small chef's salad. Just to be polite. He hadn't eaten at the Holiday Inn coffee shop before, but he supposed that it was like most chains, where everything came vacuum-wrapped in Cellophane or packed in plastic tubs.

"Natural?"

"Nope," said the sheriff.

Thumps couldn't imagine that Hockney, even in a moment of mad generosity, would let Andy anywhere near a murder.

"Suicide?"

"That's what Andy thinks."

Normally, Thumps would have been happy not to know any of the details of a run-of-the-mill suicide. They were usually badly managed things, with sad notes about not being able to go on. In Northern California, he had had to look after one where a woman took all the pictures of herself and her husband out of an album and arranged them on the floor around the bathtub before she climbed into the warm water with a glass of wine and cut her wrists.

"Your suicide have a name?" Thumps lined up the salt and pepper shakers so they formed a perfect triangle with the ceramic sugar bowl.

"Why?" said the sheriff. "You missing a friend?"

Hockney's cheeseburger came on a platter that had been decorated with lettuce leaves, tomato slices, onions, and a mound of curly french fries. Thumps's salad came in a giant bowl with a slick of ham and cheese chunks floating on an ocean of iceberg lettuce.

Hockney squeezed thin lines of ketchup on his fries. "How's your salad?"

Thumps's salad had a weary taste to it, as though it had been sitting alone in the dark too long. "Great."

"Should've had the cheeseburger."

"Can I have a fry?"

"Help yourself. You know, in Canada, they put cheese on their fries. And gravy. Call it poo-teen, or something like that." Hockney paused and looked up. "So, what about the job?"

Thumps pushed a limp tomato around with his fork. "Okay. I'm in."

"You doing it for the glory?"

"For the money."

"Welcome to the team," said Hockney, reaching into his pocket and pulling out his cellphone. The sheriff looked at the display and then put the phone back in his pocket.

"Important?"

"It'll keep," said the sheriff.

"I guess it's just a coincidence."

"What's that?"

"That Noah Ridge checks in to the Holiday Inn and someone checks out."

"Ridge isn't staying here." Hockney finished off the fries. "Big star like him goes first class."

"Buffalo Mountain Resort?"

"You'd expect that, wouldn't you?" said Hockney. "Indian-run and all."

"Shadow Ranch?"

"Tourist trap." Hockney dumped his napkin on the table. "Come on, let's go get that camera of yours."

THERE WAS A LOG-JAM of sorts in front of room 110. Deputy Andy Hooper was standing in the doorway talking to Beth Mooney.

"Hey, sheriff."

"What do we have?"

Behind Andy, through the open door, Thumps could see a man's body lying on the floor.

"Stupid bastard shot himself," said Andy.

"Maybe," said Beth.

The man was dressed in a pair of nondescript slacks and a white shirt. Thumps couldn't tell the dead man's age, but one thing was for sure: he wasn't going to get any older.

"So, was it a suicide or not?" The sheriff wasn't one to have fun with a conversation. In Hockney's world, questions were asked in order to get answers.

"Guy checks into the room on the weekend. Alone." Andy flipped a page in his notebook. "Maid finds him dead this morning. Gun on the floor beside him. One shot fired. One shot in his head. Powder burns on the side of his face."

"Suicide note?"

"Nope."

Hockney turned to Beth. "But you don't agree?"

"Maybe he's right," said Beth, looking as disagreeing as she could, "and maybe he's not."

"You know," said the sheriff, "I expect those kinds of answers from old Thumps here. I don't expect them from you."

"Suicide," said Andy. "Pure and simple."

The sheriff took a deep breath and let it out all at once. "Okay," he said to Beth. "What don't you like?"

"Doesn't look right."

"Oh," said Andy with a smirk. "Women's intuition."

Beth flashed her great smile. Anyone who didn't know her might have supposed that she had enjoyed Andy's little witticism. But Thumps knew Beth was just imagining how Andy would look stretched out on one of her tables, and how much fun it would be to cut him open.

"Jesus," said Hockney, pushing his way past Andy. "Let me see."

Beth stepped into the hallway and watched the sheriff prowl the room, Andy at his heels.

"My," said Beth, "aren't we grumpy today."

"It's the coffee he drinks," said Thumps.

"I can always take my own pictures," said Beth. "Maybe you boys should go somewhere quiet and hurt each other."

"We already did that," said Thumps.

"You didn't drink any of his coffee."

"One suicide at a time." Thumps leaned into the room. "So, what's wrong with this picture?"

Beth folded her arms across her chest so you could see the muscles in her forearms. Thumps was glad he was wearing a long-sleeved shirt. And a jacket. One of these days he was going to start working out again. Maybe in the summer.

"Why don't you tell me?" said Beth. "Ten points if you get everything right."

Crime scenes were like puzzles. There were clues everywhere. All you had to do was find them. Andy couldn't find his ass with a fly swatter, so if he thought it was a suicide and Beth didn't, Thumps's money was on Beth.

Not even the sheriff would bet on Andy.

The room was ordinary enough. Late twentieth-century maudlin with a framed print of a river flowing through a summer landscape, a queen-sized bed, a desk with a mirror so you could watch yourself work or watch yourself make phone calls, as well as two chairs, a television set, and a nightstand.

The dead guy was on the floor by the desk, but from the position of the body and the overturned chair, he had probably been sitting at the desk when he shot himself. Interesting, thought Thumps. If that's what had happened, it meant that the dead guy could have watched himself kill himself. Postmodern is what his old English professor, Edward Lueders, would have called it, which was, so far as Thumps had been able to figure, the academy's euphemism for "weird." Still, suicide wasn't a particularly sane act. Most times it was an act of despair, and Thumps had seen stranger examples than this of the ways in which people had decided to end their lives.

There were blood spatters on the desk and the wall and the mirror. Shooting yourself in the head was always a messy business. Women were generally more considerate and contained the mess to a bathtub or a bed. More times than not, they tried to get comfortable before they finished the job. Men went for drama and excess, driving their cars off cliffs at high speeds, going on a rampage with a rifle and letting the police do the job for them. Or blowing their brains out in a motel room, alone.

Thumps was standing at the desk when Hockney moved in on his elbow. "How about you take the pictures," said the sheriff, "and I'll do the looking."

"Suits me."

"But if you do find something, you'll be sure to tell me. Right?"

"I'm just a tourist."

"Suicide," said Andy, "pure and simple."

"Make sure you get some good shots of the desk," said the sheriff.

THUMPS TOOK HIS TIME with the photographs. There was a pattern with crime scene photographs. And an art. It wasn't just a matter of blasting away, making sure you got coverage. What was important was to take your shots in a manner that allowed you to see the particulars in terms of the crime scene as a whole.

For example, bodies weren't simply items in empty space. They were surrounded by an environment in which something had happened. It was natural to concentrate on the corpse, but many times the furniture could tell you as much about what had happened as a body could.

That was certainly true in this case, and as Thumps moved around the room, he began to see what Beth had seen and what Hockney wouldn't miss, no matter how much of his own coffee he drank.

"You run out of film yet?"

"Got it all."

"So, what do you figure?" said the sheriff.

Thumps glanced at Andy, who was standing near the door talking. "You want to put training wheels on this one?"

"You know, he's not a complete idiot."

"Whatever you say."

"Andy!" barked Hockney. "Go out to my car and get my cellphone."

"You can use mine," said Andy.

Hockney tossed the keys to his deputy. "And don't forget to lock it."

Beth was bent over the body, finishing up her work. Hockney squatted down beside her.

"Make any sense to you?"

"Not yet," said Beth. "But that's what makes this a fun job, right?"

"Angle's wrong," said Hockney.

"Oh, I don't know," said Beth. "He could have managed it."

"If he was right-handed." The sheriff lifted the man's left hand. "But he wasn't." Hockney pushed himself off the floor, his knees cracking as if they were heavy timbers in an old barn. "What about the desk?"

"I like the desk," said Beth. "Nice blood-spatter pattern."

"You show this to Andy?" The sheriff put his hands on his hips and leaned to one side.

"He was busy," said Beth.

Hockney gestured to the desk. "What do you suppose it was?"

"Who knows," said Beth. "Maybe a magazine. Maybe a newspaper. Maybe a briefcase."

"But that's not the important thing," said Hockney. "Is it?"

Nope, thought Thumps. What was important was that there had been something on the desk before the man shot himself. The blood showed the faint outline of a corner of something rectangular. And it didn't much matter what that something had been; what was important was that some time after the shooting, someone had taken it away.

"Any chance Andy picked it up as evidence?" Hockney said hopefully.

Beth shook her head. "Don't think so. We got here about the same time. Maid found the body and called it in. Andy asked her if she had touched anything."

"And?"

"She said she opened the door, saw the body, went to the front desk, and called your office."

"Okay," said the sheriff, "let's start at the beginning. Who is he?"

"Now that's the other interesting thing," said Beth. "We got a coin purse, a handkerchief, car keys, money in money clip, but no wallet."

So what we have, thought Thumps, is a left-handed man with no identification who shoots himself in the head with his right hand and then removes something from the desk after he dies.

"Guy must have checked in," said Hockney.

"He did," said Beth. "John Smith."

"You're kidding."

"Paid cash." Beth shrugged. "Told the front desk that he had lost his wallet."

"And?"

"Left a two-hundred-dollar deposit."

Hockney rolled his shoulders up to his ears. "You got any good news?"

"I got fingerprints," said Beth.

"Lovely." Hockney picked up the dead man's car keys and turned them over in his hand. "Absolutely lovely."

By the time Andy came back to tell Hockney he had been unable to find the sheriff's cellphone, Beth had John Smith on the gurney and ready to be loaded in the back of her station wagon. Thumps had never had the opportunity to ride in Beth's car, and he made a mental note to continue to avoid such an opportunity. "I'll know more later on," Beth told Hockney.

"Andy," said the sheriff, tossing the dead man's car keys to his deputy, "give Beth a hand with the body and then go find this guy's car."

"Parking lot's full." Andy waited to see if the sheriff was going to help.

The keys were for a Ford. Even Andy should be able to figure that out. And motels generally asked their guests for licence plate numbers.

"Don't take all day."

Andy didn't even try to keep the annoyance out of his voice. "What if I find something? Where you going to be?"

Hockney put a meaty hand on Thumps's shoulder and squeezed a little harder than he needed to. "Ansel Adams and I are going to make a house call."

SIX

U ntil a year ago, the Holiday Inn on the highway was the place to stay in Chinook. And then a subsidiary of a wholly owned corporation with offices in New York, England, Paris, and Toronto came to town and renovated the Tucker House, a limestone mansion that had been the hotel of choice for turn-of-the-century cattle barons, politicians, European tourists, and a sprinkling of famous gunfighters.

Construction started in the summer of 1875, and by the spring of 1876, just as the nation was getting ready to celebrate its one hundredth birthday and just as the Seventh Cavalry, under the dubious leadership of

General George Armstrong Custer, was crossing the Little Bighorn River, the hotel was opened for business. George Tucker hired an eight-piece band to play at the opening, the same number of musicians as were in the regimental band that played "Garry Owen" for Custer as the general moved out across the Montana plains to find the Lakota and the Cheyenne. George Tucker, a man not known for making speeches, simply welcomed everyone and bought the first round of drinks, while Custer, seeing the Indian encampment in the distance through field glasses, is supposed to have turned to his aides and said, "Hurrah, boys, we've got them!"

In the fall of 1890, the Tucker lost its top floor to a fire. No one knows how it started, but the best of the stories credited the blaze to a family of squirrels that had taken up residence in the attic and decided to play "chase" across the furniture. The paying occupant of the room had not been amused and joined the game with a broom. There was an oil lamp and a set of brocade curtains, but the story ended happily. More or less. According to most versions, both the squirrels and the guest escaped.

Through that winter, a hard season marked by blizzards and the massacre of Big Foot's band of Lakota at the hands of a revitalized Seventh Cavalry, the hotel remained vacant. But by the summer of the following year, it was open again, with two new floors.

In the years after the First World War, the Tucker fell on hard times. The hotel closed, and the bottom floor was used as a hospital, as a general store, and then as a warehouse. From the late 1940s on, it was home to travelling theatre companies, a library, and a skating rink. When McAuliffe Moran Inc. bought the property, the Tucker was showing art films in the lobby every Friday and Saturday.

Thumps had been to one movie at the Tucker. With Claire Merchant. During one of their "on-again" periods. A French film with subtitles. What he remembered most was the soft smell of damp plaster and rotting wood, and the hollow echoes of empty rooms and dead spaces. The ornate limestone exterior was still intact, but the stone had darkened down—old age and coal smoke—and summer tourists, seeing the building for the first time, imagined that it had been the site of some memorable disaster.

Thumps pulled in beside the sheriff's vehicle and got out.

"So, what do you think?"

"I think Andy is going to stick that key into every car in the lot."

"I meant the hotel."

"I know."

"Boutique," said the sheriff, letting the vowels drip off his tongue.

"It was an eyesore."

"History," said Duke. "It was history."

"Still is."

"Were you around when it was a skating rink?"

"Nope."

"Too bad." The sheriff hitched his pants and headed for the main entrance. "Those were the days."

The limestone had been sandblasted and painted with a sealant that helped bring out the veining. Brass railings had been added for accent along with a long piece of red indoor/outdoor carpet that cascaded down the granite steps.

It made sense, Thumps reasoned. If Noah Ridge was coming to town, this is where he would insist on staying.

"How well do you know Ridge?"

Thumps shrugged. "How well *did* I know him."

"He going to recognize you?"

It was a good question. Thumps wasn't sure that Noah would recognize him. Salt Lake City had been a long time ago, and in those years, thousands of people must have passed under the man's bridge.

"Maybe."

"Maybe's not an answer."

The elevator that took Thumps and the sheriff to the fourth floor was a reproduction of a turn-of-the-century lift with a door made up of slender iron rods that accordioned in and out, a faux stained-glass canopy, and rich wood panelling. Boutique or not, the corporate folk had spared no expense.

"What are you going to say to him?"

"How's 'hi' strike you?"

"I'm not paying you to say 'Hi.'"

As he walked down the hall, Thumps imagined he was in a gangster movie. That he and the sheriff were hit men on the way to a job. They'd knock on the door, and someone would say, "Who's there?" and then the two of them would take Tommy guns from beneath their trench coats and spray the place with bullets.

"Andy's not that stupid," said the sheriff.

"If you say so."

Thumps hadn't really thought about who might open the door to room 424. But even if the sheriff had asked him to guess, he would have been wrong.

"Yes?"

The winter sun coming in through the window behind the woman was blinding. Thumps recognized her voice before he could see her face.

Dakota Miles.

After all this time and there she was, standing in the doorway, looking pretty much the way she had looked when Thumps last saw her. At the train depot in Salt Lake.

"I'm Sheriff Hockney," said the sheriff in his official voice. "We're here to see Noah Ridge."

"Thumps?"

Thumps smiled. It was nice to be remembered.

"You must be kidding."

"Nope. It's me."

"The last time I saw you . . ."

"I was putting you on a train."

"That's right." Dakota nodded. "You a cop?"

"Not anymore."

The sheriff tipped his hat the way that sheriffs always tip their hats. "Thumps is helping us out."

"A consultant?" Dakota couldn't keep the smile down. "For the police."

"Sure," said the sheriff, "a consultant."

"Actually," said Thumps, "I'm a photographer."

"I guess a lot has changed." Dakota sounded sad now. And tired.

And some things are still the same, thought Thumps.

The friendly people at the front desk probably called this "an executive suite," or possibly "a penthouse." Thumps could see the corner of a galley kitchen. Somewhere farther on would be a master bedroom with a tub/shower ensuite. That was the beauty of old hotels. They were spacious compared to the cramped little boxes that you got at places like the Holiday Inn or Motel 6 or the hundreds of other look-alike chains that followed the highways west.

Thumps especially liked the windows. They were tall, stately affairs with a bevelled glass arch, the kind that opened inward, like French doors, to let in fresh air, and he wondered just when the concept of hotel windows that opened had been lost. Probably when hotel entrepreneurs discovered that windows that didn't open cost less than windows that did.

"He's out for a jog."

Thumps tried to imagine Noah out for a jog. When he knew him, the only physical exercise the man ever performed on a daily basis was talking. And he was good at it. Passionate, committed, eloquent, he could open your heart and your wallet. His looks helped. Long dark hair, a face chiselled out of stone, deep-set black eyes, he had been the darling of progressive liberals and romantic conservatives, the moneyed, well-meaning, heart-in-the-right-place sort who were committed to social change and the status quo all at the same time, who wanted to hear what Native people needed but who were loath to help in the belief that any assistance might limit free will and thwart ambition. But they were more than happy to pay for the lecture.

"I guess you're here about the death threat." Dakota pushed the door open.

"Only one?" Thumps tried a chuckle, so Dakota would know it was a joke.

"One's all it takes." Dakota said this in a flat, matter-of-fact way, but just beyond the edge of her voice was something else. Concern. Maybe anger. "Come on in," she said. "You want coffee? Tea?"

"Coffee for me," said the sheriff.

"Coffee's fine," said Thumps.

Dakota disappeared into the kitchen. The sheriff turned his hat in his hand and glanced around the room.

"There anybody you don't know?"

"Just someone from the past."

"We should sit down and talk about that past of yours one of these days."

"Nothing much to tell."

Hockney chuckled. "You wouldn't have a file with the FBI, would you?"

"Don't think so."

"Not that I'm going to look." The sheriff found a chair and hooked his hat on his knee. "Unless you screw up."

Thumps had always wondered if his time in Salt Lake had wound up in a file in Virginia. He hadn't been a member of the American Indian Movement or the Red Power Movement. Sympathetic, sure. But he had stayed away from most of the marches and the rallies.

Except for that one time when the local chapter of AIM had walked down to Temple Square to deliver two dozen long-stemmed red roses to the head of the Mormon Church. It was during one of the church's periodic conferences, and the temple grounds were filled with families taking in the sights. David Hardin, who was the head of the Salt Lake City chapter of AIM, had called the church's public relations office to let it know who was coming and what they were bringing. And why.

But paranoia runs deeper than common sense, and the church immediately called its security division, which called the Salt Lake City police. By the time the small band of Native men, women, and children arrived at the gates to the temple grounds, armed to the teeth with flowers, all the entrances had been chained shut. There were police on the rooftops of the building surrounding Temple Square, police in station wagons with police dogs, police on foot in uniforms and in plainclothes. Thumps was sure he had never seen so many police in one place at one time, though, to be fair, the long gold-foil box that Hardin had carried all the way from the Indian Walk-in Center near the railroad station to the temple grounds could have contained a Winchester carbine and a box of ammunition.

Of course, anyone who knew Native people knew they wouldn't take their families with them if they were looking for a fight, but this bit of wisdom had escaped notice by the folk whose job it was to guard the fort.

At first Hardin tried to reason with church officials, who stood behind the gates out of reach and ready to run for cover the moment the carbine appeared. He told them that this was a "thank you" march and that he wanted to present the head of the church with a dozen roses.

Leave them at the gate, the church officials politely told him. And someone will pick them up.

This give-and-take went on for a while, which allowed every television network in the city to get its cameras in place. Finally, Pauline Chee, an older Navajo woman from Shiprock, who had better things to do than to stand around and argue with frightened

White men, opened the box, took the flowers out, and shook them at the officials, while the police and the cameras stood ready for the riot to begin.

"You guys have been pretty good to us this year," said Pauline. "And we appreciate your generosity. So, here are some roses, and we're going to try to forget about what bad manners you got."

One of the officials, the smallest man of the bunch, came forward and put his arms through the bars in a gesture that was supposed to suggest goodwill, thanked Pauline for the roses, and promised that the church would continue to do what it could for Native people. "Well, then," said Pauline, "you can start by taking the chain off this gate."

"We can't do that," said the official.

"I got to use your bathroom," said Pauline. "And so does Quasty."

"That's not possible."

"'Cause she's pregnant."

In the end, the chains stayed on the gates and the Indians stayed out of Temple Square, and that night on television, the "Standoff at Temple Square," as they called it, was broadcast around the world.

Thumps was trying to remember the face of the church official who had finally come out from behind the gates to accept the roses, when he heard the hotel door behind him open.

Thumps didn't have to look at Hockney's face to see that the sheriff's eyes were bright with interest.

"Noah," said Dakota, coming out of the kitchen with cups and a pot of coffee, "this is the sheriff."

Ridge nodded to Hockney and then turned to Thumps. "I know you."

It was more a question than an answer. Thumps could see Noah flipping through the past to put a name to a face.

"Thumps DreadfulWater."

Noah had put on weight over the years. Not the pot-belly kind. Just a thick layer all over. In his younger days, his body had been a complex of mean angles and sharp edges. Ice cliffs and crags. Now he looked more like river rocks and butter. His nose was puffier than Thumps remembered. Only his eyes remained unchanged.

"I'll be in my room if you need me." Dakota put the coffee pot on the table. "You've got dinner with the mayor and the library committee at six."

Noah picked up a watch from the counter, one of those heavy masculine models with a stainless-steel band, and slid it on his wrist. "You exercise?"

Thumps shook his head.

"Nothing like it. You know Native people were some of the greatest runners in the world."

"No kidding."

"Jim Thorpe. Billy Mills." Noah flopped on the sofa and kicked off his shoes. "You're Choctaw, right?"

"Cherokee."

"Sequoyah and Will Rogers. That's pretty much it, isn't it?" Noah got up and padded into the kitchen. "Bet you're wondering about Dakota."

"She's a big girl."

"That she is," said Noah. "She's my executive assistant."

"You know," said the sheriff, butting in before either man could get warmed up, "I've always wondered what an executive assistant did."

"Depends on who the executive is," said Noah.

The last time Thumps had been in the same room with Noah Ridge, he had had the almost uncontrollable urge to hit the man. Now the old feeling was back.

"Did Dakota tell you I didn't need your help?"

"Didn't come to offer it," said the sheriff. "But this is my town. I live here. I work here."

"Nice place," said Noah. "Used to live in a town like this when I was a kid. Had a big lake just north of us. A lot of folks would come up to the lake every summer. Rich people. Fancy cabins along the shore, each one with its own private beach. Could hardly get to the lake."

"Yeah," said the sheriff, trying to be friendly, "we got a lake like that."

"The one I passed on the way into town?"

"Red Tail Lake."

"And every fall as soon as the weather turned cold, the rich folks would lock up their fancy places and head back to the city."

"Sort of like old activists," said Hockney.

"Sure," said Noah. "Some of us, at least."

"Long as the rest of you remember to mind your manners," said the sheriff, "we'll get along just fine."

Noah turned to Thumps. "Is this the 'keep your nose clean or I'll run you out of town' speech?"

"Don't guess it's the first time you've heard it," said Hockney.

"Just ask old Thumps here," said Noah.

Hockney reached down and grabbed his hat. "Well, no sense keeping you. Just wanted to stop by and say hello."

"Welcome me to town, right?"

"Sure." Hockney set his hat and shook Noah's hand, gripping it just tight enough to let the man know that he wasn't his best friend. "Welcome to Chinook."

SEVEN

Outside the hotel, the air was now dead still and frigid. Thumps could feel the cold chipping away at his nose and making his toes ache.

"That's some friend," said the sheriff as they walked back to their vehicles.

"He's not my friend."

"Well, that's good because people tend to judge you by the friends you keep."

The cars had a light sprinkling of snow. Thumps wiped off the windshield with the sleeve of his jacket.

"That woman a friend of yours too?"

"We knew each other."

"Yeah," said Hockney, opening the door to his SUV and sliding behind the wheel, "I figured that much out all on my own."

Thumps waited until the sheriff had pulled out of the parking lot and turned the corner before he headed back to the Tucker. The house phones were at the far end of the lobby.

Dakota answered on the first ring. She didn't say hello, and she didn't ask who it was. "Come on up."

"How'd you know it was me?"

"Only two people would have any reason to call me. One of them is probably standing under a hot shower, using up more than his fair share of fossil fuels."

"And the other one is freezing in the lobby."

"I'll turn the heat up."

Dakota's room was on the third floor, and it was much smaller than Noah's. No living room, no kitchen, just the standard arrangement of beds and tables. Even the window was ordinary. No arch. No bevelled glass. Just a long rectangle stuck in a wall.

"So what'd you think?"

There was a plate of fruit on the table in front of the sofa and a pot of tea.

"Of what?"

"Noah. Me. Take your pick."

The fruit plate was an artistic fan of sliced apples, bananas, blueberries, cantaloupe, pineapple, and watermelon. Thumps hadn't seen a cantaloupe at the supermarket for almost a month, and he had no idea where the hotel would have found a watermelon.

"Noah's looking good."

"He's put on weight."

Thumps helped himself to several slices of watermelon and three chunks of pineapple. "You look good."

Dakota nodded. "But you didn't come back to tell me that. And you didn't come back for the fruit."

No, Thumps thought to himself, I didn't come back for the fruit. "I'm surprised, that's all."

Dakota walked to the window and looked out. "Some days when I wake up, so am I."

Dakota was thinner than Thumps remembered, and she had cut her hair. It had been long before, the kind of hair you could braid and still come away with length. It was close-cropped now, almost severe, as if she was in mourning. But then again, maybe she was.

That was how Thumps remembered her. In mourning. Dakota and Lucy Kettle had been friends. More than friends. Less than lovers. Sisters. Not that those designations meant anything. Friends could become enemies. Lovers could leave. Sisters could move away and never call. Dakota and Lucy had been more than all of those. When Lucy disappeared and didn't return, Dakota crawled away into a deep depression. And then she crawled into a tub. Along with a bottle of pills.

Noah had found Dakota one of those happy endings that you hear about from time to time. Thumps had visited her in the hospital, had sat with her that first week when no one was sure if she would live. And after she recovered her strength, he had taken her to the train station. The last time he saw her, she was headed home to Albuquerque. Either she hadn't made it. Or she had come back.

"Don't try to figure it out." Dakota sat down on the sofa. "It won't make any sense."

"Try me."

Dakota and Noah had been lovers. It hadn't been a secret. Nor was it a secret that Noah wasn't monogamous. Thumps imagined that power gave some men the illusion of privilege, in the same way that wealth gave some men the illusion of power. Noah liked to joke that strong men had the right to breed. It was all about sex, he said. Love was just something White culture made up to hide the fact that we were all animals.

"I went home. Stayed for a couple of months. And then I came back. There's nothing much else to tell."

Thumps poured himself a cup of tea.

"The movement was my life. I came back for that."

"And Noah?"

"Noah was just the face that the movement wore." Dakota's eyes caught his. "It could have been yours."

"Not likely," said Thumps.

"That's right," said Dakota. "You didn't believe in it."

"I didn't believe in Noah."

"Noah wasn't the movement."

"So, you and Noah . . . ?" Thumps let the question dangle in mid-air.

"Yeah. We tried it again after I came back." Dakota put her hands in her lap. "Then I grew up. What about you?"

"Everybody grows up."

"Some don't."

"You ever get married?"

Dakota shook her head. "Thought about it from time to time. You remember Mrs. Tomioka?"

Thumps came up blank.

"Lucy's next-door neighbour."

"The crazy Japanese woman?"

"She wasn't crazy. She was eccentric. She liked to tell Lucy and me that when women get to a certain age, they begin to remind men of other women they've known. And from there on out, marriage wasn't worth the bother."

"Did she have an alternative?"

"Yeah," said Dakota. "Dildos, hot baths, and dark chocolate. How about you?"

"Me?"

"Marriage?"

"No."

"You don't sound so sure."

"Came close once." Thumps pushed the memory of Anna back into the shadows. "But it didn't work out."

Dakota walked to the closet and took out a heavy

wool jacket. "I have to check in with the people at the church to make sure everything is ready for tonight. You want to walk with me?"

"Sure."

"But no shop talk. I want to hear about you and what you've been doing."

THE READING, THUMPS discovered, was to be at the United Church on Main, a newer building with good acoustics. When the Chinook Jazz Festival came to town, the United Church was one of the main venues. Thumps turned his collar up and took the long way around. In the fall, when the leaves ran crimson and yellow, the path along the river was wildfire and blood. Now it was a bleak walk, the river ash grey, the sky bone white. Autumn brought with it banks of towering clouds in soft pastels. Winter brought a cold corpse laid out on the horizon.

"So, you used to be a cop?"

"Northern California."

"I never imagined you as a cop."

"Some things just happen."

"But you're not a cop anymore."

Thumps picked up a rock and skipped it off the ice into the open water. "Nope. I'm a photographer."

"You're the one who's going to take the pictures?"

"That's me."

Thumps and Dakota had dated when they were both in Utah, but her first love had been the movement, and he had never been able to get closer than sex. It was as much his fault as hers. Fanaticism, even in its most benign forms, made him uncomfortable. There were good causes and bad causes, but in either case you were expected to suspend your disbelief. It was hard enough for him to do this at movies. In real life, it had proved to be impossible.

"You don't like Noah, do you?"

"Don't have to like him to take his picture."

"Have you read his new book?"

"Nope."

"I'll get you a copy."

The river curved around the edge of the downtown, passed under a series of stone and steel bridges, and ran out into the countryside as a string of beaver ponds before it regrouped and headed for Turtle Lake.

"Why'd Noah come to Chinook?"

"I thought I said no shop talk." Dakota stopped and watched the river. "It's almost frozen."

"I was just curious."

"Now you sound like a cop." Dakota put a hand on Thumps's shoulder and let her glove brush his cheek. "I better get to the church."

Thumps watched the river slide under the ice plates. Something wasn't right. Maybe it was the cold. Maybe it was simply the surprise of seeing Dakota after all these years. Whatever the reason, he could hear his instincts whispering that cold weather wasn't the only dangerous thing that had just arrived in Chinook.

EIGHT

The United Church on Main Street was supposed to be an inexpensive reproduction of a famous church somewhere on the east coast. Boston maybe. Or Baltimore. The original was probably architecturally pleasing in the way old churches tended to be, but this copy, with its stone-veneer face and its aluminum-siding body, looked like a politician in a wash-and-wear suit.

The inside wasn't any better. Plywood benches, dead dog brown carpet, and tall windows with stained-glass patterns painted on plastic panes.

On the walk from the river to the church, neither

81

Thumps nor Dakota had said anything much. A memory here and there. Nothing more.

"Can we have dinner later?"

Thumps nodded. "Sure, if you're free."

Dakota leaned in and touched his cheek with her lips. "I will be."

Thumps stood on the steps, watching his breath turn frosty, and went through his options. He could go home, crawl into bed, and warm up. Freeway would like that. The cat's schedule consisted of waking up at around six in the morning, complaining, eating, visiting the kitty litter, and then going back to sleep for the rest of the day. If she had someone to sleep with, so much the better. Especially if that someone would raise the covers just a little so she could crawl in and curl up behind the crook of a leg.

Or he could leave town.

The latter choice had the most immediate appeal. He could throw his gear in the car, chase the sun south, and come back when the past had left town. Seeing Noah and Dakota again had raised old ghosts, ghosts that he had no intention of entertaining.

"You DreadfulWater?"

The man standing by the door to the church was a stranger. Short black hair, dark eyes. Fit. The way Thumps imagined he had looked at thirty-five. The man was wearing a navy blue suit with a white shirt and a tie that looked to have been made out of the same material as the suit. Along with a down-filled parka with a fur-trimmed hood.

"You DreadfulWater?"

"Nice parka."

"It's been tried," said the man.

Thumps smiled. "I'm DreadfulWater."

The man kept his hands in his pockets. "Spencer Asah."

"Asah?" Thumps looked at the man closely.

"Kiowa," said Asah.

"Cherokee," said Thumps.

"Aren't we supposed to share family histories about now?"

Thumps jammed his hands into his pockets. "So, what can I do for the FBI?"

Asah smiled. "What gave me away? The white shirt, right?"

"Didn't know any of you were any of us."

Asah took a stick of gum out of his pocket and offered it to Thumps. "Have you ever had the 'if you admire it, it's yours' routine work?"

"You want some coffee?"

"Am I buying?"

Al's was empty. The lunch regulars were gone, and it was that time of the day when Al retired to the backroom with the newspaper and put her feet up on a milk crate. And when she put her feet up, she did not want to put them down.

"I've got it," Thumps shouted into the backroom. "Don't get up." He reached across the counter, grabbed the pot and two cups. "Just coffee."

Asah slid into one of the booths. "Nice place."

"Good food." Thumps poured two cups. "This about Noah Ridge?"

"I hear you two are friends."

"You really with the FBI?"

Asah took out a black leather case and laid it open on the table. An Indian to follow an Indian. The bureau's idea of a good idea. "How well do you know Noah Ridge?"

Thumps had played this game before. He had liked

it when he was a cop. Now that he was a photographer, it wasn't as exciting. "Did know. It was a long time ago."

"And now he comes to town."

Thumps shrugged. "Book tour."

"That's what I hear." Asah spooned sugar into his coffee.

"You going to arrest him?"

"Nope," said Asah. "I'm just here as an observer."

"Bullshit."

Asah was smiling now. "You know I can't talk about bureau business."

Thumps had met a number of federal agents during his years on the California coast. None of them had had a sense of humour. The ones who had come to the coast that one summer to help with the Obsidian Murders had been grim-faced and officious. Thumps wasn't sure how much help Asah was going to be in Chinook. The ones in California hadn't been any help at all.

"So, why are you telling me any of this?"

"We're both from Oklahoma," said Asah. "Maybe we're related."

"Sure."

Asah finished his coffee and pushed a card across the table. "That's my cell. Since we're family, maybe you'll give me a call if you think of something."

"The Tucker?" Thumps wanted to say something about his tax dollars. "Government work must be sweet."

"I have to stay close," said Asah. "In case something exciting happens."

THUMPS STAYED IN THE BOOTH and worked things over in his head. So far as he knew, Noah hadn't broken any federal laws, and Thumps had trouble imagining the bureau sending an agent all the way from Denver to babysit an over-the-hill activist. Something else was going on, and it didn't appear that Asah was about to tell him. Which suited Thumps just fine. As far as he was concerned, he didn't want to know.

THE OLD LAND TITLES BUILDING was a tall two-storey brick affair that tripled as Beth Mooney's medical practice, the county morgue, and the three-bedroom apartment that Beth and Ora Mae Foreman shared. The morgue was in the basement. The office was on the ground floor. The apartment was on the second floor with a view of the river and the mountains. Thumps tried to limit his visits to the two floors above ground. He had been to the morgue on a number of occasions and had always left with the promise that he would not return.

Thumps pressed the buzzer and waited.

"Yes?"

"It's me, Thumps."

"Second floor."

Thumps had a fondness for older buildings with high ceilings, but they did mean longer staircases. The Land Titles building had an elevator, and each spring Beth and Ora Mae talked about getting it fixed. Thumps suspected that Beth liked climbing stairs.

Beth was waiting for him. "Took you long enough."

"See the elevator isn't fixed yet."

"Walking is good for you." Beth turned back into the apartment. "You want something to drink?"

Thumps stood on the landing for a moment, bent over, his hands on his knees. "Sure."

The last time Thumps had been to the apartment, Ora Mae was painting the walls dark yellow. Now they were sea green. The faint smell of wet paint was in the air.

"What happened to the yellow?"

"You mean what happened to the taupe."

"Taupe?"

"The yellow was two colours ago."

Ora Mae worked at Wild Rose Realty, where she sold anything with a roof. But her passion was home decorating, particularly painting.

"You know if you get too much paint built up, it will begin to crack."

"Painting makes her happy," said Beth. "You want to tell her to stop painting?"

No, Thumps thought to himself, he didn't want to do that.

"So, you here to see me or Ora Mae?"

"You."

"Last time you wanted to see me, it was about a dead body." Beth put a pot of water on the stove. "We talking about the guy at the Holiday Inn?"

"I was just curious."

"Funny," said Beth. "You don't look like a cop."

"I'm working with the sheriff."

The kettle on the stove was beginning to gurgle. "Coffee or tea?" Thumps looked out the window. A snow squall had snuck in, and the streets were beginning to disappear.

"Tea, please."

"Good choice," said Beth, putting on a thick red sweater. "But if you're going to waste my time and drink my tea, the least you can do is help."

THE BASEMENT IN the Land Titles building was not Thumps's idea of help. Raking leaves was help. Shovelling a walk was help. Jump-starting a car was help.

"I have to get ready for the reading," Thumps said as he followed Beth down the stairs.

"That's not until tomorrow."

Thumps could feel his feet slow down as they got to the first floor. "Yeah, but I should probably go home."

"Don't be a baby."

"No, I have to . . . shower and . . . shave and . . . check my cameras."

Beth pulled the door open. Thumps felt the rush of warm, moist air lurch out of the black hole in front of him.

"Tell you what," said Beth, "I won't do any cutting. Okay?"

Thumps began breathing quickly, short, shallow breaths through his mouth. Drinking the tea was now out of the question.

Beth hit the light switch. "See? All nice and bright."

The stairs to the basement were metal and they made a sharp, clanging sound that Thumps had come to associate with danger. The only windows were set high on the walls and painted black. But it wasn't the sound of the stairs or the dark windows that made Thumps's skin move. It was the desperate sense of loneliness.

And the smell.

"Okay," said Beth. "Where should we start?"

Thumps felt his stomach heave. "How about we look at his belongings."

"Sure." Beth took a sip of her tea. "We can sneak up on the corpse later."

* * *

JOHN SMITH'S BELONGINGS consisted of the clothes the man had been wearing and a small suitcase that contained a shaving kit, a pair of pants, two shirts, two pairs of underwear, and two pairs of socks. Thumps had hoped to find something to tell him who the man was, a prescription bottle, a letter, something with a name on it.

Beth sat on a stool and watched Thumps sift through the dead man's things. "So, you think John Smith is an alias?"

"What do you think?"

"Oh," said Beth, "I think he was having an affair with Pocahontas and didn't want anyone to know."

"This it?"

"When I left, Andy was still looking for Mr. Smith's car."

"Did you tell him it was a Ford?"

"Oh, dear," said Beth, tilting her head to one side and batting her eyes, "that's what I forgot to do."

The labels on the clothes read "Cabela's, World's Foremost Outfitter, Outdoor Gear Since 1961."

"Fancy that," said Beth.

"What?"

"Ora Mae and I stopped by their store."

"Cabela's?"

"When we went through Nebraska. They've got this giant store in the middle of nowhere."

Thumps held the cotton pants up. They weren't new, and neither was the thick leather belt. "Doesn't look like Ora Mae's kind of thing," he said, remembering that Ora Mae preferred the designer side of the aisle.

"It's not," said Beth, "but the store was worth the stop. It's got to be a couple of acres with log beams and rafters. Upscale in an outdoor sort of way. They've got this artificial mountain at the back with stuffed animals standing on the slopes. And next to the mountain they have a trout stream with live trout."

"A trout stream?"

"The clothes are a pretty good deal. If you like cotton."

"With live trout?"

Beth picked up the gun and handed it to Thumps. "If you're going to shoot yourself, this is the gun to do it with."

Thumps looked at the gun for a moment and then

slipped it back in its holster. "You want to do me a favour?"

"It's what I live for."

"The dead guy . . . the corpse . . . could you check his leg?"

"I thought you'd never ask," said Beth. "What am I looking for?"

Thumps backed away from the table to a safe distance. "His right leg. Near the ankle. On the inside."

Beth went to a set of stainless-steel doors, opened the one on the left, and pulled out the long metal tray. She unzipped the body bag. "This leg?"

Thumps turned away and stared at the stairs.

"It's just a leg," said Beth. "And look at this."

"What?" said Thumps, without turning back to the table.

"Aren't you the clever one. It looks like a callus. Just above the ankle, as though something has been rubbing against the skin."

"New?"

"Nope. He's had this for a while. You want to share?"

"Just a hunch," said Thumps. "You got the fingerprints ready to go?"

"I do."

"You might want to run them through the FBI database."

"He's got a callus on his leg, and you think he's a fugitive?"

"No," said Thumps, wondering if Hockney had dragged him into a mess that he wouldn't be able to get out of easily, "I think he might be a cop."

NINE

The smart thing, Thumps told himself as he pointed his Volvo west, was to go home, turn off the phone, get into bed, and disappear under something warm and soft and dark. And stay there until spring.

Instead, he was on his way to Buffalo Mountain Resort to try to find Claire, though he wasn't sure exactly why he was doing this. Maybe it was because they hadn't talked since Thumps had taken off for Canada. Before he left, they had had a minor disagreement about Claire's son, Stanley, or Stick as he was known to his friends. Thumps had suggested, in a positive way, that Stanley was arrogant and lazy—which he was—and Claire had suggested that Thumps mind his own business. It had been his own fault, stepping between a bear and her cub, and since Claire always put work and Stanley before romance, if amends were to be made, Thumps would have to make them.

Sometimes his relationship with Claire was more trouble than it was worth. She was loving enough when she remembered and when she made the time, but getting her attention focused on something other than work took more effort than it should.

Thumps looked at the sky through the windshield. With any luck, he'd get snowed in at the resort, and he and Claire would have to hole up in one of the condominiums that the tribe hadn't sold yet, a unit with a whirlpool tub and a panorama of the mountains. A unit with a lock on the door and no Stanley banging around in the refrigerator, demanding to be fed. Best of all, he wouldn't have to bother with Noah Ridge and the dangerous baggage the man dragged along behind him.

The Volvo didn't like the look of the sky either, and as they hit the first grade, the car started chug-chugging and drifting toward the shoulder, as if it were running out of breath and needed a rest.

"Don't even think about it," he said, and he leaned into the accelerator.

Amazing how the past could swing around and find you. Thumps hadn't thought about Utah or Noah Ridge or Lucy Kettle or Dakota Miles for years. And here they were again. Almost larger than life. And as he coaxed the car into the mountains toward the promise of snow, pieces of those years began working their way out of the ground like old bones that hadn't been buried deep enough.

Thumps had watched those years from the sidelines. Close to the action, but never on the field. He vaguely remembered growing his hair long, could recall owning a four-strand bone choker and a beaded belt buckle. Had he really worn them? But when Noah began talking about commitment and pride and today being a good day to die, Thumps had stepped away. He had no quarrel with Noah's contention that the government's attitude toward Indians hadn't changed in two hundred years or that the Bureau of Indian Affairs and the Department of the Interior had done little to protect Indians and Indian resources, but the simplistic brand of evangelical rhetoric that flowed out of Noah whenever the media came around always left Thumps uneasy and looking for cover.

It had been a strategy that combined lost pride and tribalism with the realities of racism and, Thumps's concerns aside, it had played well on the reservations and in the world press.

There was no question that the government had crawled into bed with business, passing out leases on Indian land to private companies for oil and coal and gas exploration like loot bags at a party, or that these same corporations had returned the favour, pouring money into political campaigns, so that the cycle of chicanery and profit could be maintained.

After all, levels of corruption always rose to the level of profit.

But that had begun to change. Maybe it was because organizations such as the Red Power Movement and the American Indian Movement had brought national attention to a national problem, or maybe it was because Native people had finally had enough of the lies that flowed out of Washington like a river. Whatever the reason, after years of watching their land base dwindle, tribes suddenly dug in their heels, hired lawyers, and went to court to stop the pillage. And they had been surprisingly successful. Not that these wins had stemmed the clamour for the mineral deposits or for the stands of timber or for the fisheries that Native people controlled. As long as Indians controlled one square acre of land, Noah argued from his public pulpit, there would be a White man trying to steal it.

Maybe that's what separated humans from animals, a willingness to steal from each other. Then again, Thumps remembered watching a nature show in which a lion made off with the carcass of an antelope that a leopard had killed. So, maybe there was no difference after all. Maybe the old stories were right.

COOLEY SMALL ELK was waiting for Thumps when he got to the main gate at Buffalo Mountain Resort.

"Hey, Thumps."

Cooley rolled over to the car like a boulder coming down a mountain. He had on a thick leather parka which made him look even larger, if that was possible.

"You looking to buy," said Cooley, "or just looking?"

"Thought they were going to bring in an automatic gate."

Cooley put a hand on the roof and leaned in. Thumps could feel the car struggling to keep its balance.

"They did, but someone broke off the arm. So, they hired me back."

Thumps grabbed the edge of the seat so he wouldn't fall out the window.

"Claire around?"

"She's at one of those meetings," said Cooley. "Hey, did you hear about my new business?"

Thumps couldn't recall that Cooley had ever had a business, let alone a new one.

"Here you go." Cooley handed Thumps a card that read, simply, "Small Elk Security."

Thumps turned the card over. There was nothing on the back. No phone number. No fax number. No email address.

"Security, eh?"

"That's right. If you need something looked after, give me a call."

"There's no phone number."

"Yeah," said Cooley. "I know."

"You're probably going to need a phone number."

"It changes a lot," said Cooley, "so if I get a client, I just write it on the back."

Thumps could still remember the days when his phone bill got paid last. Or not at all. "Well, that's a good business," he told Cooley. "And you got the looks for it."

Cooley stepped back from the car so Thumps could see all of him all at once. The Volvo bounced to its feet and took a deep breath.

"My girlfriend says everyone feels safer when they're standing next to a big guy."

"You think I could go up to the office and hang around until Claire finishes her meeting?"

"You go away on trips, right?"

"Sometimes."

"Next time you go, you should think about hiring someone to watch your house."

Thumps tried to think what there was in the house worth stealing. The cameras, maybe, although the digital revolution had made most of his equipment next to worthless. He remembered when personal computers came into their own, and electric typewriters became obsolete overnight.

No one would steal a grumpy cat, so Freeway was safe.

"Sure," said Thumps, "and I'll pass the word around."

"Tell them I've been trained by Vladimir Vasiliev."

If Thumps was going to have to wait to see Claire, sitting in the car and talking to Cooley wasn't such a bad way to spend the time.

"Vladimir?"

"Vladimir Vasiliev." Cooley waited for Thumps to recognize the name. "The Russian Martial Art System."

And then again, sitting in the lobby of the resort and thumbing through old magazines would be okay too.

"He used to be with a Russian Special Operations Unit." Cooley took one step to the side and assumed a fighting pose. "I just finished the DVD on strikes. Hop out and I'll show you a couple of moves."

Cooley spun around and slammed his elbow into a

nearby aspen. Thumps eased up on the brake and let the car roll forward out of harm's way.

"Maybe later."

"Sure," said Cooley, "and as soon as the new gate arm comes in, I'll be available for security work full-time."

The Volvo limped up the road to the main complex, favouring the side Cooley had crushed. In his rear-view mirror, Thumps could see the aspen. It was still quaking, and he wondered if the gate arm had been a casualty of Cooley's training.

BUFFALO MOUNTAIN RESORT had become what ambitious projects with high expectations generally become. Disappointments. Not failures. Just disappointments. Claire and the tribal council had hoped that the high-rise condos with their panoramic views of the Rockies and the casino with its glitter and bells and lights and easy cash would provide the tribe with a reliable economic base.

That hadn't happened.

Not that it wouldn't. Eventually, perhaps. But the last time Thumps spoke to Ora Mae, only about half of the condos had been sold and many of those had gone to speculators who expected to rent them back for exorbitant rates to people on vacation. Fewer than ten percent of the units were actually occupied by warm bodies, and that made the concrete and glass structure feel more like a hotel than a second home.

The casino had been a success. A nice condo in a good location might be a prudent investment, but if the number of people who drove up to the resort on the weekend or the caravan of buses that arrived daily was any indication, people would rather take a chance than play it safe.

Thumps had decided that he didn't like any of it very much. There was something about having a condo-casino complex stuck in the middle of a perfectly-fine-as-it-was forest that rubbed him the wrong way. Maybe it was the photographer in him who was tired of seeing fences and power lines and highways on the ground glass, or maybe it was the knowledge that no matter how successful the resort was, money wouldn't necessarily make the lives of people better.

Then again, Thumps reflected, as he eased into a parking space next to the administration office, a little money now and then wouldn't make his life any worse.

So, the resort was bringing in money. Just not in the bucket loads that Claire had hoped for and not in any dependable fashion. Which meant the tribe could never plan, only react.

Which is what Indians did. Or at least, that's the way it appeared. Life on the reservation, so far as Thumps could see, was a series of reactions. Reactions to governments that wanted to dispense with treaties. Reactions to corporations that wanted to get at the natural resources the tribes controlled. Reactions to benevolent organizations that wanted to help Indians become White. Vine Deloria Jr. had said it best in his book *Custer Died for Your Sins*, when he argued that Indians were transparent, that Whites looking at Native people knew exactly what Indians needed and how they felt and what could be done to help them. Thumps had read Deloria's book at university, and while he felt that the man had used a rather general brush to paint his landscape of North American politics and policies, he hadn't been wrong.

* * *

CLAIRE WASN'T AT the administration office. She was at the condo complex. Thumps caught up to her on the sixth floor in one of the two-bedroom units, standing on the balcony, looking out at the Rockies.

"If you were in the market for a condo," said Claire, without turning around, "would you buy this one?"

Thumps did not believe in extrasensory perception. "You saw me walk over from the office."

"What about it?"

Thumps looked around. He had a vague memory of seeing a model called the Cascade, a luxurious three-bedroom with cathedral ceilings and a glass wall that looked down the Rockies. This wasn't a Cascade.

"How many bedrooms?"

"Two."

"Feels small."

"We've sold only one of these."

"Maybe you should lower the price."

Thumps had said this as a joke, but when Claire turned to face him, he could see that she wasn't in the mood for humour. Thumps was reasonably sure that he hadn't had enough time to piss her off.

"So, what's he done now?"

"Who?" Claire lied poorly. It was one of the qualities that Thumps liked about her.

"Stick."

"Stanley."

Stanley Merchant, or Stick as he was known to everyone except his mother, was Claire's only child. Which was an argument all by itself for multiple-children families. Stick was smart. And he was arrogant. Worse, he was young and still stupid enough to think that the first two attributes were attractive features.

"So, what's Stanley done now?"

"You didn't come out here to ask me about my son."

No, Thumps agreed, he hadn't, but it was clear that he was going to have to get Stick out of the way before he could move on to the matter at hand.

"It couldn't be that bad."

Claire sat down in a large, overstuffed chair upholstered with material that looked like a Tuscany grape arbour.

"Sometimes I think he needs a father."

"He doesn't need a father," said Thumps. "He's got a great mother."

Normally, Claire would have taken his head off for

being condescending, but sometimes flattery and the truth are one and the same.

"Two weeks ago, he came home with a cut lip."

Thumps clamped his teeth on his tongue.

"It's not funny. Then he came home limping."

"Did you ask him?"

"Of course I asked him."

"And?"

"He said he was playing basketball."

So far as Thumps could remember, Stick hated sports, was happiest sitting in front of a computer monitor.

"When did he take up basketball?"

"The other day, he came home with his eye swollen. He could hardly see."

Now that, thought Thumps, keeping a firm grip on his tongue, was serious.

"I'd like you to talk to him."

"He won't talk to me."

"You're a man," said Claire.

The last thing in the world Thumps wanted to do was to have a man-to-man talk with Stick. Well, maybe not the last thing, but it wasn't high on his list of fun activities. Claire, on the other hand, was right up there with warm fires and good food.

"It's probably nothing," said Thumps. "He's not telling just to bug you."

Thumps could see that Claire was unmoved by this logic.

"Okay, I'll talk to him."

Claire nodded, but she didn't smile. "Don't tell him I asked."

Thumps had hoped he could bring Noah's name up in the middle of a conversation that had nothing to do with Noah, but he could see Claire wasn't about to make the space or the time for that.

"Noah Ridge is in town."

Claire snorted. "Is that a question?"

"Was just surprised to see him turn up in Chinook."

Claire cocked her head and looked at Thumps as though he were something shiny and she were a crow. "You think the tribe invited him?"

"Just curious."

"Hell," said Claire, "I'm surprised he has the balls to show his face around here at all."

There were only two answers that Thumps had expected. Yes, the tribe had invited him. Or no, the tribe had not invited him.

"You know him?"

Claire shook her head. "Never met the man."

"But . . . ?"

"Ask Grover Many Horses. I would imagine he's pretty hot about Ridge coming to town."

Somehow the conversation had taken a turn when Thumps wasn't looking. "Grover Many Horses?"

"Grover was her brother."

"Whose brother?"

"Lucy Many Horses."

Thumps could feel the hairs on the back of his neck stiffen. "Lucy?"

Claire nodded. "It happened years ago. In Salt Lake City. She worked with Ridge."

"Lucy Kettle."

"That was her father's name," said Claire. "But her mother's family is from here."

TEN

Thumps could remember that even as a child, he had not been fond of surprises. There was a certain disorder to them. A certain confusion. Even good surprises were somewhat annoying. Discovering that Lucy Kettle was from the reservation and that she had a brother who might not be well disposed toward Noah Ridge was a rather large surprise.

As Thumps drove back to town, he began playing out several scenarios, most of which featured Grover in the role of the avenging angel, striding into the church while Noah was reading from his good book and blowing Ridge's head off.

Fantasies aside, one could argue that Noah Ridge's showing up in a town such as Chinook was nothing more than a surprise with a good explanation. And a gullible optimist might be willing to believe that Lucy Kettle's brother living near said town was simply a coincidence. It helped if you eliminated the postcard with the death threat, Noah's past, and an FBI agent who was just wandering around taking in the sights. The sheriff wouldn't believe it. Not for a minute. Neither would Spencer Asah. But someone might.

And then there was the dead guy in the motel. John Smith might have nothing at all to do with Noah or Grover or Dakota or Lucy Kettle, but Thumps had the nagging feeling that all these pieces were on a collision course with each other, and that the sound of the crash might just wake up the dead.

How had it happened? Thumps had started off the day cold, tired, and in a bad mood. He had reluctantly said yes to Hockney's offer to play deputy for a few days, and here he was driving all over hell chasing suspects. Well, not suspects exactly. Information. Almost as bad. As if he were still a cop. As if he still enjoyed the game.

Worse, now he had to talk to Stick. Maybe the boy would turn out all right in the end. Maybe he was a late bloomer, one of those kids who did nothing until they hit thirty. Or forty. Not that Thumps cared one way or the other. But Stick was tied to Claire—a package, if you will—and if Thumps wanted to have a relationship with the mother, he knew he had to deal with the son.

Thinking about Claire and her son had the same effect on Thumps as thinking about Noah Ridge, and when he looked down at the speedometer, he discovered he was well over the speed limit. It would be a fine irony if his curiosity and concern landed him a ticket. Not that he had any money. The trip north had been expensive, and the lack of cash was why he had said yes to Hockney in the first place.

The sheriff was another annoyance.

Thumps had to smile. Claire, Stick, Noah, Hockney. Might as well add Freeway to the list of people who annoyed him. Not that the cat was people in the Judeo-Christian sense of the universe.

Maybe the fault was in him. Maybe it was one of those days where everything annoyed him. Maybe he should try to be more understanding, more giving.

THE TURNOFF FOR Moses Blood's place was a dirt road that was easy enough to find during the day and almost impossible to see in the dark. Thumps found it on the second try. Moses liked to refer to the two-mile track of potholes and gullies as a driveway, but then Moses had a sense of humour. As Thumps tried to keep his oil pan intact and his springs from bottoming out, he wondered how much Moses knew about Lucy Kettle and particularly about her brother, Grover. If anyone on the reservation did know, it would be Moses.

As Thumps started down the side of the coulee, he could see Moses's house in the distance and the tangle of old trailers behind it. Trailers were common-enough sights on the reservation. People bought trailers, and people sold trailers, and when a trailer was too old to be bought or sold, it made its way to Moses's fifty acres of bottom land and arranged itself among the other trailers.

If the trailers had had horns and a tail, from a distance, Thumps might have mistaken them for a herd of buffalo.

He had asked Moses about the trailers more than once, and the old man had always seemed pleasantly surprised by Thumps's interest.

"They're just resting," Moses told him. "They'll move on when they feel like it."

Stick's Mustang was parked in front of the house. Thumps sat in the car where it was warm and measured the distance from where he was to where he wanted to be. Next to Moses's wood stove. And then he undid the seat belt, vaulted out of the car, and walked briskly across the snow as it cackled at him underfoot. Just as he got to the house, Moses opened the door and held out a cup of tea.

"Oki," the old man said. "Come on in. I've been expecting you."

MOSES'S HOUSE WAS TOASTY, and Thumps could feel happiness filling his body for the second time today. The tea helped. It was hot and sweet, and Thumps

ignored the bits of twigs and leaves and flowers floating just off the bottom.

"You want to watch some television?" Moses
handed Thumps the remote control. "They got some
pretty interesting stuff on television these days."

Moses had the biggest television set on the reservation, and every Saturday night, during hockey season,
his house was packed.

"The other day they had this guy who tried to kill
the president." Moses brought up the movie schedule.
"He was mostly dark blue with lines all over his body
and every time someone tried to shoot him, he would
disappear into smoke."

Thumps put his nose into the cup and inhaled the
warm vapours.

"And there was this other guy who had these steel
claws come out of his hands whenever he got upset and
a woman who could control the weather."

A Mormon bishop on his way from Cardston to
Salt Lake City had stopped by Moses's house one
afternoon to say hello and asked what a Native elder
was doing with a large-screen television in his house.
Couldn't see the small one, Moses told him.

"Boy, we could have sure used that kind of a woman last summer."

"Stick around?"

"You bet. He's out back talking to the Nephews."

The Nephews, Thumps remembered, was what Moses called the bank of computers that Stick had cobbled together in one of the trailers. Evidently trailers and computers talked to each other because, somehow or other, most of the orphaned computers from the band offices and elsewhere found their way to the orphaned trailers.

"Of course, being able to turn into smoke and disappear is pretty handy too." Moses went to the stove and poured himself another cup of tea. "Politicians do that all the time. It's sort of what Lucy did."

Moses looked slow, but Thumps knew from personal experience that no one could make a turn in the middle of a conversation faster than the old man.

"Lucy Kettle, right?"

"That's what you came to talk about, isn't it?"

"You knew her?"

"Oh, sure," said Moses. "Only her name was Many Horses. Kettle was her dad's name. He was Cheyenne or something like that."

"What happened?"

Moses looked up from his tea. "Nothing."

"I knew her."

"I know," said Moses.

"But I thought she was from Oklahoma."

"Oh, that," said Moses. "That's just kids and parents. Her and her mom used to fight all the time, so Lucy took her dad's name and put her mother's name away, and then one day she disappeared. Like that guy in the movie."

"What about her brother?"

"Grover?" Moses leaned back in the chair. "He's a pretty good boy. Got a temper, that one. But he's real good with horses. He can talk to them, and they talk to him."

"You know where I can find him?"

"Nope," said Moses, "but Stick might know. Come on. Let's go see what the Nephews have to tell us today."

THUMPS HAD FOLLOWED Moses to the trailer that held the computers several times, and each time the old man seemed to take a different way. He'd enter the door of

one trailer, walk through it to the back door, come outside for a moment, and then climb back into another
trailer, and make his way from that one to another one
until, as if by magic, they would arrive at a trailer that
was marked with a sticker that warned about possible
radioactivity.

"Don't worry," said Moses as he always did. "It used
to be one of those X-ray things."

"I know," said Thumps.

"That X-ray would shine a light right through you."
Moses patted the side of the trailer. "But it's okay now."

Stick was sitting in front of a row of monitors playing
a game. Thumps had no idea which one it was. They
all looked the same. Once, he had bought something
called *The 7th Guest*, which turned out to be bizarre and
boring, a game that was little more than a set of puzzles
with graphics set against creepy music. How anyone
could sit in front of a screen for hours and be entertained
by something so mind-numbing was beyond him.

Of course, Thumps wasn't sure there was any great
difference between video games and television. At least
with the video games you got to move your fingers.

"Look who's come to visit us."

Stick didn't even turn. "Shut the door."

Thumps was in favour of that. Moses sat down next to Stick and looked at the screens.

"Are you winning?"

"See that guy there?" said Stick, pointing to a blue blob with a flash of yellow. "That's Custer."

"Yes," said Moses. "That's him all right."

Thumps moved in and changed his angle. "The Battle of the Little Bighorn?"

Stick smirked. "Battle of the Washita. Don't suppose you've ever heard of it."

Thumps didn't actually dislike Stick. But the combination of youth and arrogance was wearing. The kid wasn't stupid, but he was annoying, and today annoying was a mortal sin.

"November 27," said Thumps, "1868. Custer and the Seventh Cavalry ride into Black Kettle's village. Black Kettle and his wife were killed. More than fifty Cheyenne women and children were taken prisoner. Custer burned the village and shot all the horses."

Now Stick looked annoyed. Good.

"Yeah, but the Cheyenne wiped out Major Elliott's detachment."

"Her father was Cheyenne," said Moses. "Maybe she was related to Black Kettle."

"Maybe," said Stick, turning back to the game. "All the stuff I found is there."

On the floor next to Stick was a box filled with paper.

"All this on Lucy Kettle?"

"Lucy Kettle. The Red Power Movement. The FBI. Some interesting shit."

Thumps looked at the box. The easy thing to do would be to take the box and let things lie. "Talked to your mother."

Stick didn't even look up. "Thought she dumped you."

"Asked me to have a man-to-man talk with you." Thumps felt a smile coming on as he said "man-to-man."

"You're not my father."

"Always nice to have people who care for you," said Moses.

"He doesn't care for me," said Stick. "He just wants to have sex with my mother."

"Sex is good too," said Moses. "Calms you down. Helps you get to sleep."

Stick's eye was black and purple, and it was still swollen. Thumps had seen injuries like this before.

Especially with drunks who tumbled out of the bars in the early hours of morning full of rage and immortality.

"You know there's no profit in pissing her off."

Stick looked up from the monitor. "Tell her you hit me. That'll make her happy."

It was a family trait, Thumps decided. There was no give in either one of them. No elasticity. No compromise. Just hardpan and stone.

"You should think of Thumps as your uncle," said Moses. "Always good to talk things out with an uncle."

Stick made a growling sound and retreated to his computer world.

Moses patted Stick on the back. "Don't forget that time your uncle helped you."

"He got me shot."

"But he saved your life."

"He got lucky."

Lucky was what Stick had been, Thumps remembered with some annoyance. The kid had been a suspect in the shooting death of a computer programmer at Buffalo Mountain. He hadn't killed the man, but instead of turning himself in, he took off, thinking he was going to solve the case himself, and wound up getting shot by Andy Hooper. Thumps could still remember that night, waiting in the hospital, wondering if Claire's only child was going to die before he even began to live.

Moses stooped down, picked up the box, and handed it to Thumps. "Hard to be polite when your eye hurts."

Thumps sighed and took the box.

"Let us know if this helps to solve the mystery."

"What mystery?"

"What happened to Lucy," said Moses. "We've been wondering about that for years. Always hard to understand the present if you don't understand the past."

MOSES WALKED THUMPS back to his car, telling the story of each of the trailers they passed through.

"Pat Pretty Weasel bought this one in Edmonton from a guy who worked oil rigs. There were oil stains everywhere and when Pat pulled up the carpet, he discovered that the underlay had at least four barrels of heavy crude in it.

"Roxanne Heavy Runner's mother used to live in

this one. When her mother passed, Roxanne was going to live in it, but the memories were too strong, so she got a house at the townsite instead. Her mother used to make the best tea on the reservation. You can still smell it.

"This one belonged to Floyd Small Elk. He was killed in the bedroom. Cooley brought this out and left it with me and asked me to park it where it would get lots of sunshine."

As they moved from trailer to trailer, Thumps caught glimpses of the sky. It was darker now, heavy with sorrow and snow, and it reminded him of the sky on the Northern California coast all those years ago. They had found Anna and Callie under such a sky.

"Your car doesn't look too happy," said Moses.

There were tiny icicles forming on the Volvo's wheel wells, and the front bumper was shivering. "It doesn't like cold weather."

"You should take it someplace warm."

Thumps put the box on the hood. "What am I supposed to do with this?"

Moses watched a flock of geese in the distance. "You know, sometimes an old story comes along and you can't remember how it goes. Sometimes it helps to hear a story again."

Thumps picked up the box and walked to the side of the car. "This is a lot of paper."

"It's recycled. The other side has band-meeting stuff on it." Moses opened the back door. "They say some good things about her, and they say some bad things too."

"Any of it true?"

"All stories are true."

Thumps put the box on the seat and shut the door a little harder than usual, to let the car know he wasn't in the mood to hear complaints.

"So, she never came back."

Moses dragged the toe of his boot across the ground so that the dark earth showed through the thin layer of snow. "Not yet."

ELEVEN

Archimedes Kousoulas owned the Aegean, the only bookstore in Chinook worth the mention. For years, the Aegean had been the *only* bookstore in town, but a hole-in-the-wall storefront affair called Gone with the Wind had opened next to the barbershop on Main, and one of those chain things had set up shop in the mall. Gone with the Wind dealt in used paperbacks, mostly romance and adventure fiction, while the store at the mall sold the latest bestsellers, books with large advertising budgets, books that had been turned into movies. Books that people who didn't read books bought for other people who didn't read books. Thumps had gone there once, looking for a good book on digital photography, and made the mistake of asking one of the assistant managers for a recommendation.

"Do you have a title?" the clerk had asked him.

"No, I'm hoping you can recommend a book."

"We don't really do that."

"But you sell books on digital photography."

"Absolutely. And if you know the title you want, we can find the book."

The Aegean had originally been a Carnegie library. But when a new library had been built in the late '80s, the old building had been put up for sale. It should have sold right away, but it had been in terrible condition. The roof leaked. The windows had rotted. The foundation had shifted. The plaster had crumbled. The wiring and plumbing had to be replaced. There was a certain majesty to the old edifice, but most people could see the building for what it was.

A money pit.

So, most everyone in town was surprised when Archie bought the old library and slowly but surely coaxed it off its deathbed and brought it back to health.

Walking into the Aegean was always a surprise. For a variety of intangibles—the soft, shafting light, the high ceilings, the endless shelves of books, the narrow mezzanine that ran the circumference of the main room—the inside of the building always felt more spacious than the outside would suggest. Whatever the reasons, stepping into the bookstore was like stepping out of one universe and into another.

Archie was on the mezzanine putting books on shelves.

"Hey, Archie."

"Thumps!" Archie put the books on the floor, came clanging down the spiral staircase, and dragged Thumps to the large library table in the middle of the room. "What do you think?"

Spread out on the table was a series of crude drawings.

"What are they?"

"Ideas," said Archie, holding one up. "For the photographs."

Thumps had to look closely to figure out what was happening. "So, this is supposed to be Ridge standing in front of . . . an American flag with his arms . . . crossed."

"Right," said Archie. "Everybody likes patriotism.

And here's one of him standing in front of city hall."

Thumps could feel his eyes folding shut as Archie picked up each sketch and explained the pose.

"Herb Stockley said we could use his 1957 Pontiac Star Chief convertible for this shot."

"Archie . . ."

"You don't have to use all my ideas." Archie slipped the drawings into a manila envelope. "Just the ones you think are good."

Thumps took the envelope because Archie was a friend and because there was nothing else he could do. "Thanks."

"Guess what else?"

Thumps had his own set of questions, but there was a ritual to life with Archie, and in that ritual Archie's questions came first.

"A postcard?"

"Nope."

"A book?"

"Nope."

"Can I stop now?"

"Wait till you see it," said Archie, looking pleased that Thumps had not been able to guess.

Archie's first love was books, but he wasn't

monogamous. He collected early postcards, vintage photographs, old maps. Posters. So long as they had a western theme, which for Archie meant cowboys and Indians.

"I found it in a shop in Seattle." Archie went to one of the large map files. "You don't find one of these just any old day."

It was a poster, and it showed a large steamship in the background, all black and white and red and bright, knifing through an emerald green sea while in the foreground, surrounded by the silhouette of palm fronds, an Indian in a full headdress clutching a spear peered out of the jungle at the approaching ship. "Cosulich Line Trieste" was printed in bold letters across the bottom. In the lower left corner was "A. Dondou," which was, Thumps supposed, the artist's name, while in the lower right corner was "Arti Grafiche S. D. Modiano-Trieste."

The Indian was etched in red so you could see him amidst the foliage.

"Late 1920s?"

"Maybe early '30s," said Archie. "The company's not in business anymore, but when it was, it specialized in cruises to the Americas."

130

"So, that's how they imagined the Americas."

Archie shrugged. "That's how everyone imagined the Americas."

"Is it for sale?"

"Depends."

"On what?"

"The pictures you take of Noah Ridge."

Thumps watched the ship breaking through the waves and the Indian hiding in the woods, waiting for the tourists to arrive. New World fantasies. Old World fears. He wondered how many tickets this poster had sold.

"It's nice."

Archie's head snapped up. "That's how you thank me? 'It's nice'?"

"You bought this for me?"

"Of course I bought this for you. You're my friend, right? You need a poster like this for your house. Something to brighten up the place."

"Thanks."

"Don't go thanking me yet. You have to earn it first."

Of all Archie's endearing qualities, his endless energy was Thumps's favourite.

"I'll take the pictures of Ridge. But not in front of an American flag. Okay?"

"You're the boss. Hey, maybe I should be your assistant."

"That'll cost you two posters."

The Indian in the poster was pushing the fronds to one side to get a better look. And well he should, for as far as Thumps could see, the ship headed for him was deserted. There was no sign of passengers anywhere. No happy folks on deck with flags and cameras. No festivities to mark its arrival. Just a silent, swift cruise moving across the face of the water like a missile.

"Who arranged for Ridge to come to Chinook?"

"The publisher."

"You talked to them?"

"Who else would send him?"

No matter which way Thumps turned it, Noah's arrival didn't make sense. "When was the last time a writer came to Chinook as part of a book tour?"

Archie cocked his head. "You trying to tell me I don't know what I'm doing?"

"No."

"It's not easy bringing culture to Chinook."

"I know."

"Did you also know that no one on the library committee gets any pay?"

"You're doing a great job," said Thumps.

"Tony Hillerman."

"What?"

"He came through town when he was on his last book tour. He signed books right here in the store." Archie went to a cabinet and rummaged through the files until he found what he was looking for. "See?"

The flyer was part of a press packet for one of Hillerman's novels. There was a picture of the author and a picture of the book cover, a series of reviews, along with information on the publicity campaign.

Thumps looked at the flyer for a moment and then handed it back to Archie. "He was on a twelve-city tour."

"He's popular," said Archie.

"And do you know where *he* went?" The cities were listed. Thumps waited to see if Archie was going to bite.

"Okay, Mr. Smarty-pants, Chinook wasn't on his tour. Happy?"

"What happened?"

"Hillerman was in Calgary on his way to Denver. But there was a pilots' strike, so he drove down and wound up stopping here." Archie gestured to the glass cases where he kept the first editions. "He signed every book I had. Great guy. Real friendly. Said he was going to see about putting Chinook on his next tour."

Thumps laid the flyer on the table. "Hillerman's a major writer. His publishing house flies him around the country, east coast, west coast, most of the major stops in between. You know where Noah is going?"

"Albuquerque, Denver, and Salt Lake City."

"That's it?"

"Mysteries always sell better than non-fiction."

"You just made that up." Thumps looked at the Hillerman flyer again. "So, they fly Noah to three cities that make sense and one town that doesn't."

"They didn't fly Ridge anywhere."

"What?"

"He drove. Said he wanted to be close to the land, see the country."

"He drove to Chinook?"

"More people should drive around and see the country," said Archie. "I'm thinking of taking a horse trip back into the mountains. You want to come?"

"This about the Aztec gold?"

"I've got a hunch I know where it is."

"What about Noah Ridge?"

"After," said Archie, putting the poster back in the drawer. "We'll go find the gold after."

Thumps looked around the room at the rows of books all neatly arranged on shelves. He took a deep breath. Then he took another. There was something about standing in the middle of such an ostentatious display of order that made him feel calm, that made him feel at peace.

"I need a favour."

"Sure," said Archie. "How much do you need?"

Thumps shook his head. "I need you to make a couple of phone calls."

FREEWAY WAS WAITING for him when he got home, and the cat was not happy. As soon as he came in the front door, she crawled under the sofa and refused to come out. Even shaking the carton of kitty treats didn't dislodge her from her lair. So far today, Thumps mused, he hadn't been much of a hit with the females of at least two species. And there was still dinner with Dakota, still time enough to annoy someone else.

Thumps set the box that Moses had given him on the table. It was mostly copies of newspaper articles. As Thumps glanced at each piece, he could feel the whole story coming together around him. When he had been a cop on the Northern California coast, he had been able to do that with a crime scene, see things in relief as though he were standing in the middle of a diorama and could look in all directions at once.

Halfway through the box, he picked up the phone. The front desk put him through, and Dakota answered on the second ring.

"You're late."

Thumps froze.

"I'm kidding."

"I know. You still want dinner?"

"Yes," said Dakota softly. "I'd like that."

Me too, thought Thumps. "When?"

"Later?"

"Sure."

"I have to go over some stuff with Noah."

"Pick a time."

"And I had a late lunch."

"How's nine?"

"Nine's good," said Dakota.

Thumps hung up the phone and lay back on the sofa. Through the window, he could see a corner of the sky, and he tried to imagine that a warm front was on its way in.

"I forgive you." Thumps rattled the treats once more and dropped the box on the floor. When the cat got over her snit, she could damn well open it herself. Then he dragged the afghan off the back of the sofa and pulled it over his head.

IT WAS SEVEN-THIRTY when he woke. Evidently, Freeway had relented because the cat was curled up behind his legs, snoring away. Thumps hadn't planned on falling asleep, had the nagging feeling that he might have gone on sleeping right through his dinner date with Dakota and straight on until morning had not something wakened him.

What it was that had roused him he couldn't say. It might have been a noise, a car coming down the street perhaps or a siren in the distance. Or the sound of snow hitting the sidewalk. The more he tried to remember, the more the moment vanished, until he was left with only the vague impression of someone leaning over and whispering something in his ear.

The articles he had read were still in a neat pile on the table. Thank goodness for small mercies. He could have knocked the papers over with his foot, or Freeway could have decided to rub her cheek against the stack until she pushed everything onto the floor.

Thumps took the next article out of the box and settled back against the cushions. Freeway rolled over on her back, but she wasn't going anywhere. Most of the stories had been about Lucy's disappearance and about Noah Ridge and the parade of hot leads and dead ends that had marked the case from the beginning. But the story that Thumps held in his hands was not about Lucy. It was about a raid that the FBI had conducted on a house in Salt Lake City. The bureau, acting on a tip, had gone in looking for three AIM activists who were wanted in Colorado for robbery and attempted murder and who were believed to be hiding in the house.

And the boys from Washington had gone in with guns blazing.

Thumps didn't recognize the names—Clinton Buckhorn, Wilson Scout, and Wallace Begay—but he remembered the event. By the time the smoke cleared, Buckhorn, Scout, and Begay were dead, as were two FBI agents.

Thumps had forgotten about that particular mess and the conspiracy theories that had been floated about the raid and Lucy's disappearance.

Along with the photographs of Buckhorn, Scout, and Begay, there was a picture of Lucy and the agent in charge standing toe to toe, wagging fingers at each other. Lucy looked fierce in the picture, the way she had always looked. And dedicated. That was how Thumps remembered her. She never went looking for a fight the way Noah did, but she was always ready to go to battle if that's what it took.

Thumps was looking at the picture and marvelling how photographs allowed you to hang in time, neither moving forward nor moving back, when he heard the voice again. This time it was clear, and as he sat on the sofa listening to Freeway chase squirrels in her sleep, he could feel a cold chill move through his body.

And it wasn't the weather.

TWELVE

Thumps hadn't expected to find the sheriff's SUV parked in front of the Land Titles building. But there it was. Beth answered on the first ring.

"It's me."

"So it is," said Beth, sounding almost festive. "Downstairs."

Thumps tried to remember if he had ever been "downstairs" twice in one day. He didn't think so, and he wasn't particularly happy that that was about to change.

Beth was standing by the autopsy table talking to the sheriff and Special Agent Asah. Everyone looked happy, and if Thumps hadn't known better, he might have thought that he had happened on a party.

"I know why I'm here," said Hockney, looking right at Thumps. "And I know why Mr. Asah is here. Hell, I even know why Beth is here."

"I live here," said Beth.

"Mitchell Street," said Thumps.

"That's the password, all right," said the sheriff.

Special Agent Asah wasn't quite so congratulatory. "How in hell did you know that?"

"Oh, our Thumps is a clever duck," said Beth, who was having more fun than her line of work should allow.

Thumps shrugged. "Andy find the car?"

"He did," said Hockney. "And I'll bet you can tell me what he found."

Thumps paused for a moment, enjoying the short film that was playing in his head, starring Andy Hooper wandering the parking lot of the Holiday Inn in a snowstorm, shoving the key into frozen locks. "Street's wallet."

Hockney scratched his stomach. "You should have been a cop."

"You drive a long distance, the last thing you want

to do is sit on your wallet," said Thumps. "Where'd Andy find it?"

"Glovebox."

"Gas receipts?"

"On the passenger seat," said the sheriff. "One for a station in Missoula and one for a station in Whitefish."

Agent Asah flipped open his little black book. "Special Agent Mitchell Street, Omaha office."

"Nebraska?"

"Man was retired and living in Missoula," said Hockney. "But before Omaha and before he went fishing, he headed up the Salt Lake City field office. Same time as all that trouble." The sheriff paused in case Thumps wanted to add something. "Don't suppose you knew him."

"Nope."

"So, you didn't kill him?"

Hockney was good. He'd slipped that question in without breaking stride.

"So, he was murdered."

"Well," said Beth, "he could have shot himself."

"But we had a little vote," said the sheriff, "and murder won." Hockney took off his hat and checked the brim. "Want to guess what else we found?"

Thumps glanced at Beth to see if she was going to give him a hint. The sheriff slid the bag across the table. Inside was a book. *Ghost Dance: The Red Power Movement in America.* By Noah Ridge.

"Street was FBI," said Asah, "so now it's a federal matter."

"Man was retired," said the sheriff. "That makes him mine."

Asah folded his arms across his chest. "Bureau won't see it that way."

"This is fun." Beth looked over at Thumps. "Don't you think this is fun?"

Through the plastic, Thumps could see a piece of paper sticking out of the book.

"Go ahead," said the sheriff. "You like a good read, don't you?"

Thumps opened the book and took out a black-and-white Xerox of a certificate.

"That there's a bearer bond," said Hockney. "For fifty thousand dollars. Course, it's a copy, so you can't cash it."

But that wasn't what caught Thumps's attention. It

was the note someone had written across the face of the bond. "See you in Chinook, kemo-sabe."

"A real coincidence, don't you think?" said Hockney. "First the postcard and now this. Don't suppose you know who this kemo-sabe is?"

"I'm going to question Ridge," said Asah. "Any objections?"

"Got nothing to link Mr. Street to Mr. Ridge," said Hockney.

Thumps held the Xerox up to the light. "They were in Salt Lake together."

"Yes, they were," said Asah. "Street didn't come here for the food. We got the book and the note and one dead FBI agent."

Right, Thumps thought to himself, the only things missing are a motive and a weapon, fingerprints, a couple of witnesses, and a signed confession.

"That might get you fed in Washington or New York City," said the sheriff, "but it won't even buy you a cup of coffee around here."

Asah might be young, but he wasn't that young, and Thumps could see that the man wasn't about to turn a murder investigation of a federal agent, retired or not, over to a hick sheriff, no offence, in a hick town.

"Okay," said Asah, trying to be friendly, "what would you do?"

Hockney put a beefy hand on Thumps's shoulder, and for an instant, Thumps wondered if this was how his Volvo felt when Cooley leaned on the car. "Thumps here has a date with Mr. Ridge's executive secretary. Isn't that right?"

Thumps stiffened. How in the hell did the sheriff know that?

"They're old friends," Hockney explained to Asah. "Got a lot of catching up to do. Isn't that right?"

So, it had been a guess. And a damn good one.

"That right?" said Asah.

"I'm hungry," said Beth. "Anyone want to take me to dinner?"

"I was thinking maybe Thumps could mention our friend here."

"And see what happens?"

"Couldn't hurt," said the sheriff, laying the bond on the table. "Maybe Ms. Miles knows what the hell this is supposed to be."

"Someone's idea of a joke," said Asah. "You can get shit like this at any novelty store."

"Let me make sure I understand the plan," said

Thumps. "After the waiter lights our candle and we look at the menus, you want me to drop a hint that there's a dead ex-FBI agent at the morgue whom the police think Noah killed. Is that about it?"

"Course, we could just haul them both in," said the sheriff.

"I like that," said Asah.

The sheriff was bluffing. Thumps wasn't so sure about Asah.

"Where you going to take her?" said the sheriff. "In case we have to find you."

"One of you paying for the meal?" said Thumps.

"Keep the receipt," said Hockney. "You never know what the FBI might do for you."

THUMPS STOOD ON the street and let the wind and the cold blow the smell of the morgue away. So, Noah Ridge the activist comes to town, and Mitchell Street the FBI agent comes to town. All at the same time. And Street winds up dead in a motel room. Thumps had thought of mentioning Lucy's brother to Hockney, and he wondered when Grover Many

Horses was going to arrive on stage, hot from hell with Atea by his side, to quote Shakespeare. Then there was Dakota Miles, and Thumps himself, for that matter. All they needed was Lucy Kettle's ghost prowling the parapets and they had the makings of a first-rate piece of Jacobean drama.

And that was before they got to the postcard. And the bond.

And the note.

Not that any of it made much sense. After all these years, why would Mitchell Street give a damn about Noah Ridge? Why would he buy a copy of Ridge's book and drive all the way from Missoula to Chinook? To go to Ridge's reading? Hardly. And why had Noah come to Chinook in the first place?

Thumps pulled his jacket tight around himself. The weather and the stench had fought each other to a draw, leaving Thumps cold and musty. Time for a long, hot shower and a change of clothes. Time for a firm resolution to let the sheriff and Special Agent Spencer Asah do their jobs. Without his help. Dakota Miles might well have some of the answers to some of the questions, and then again she might not. But tonight all Thumps wanted was a little companionship and a good meal.

The sheriff, on the other hand, was not going to have either. Hockney had been concerned about winding up with a dead activist. Instead, he had wound up with a dead FBI agent. And it was no contest as to which was worse. Mitchell Street might have been retired, but the bureau was not going to split hairs. Active agents and retired agents were all the same to Washington. And when one died, the bureau would want to know why. Thumps guessed that Asah had already called someone and that any time soon the sheriff was going to be knee-deep in suits.

Thumps was halfway down the street before he realized he couldn't see his car, and for one annoying moment, he imagined that someone had stolen the Volvo. But no, there it was, huddled in behind Hockney's SUV, trying to stay warm.

Thumps slid in behind the wheel, leaned over, and patted the dashboard. If anything, the inside of the car was colder than the outside.

"Let's go home."

The car didn't groan or complain as it normally did.

It also didn't start. In fact, it didn't even try to start. Thumps turned the key again. Nothing. Not even a hint that the spark plugs and the cylinders were talking to each other.

"Come on."

Nothing. Nothing. Nothing.

Thumps pumped the accelerator and tried again. Nothing. Just to irritate himself, he tried turning on the lights. Nothing. Hadn't he bought a new battery two years ago? Or was it three? Or four?

Not that it mattered.

As he walked down the street, heading home, he wondered if the battery had committed suicide or if the car had killed it on purpose. Which for a moment brought him back to Mitchell Street lying dead on a motel floor. But that was, as the song said, someone else's misfortune and none of his own.

THIRTEEN

Robert Frost might have enjoyed the woods on a snowy evening, but that was because he didn't have to walk through them. He had a sleigh. And all sorts of warm things piled around him. Neither had Frost written the poem on the coldest evening of the year, while riding in said sleigh. He had most likely been indoors, probably in front of a crackling fire or under an arbour in the heart of summer.

He certainly didn't have to contend with a surly car and a dead battery.

By the time Thumps arrived home, defrosted himself under the shower, and got dressed, he was late.

Part of his tardiness was the walk, and part of it was trying to decide on clothes. Not that he had many, but limited options didn't make the decisions any easier. He was torn between cowboy casual and dress casual, and finally decided on combining the two, leaving the house in a pair of jeans, a black-and-grey sports shirt with tiny yellow highlights, and a black blazer.

He had bought the shirt and jacket at Harry Rosen, an upscale men's store in Toronto on Bloor Street. Thumps had a weakness for elegance, and Rosen had everything for the folks who could afford the best: Armani, Canali, Brioni, Kiton. You could have your suits and shirts and even your ties custom-made or, as they said at Rosen, "bespoke," which for some reason reminded Thumps of "betrothed." And while you contemplated your purchases, you could sit at a coffee bar in the middle of the store on the second floor and have an espresso or a cappuccino or a glass of Perrier.

Free.

Harry Rosen was not the kind of place that Thumps could afford to visit, but with the Canadian dollar rapidly losing ground at that time to its U.S. cousin, he was delighted to discover that he had, in essence, walked into a half-price sale.

Part of the charm of the store was the sales staff. They seemed to appear when you had a question and disappear when you just wanted to look. Thumps wondered if they had been trained to do that or if they had been hired because they could. And all the customers, it seemed, had their own personal sales-person. Thumps wound up with a young man named John, who gave him a tour of the store, made him a cappuccino, and advised him on the essentials of a wardrobe. Not that Thumps had one, but he played along, partly because he was embarrassed about his knowledge of clothes and partly because he was hav-ing such a good time.

Most of the salespeople at Rosen were men, but there were a few women. Thumps assumed that they were there to help the wives of successful men who were too intimidated or too lazy to shop for them-selves, but he was wrong. As he stood in the middle of a three-way mirror contemplating an Ermenegildo Zegna sports shirt and an Arnold Brant cashmere blazer, trying to see his front and his butt at the same time, a tall, striking blonde with long, hard legs and a firm body—what the fashion folks would call "statuesque"—came by and made a low sound that was somewhere between a growl and a sigh.

"That was Rhonda," John told him as the woman floated down the escalator. "She likes the outfit."

As he waited for John to write up the sale and hoped that Rhonda would pass by again, he told himself that he would need such an outfit for those occasions when he was exhibiting his photographs around the world. That hadn't quite happened yet, but dinner with Dakota Miles was as good an excuse as any to dress up and practise pretending that he was a successful artist.

As he trudged over to the Tucker, Thumps was sorry that he hadn't bought the navy wool overcoat that he had seen at Rosen. His red windbreaker had all the elegance of a football jersey, and because of the weather and a car that had decided to play dead, he had had to wear his workboots, which made him feel more like a fly fisherman in waders just come off the river than a man about town. His dress shoes were stuffed in the pockets of the jacket, and the plan was to dump the boots and the jacket somewhere long before anyone saw him.

Sometimes plans don't work out.

Thumps would have preferred that the lobby of the Tucker be deserted. He was sure there was a coat check somewhere that would be happy to take his jacket and boots, and if he could find it quickly, so much the better.

"Thumps!"

Archie was standing in the middle of the lobby. Along with Helen Hoy, Chinook's perennial mayor; Vernon Rockland, who owned Shadow Ranch, a resort complex in the foothills just west of town that catered to the rich and famous; Beverly Nickerson, the president of Chinook Community College; and Milo Tashkent, who owned the town's only daily newspaper, the *Chinook Tribune*.

And Noah Ridge.

Archie trotted over and dragged Thumps back to the group. Thumps could feel the windbreaker get tighter and brighter, could feel the mud and snow slough off his boots onto the marble floor as he went.

"Have you met Mr. Ridge?"

Noah smiled at him, and Thumps smiled back. But they didn't shake hands.

"Thumps and I are old friends," said Noah.

Archie was on Thumps in a flash. "You don't tell me this?"

"It's a long story."

"We're having dinner out at the ranch," said Rockland. "Informal thing. You're welcome to join us."

Not that anyone looked particularly informal. Archie was wearing his suit. The mayor was dressed in a black shift that looked to be silk and a fitted silver grey jacket. Nickerson had on a dark red and green batik dress that reminded Thumps of Christmas, and Tashkent was going to dinner in a brown sports jacket and olive slacks.

Even Noah was dressed for the occasion, all in black.

"Thanks," said Thumps, opening his jacket just a little so everyone could get a glimpse of the blazer, "but I have some work to do."

"Never thought of dinner with Dakota as work," said Noah.

So, Noah knew. No reason he shouldn't. It wasn't

supposed to be a secret. But for some reason, Thumps didn't like it.

"Did you hear about the body at the Holiday Inn?" said Archie. "Terrible."

"Be a story in tomorrow's paper," said Tashkent. "I'm talking with the sheriff in the morning."

And sometimes plans worked out in unexpected ways. No sense using Dakota as the messenger, thought Thumps. Now was as good a time as any.

"Yeah," said Thumps, "guy's name was Mitchell Street. Looked like a suicide at first."

"But?" said Tashkent, who was suddenly very interested.

"Murder," said Thumps. "They're pretty sure it was murder."

If Noah recognized the name, he was hiding it well. Thumps watched his face as he let the details slip. But he didn't mention that Street was a former FBI agent or that the dead man had had a copy of Ridge's book with him. He'd leave those matters for the sheriff to share with Tashkent in the morning. If he wanted to.

"Sounds exciting," said Noah. "But I'm hungry."

"The cars are out front," said Rockland. "We can leave any time."

"Okay, we got to go." Archie grabbed Thumps's sleeve. "But tomorrow we do the photographs, right?"

"Any time," said Thumps as he watched Noah and Archie and the official entourage head for the doors. "Any time at all."

THE HOTEL WAS only too happy to take Thumps's jacket and boots. Especially since Mr. DreadfulWater and his guest were going to be eating in the Mother Lode. Thumps hadn't planned on eating at the Tucker, but with Noah dining at Shadow Ranch and no car, the choices were limited. He had never eaten at the Tucker before, and after he and Dakota had been seated and Thumps had glanced at the menu, he knew he probably wouldn't eat there again.

You can tell a great deal about a restaurant by the menu. Restaurants whose menus listed their dishes in French or Italian first with English subtitles and that used fine parchment inserts on which the offerings had been printed in raised letters by an offset press generally made up for such expenses in the price of the meals. The other trick, Thumps remembered, was to look at the appetizers. Triple the price of the appetizers and you'll have a fair idea of what the entrees will cost.

"Are you trying to impress me?"

It wasn't a growl and it wasn't a sigh. Thumps wasn't even sure that it was a compliment.

"I got it at Harry Rosen. In Toronto."

"I meant the restaurant."

"My car broke down."

Dakota hadn't seemed in a happy mood when Thumps had arrived at her room. Now, here she was sitting across from him in a swanky restaurant, laughing.

"Really, it did."

"I believe you," said Dakota. "It's just what a girl wants to hear."

Their waiter for the evening was Stephen, who had a French accent and was from Montreal.

"Some bread," he said, placing the basket in the middle of the table. "May I start madam off with a cocktail?"

"No," said Dakota, "just water."

"Evian, Perrier, or Pellegrino?"

"Tap," said Dakota.

"We also have Aberfoyle Springs water from Canada."

"Plain water," said Dakota, "no ice."

Thumps had thought about ordering a soft drink, until he turned the menu over and discovered that the back was taken up with a succinct and sanitized history of the Tucker that featured the story of the squirrels and the fire but made no mention of the hospital and the skating rink. Five dollars, Thumps decided. Soft drinks here would cost at least five dollars.

"Is water okay with you?"

"Perfect," said Thumps. "But have what you want. My treat."

"This a date?"

"No." Thumps tried to think of something more neutral. "It's a reunion."

"I like that," said Dakota. "So, we'll go Dutch."

Stephen wasn't gone long. "Can I answer any questions about the menu?"

"I'll have the steak," said Dakota. "Medium rare. Peppercorn gravy."

"Me too," said Thumps.

"And an appetizer for madam?"

"Just the steak."

Stephen waited for a moment, in case Dakota had misunderstood the question. "We have a superb foie gras."

"Steak."

That was the great thing about expensive restaurants. The service staff were trained to ask questions in a way that allowed only one right answer. So you wouldn't make a mistake and embarrass yourself.

"May I suggest a wine for your meal?"

Dakota looked at Thumps.

"We have an excellent Merlot."

"I think the water will do us," said Thumps. He could see from the expression on Stephen's face that this was another wrong answer.

"So," said Dakota as she watched Stephen retreat to the kitchen, "what would your girlfriend have ordered?"

Thumps felt the blood rush to his face. He didn't much like being caught off guard like that. "I don't really have a girlfriend."

"Normally, I would have ordered the pasta because it's the cheapest thing on the menu."

Thumps could feel a smile forming. Claire would have ordered the pasta too. And for the same reason.

"But tonight's a celebration, isn't it?" Dakota held her glass up. "To the reunion."

"To the reunion."

"You want to ask me now or later?"

Thumps looked around quickly, hoping that Stephen was on his way over with another rhetorical question.

"You didn't invite me to dinner just so I'd have sex with you, did you?"

There were some questions for which there were no right answers.

"Good," said Dakota. "Let's get the questions out of the way, so we can enjoy our evening."

The Dakota Miles that Thumps remembered from Salt Lake City had been quiet, deferential. The woman sitting across the table from him was anything but that, and Thumps wasn't sure whether he liked the new version or missed the old one. Not that it mattered. Whatever Dakota had been in the past was in the past.

"How about I ask the questions," said Dakota, "and you can answer them."

"Dakota . . ."

"Come on. It'll be fun."

Not that Dakota was having much fun at all. Now he could hear it clearly. Sorrow. In her voice. And he could see it in her eyes.

"First question. Why did I come back?"

"You already answered that one."

"Did I?"

"You came back for the movement."

"Noah should have left me in that tub." Dakota broke a dinner roll in half. "I guess I've never really got over Lucy. How about you?"

"Didn't know her very well."

"She was a warrior. Liked to set men straight. Especially Noah." Dakota poked at the butter with her knife. "She was like a sister. When she died, I wanted to die too."

Thumps dove into his memory and came up empty. "I thought she disappeared."

"You didn't believe that witness protection program crap Noah was spreading around, did you?"

Dakota shook her head. "All her things were still in her house. That leather jacket she wore everywhere was in the closet. She wouldn't have left it behind."

"But the clothes weren't the issue."

"No." Dakota closed her eyes. "Okay, second question. What does an executive assistant do?"

"I wasn't going to ask that."

"First, she doesn't fuck the boss."

Dakota began picking at the skin at the side of her fingers, pulling off little strips nearest the nail. It was an old habit. Thumps had seen her work on her fingers before, especially when she was under stress, but it still made his scalp crawl.

"Dakota . . ."

"And the boss doesn't fuck her."

"Look, you want to go someplace else?"

"Like my room?"

Where the anger had come from, Thumps didn't know, but it carried across the table and filled the room.

"Sorry." Dakota leaned back in the chair. "I didn't mean that."

"It's okay."

"Some reunion, eh?"

"I hear the steaks are good."

"I run Noah's life. I run RPM. That's what I do. Noah's the poster."

"So, why do you need Noah at all?"

"She would have called me," said Dakota. "She would have let me know she was all right."

Out of the corner of his eye, Thumps could see Stephen coming to the rescue, steaks in hand. "Pepper," he said, leaning across the table. "Does madam want some fresh ground pepper?"

Dakota didn't laugh, but she did smile, and for a moment, Thumps imagined that she had been able to chase away the sorrow and the anger.

"I want to go home," she said, taking a breath and letting it out. "I'd like you to take me home."

THEY DIDN'T TALK in the elevator or as they walked down the hallway to Dakota's room. When they got there, Dakota opened the door and turned back to Thumps.

"I've got something for you." Dakota slipped into

the room and came out with a copy of Noah's book. "He autographed it."

Thumps opened the book. On the title page, Noah had written, *May the Red Power Movement open your conscience to a new dawn.*

"You want to come in for a while?"

"Sure," he said. "But I think I've done enough damage for one evening."

Dakota ran her hand across his lapel. "Nice jacket."

"It's cashmere."

"That's what I like about you, DreadfulWater."

"My clothes?"

"That you always know the right answers."

THUMPS SAT IN THE LOBBY of the Tucker and put on his boots and his windbreaker. He had wanted to say yes to Dakota's invitation. Yes to staying a while. Yes to coffee. Yes to whatever. Yes, yes, yes. After all these years, after all she had been through, Dakota was still vulnerable. And for reasons that he did not want to dwell on, Thumps found this attractive. But he had had enough experience with anger and sorrow to know that no good could come from taking advantage of someone's pain.

Dakota had been right. He had wanted to ask questions. Not the ones she had asked. Maybe tomorrow he'd ask them. Maybe tomorrow he'd get answers. But not tonight. With the bright stars high in a black sky, Thumps tried to pretend that he was wearing Asah's parka as he began the long walk home.

FOURTEEN

reeway had a bad night. She tossed and turned, and when she got tired of that, she practised pressing her claws against Thumps's thighs or trying to lick his calves raw. By the time the winter sun rolled up on the horizon, he was exhausted and the cat, who had worked very hard at keeping both of them awake, was sound asleep.

He was sitting in the kitchen, trying to muster the strength to make coffee, when someone began banging on the door. Thumps looked out the window. It had snowed during the night, and the world was white.

Maybe it was Santa at the door, unable to find the chimney, needing to use the bathroom.

In fact, Thumps would have preferred Santa.

"Good, you're awake." Hockney had the right shape, but he didn't have jolly old Saint Nick's general disposition. "You look like hell."

"The cat had a bad night."

"You sleep with animals?"

"Beats sleeping alone."

"Not my problem," said the sheriff. "Come on."

Thumps vaguely remembered agreeing to be a sort of temporary deputy for the sheriff and the sheriff agreeing to pay him for the effort.

"You're going to have to do better than that."

"It's Noah Ridge."

Hockney's face wasn't giving anything away.

"Is he dead?"

"No."

"Then I'm going back to bed."

"He's in the hospital."

Thumps slept most of the way to Chinook General. And he would have been perfectly happy to go on sleeping had not the sheriff shaken him awake.

"You better shoot that cat," said the sheriff as they walked into the main lobby. "Or get a dog."

"Dogs are just as bad."

"Not if you don't let them in bed with you."

The nurse at the front desk was much too bright and cheery. Her voice had all the qualities of a robin singing on your windowsill. Noah Ridge was in the emergency room.

"Follow the red line," she chirped. "He's in the second cubicle with his bodyguard."

Hockney's head turned slowly from the nurse to Thumps and then back again. "His what?"

The sheriff's tone of voice slid off the nurse's back like water off a duck. "His bodyguard," she said as though bodyguards were common accessories for emergency room patients.

"Great," growled Hockney.

For some reason, Thumps had assumed that the nurse had mistaken Spencer Asah for a bodyguard. An easy-enough mistake to make, seeing how Asah dressed. But when they got to the emergency room, Thumps discovered he was wrong.

"Hi, Thumps."

"Hi, Cooley."

"Hi, sheriff."

"Noah Ridge," said the sheriff. Simple and blunt.

"Do you have an appointment?"

Thumps half-expected that the sheriff was either going to laugh or pull out his gun and shoot Cooley. He did neither.

"Thumps," said Hockney.

"Yeah, sheriff?"

"You know what's going on?"

"Cooley has his own security company." Thumps tried to sound matter-of-fact.

"Small Elk Security," said Cooley.

The sheriff turned back to Cooley. "Noah Ridge hired you to protect him?"

"Not exactly," said Cooley.

Hockney waited for the rest of the answer, but Thumps knew that waiting wasn't going to do any good. Getting any kind of elaboration out of Cooley required that you ask the right questions.

Thumps backed up and started at the beginning. "Noah didn't ask you to protect him?"

"Nope."

"And he doesn't know that he is now under the protection of Small Elk Security?"

"Not yet."

"So, currently your services are . . . free?"

Cooley hooked his fingers in his belt and pulled his pants up. "It's one of those complimentary things."

"But if he likes your work, he may endorse the company or even hire you officially."

"Those are good ideas," said Cooley. "Maybe you could mention them when you see him."

"We'd like to see him now," said the sheriff.

"Someone tried to kill him this morning," said Cooley. "You can't be too careful."

NOAH RIDGE WAS lying on the examining table. One eye had been blackened and his lip was cut.

"Looks like you found a little trouble," said Hockney.

"Tough town you got here, sheriff," said Noah. He sounded okay, but Thumps could see that the effort to talk was painful.

"You know what happened?"

"I was jogging. Somebody took me from behind."

"Did you see who it was?"

Noah tried rolling over on one side but gave up immediately. "Just a glimpse."

"Would you recognize him again?"

"No," said Noah. "It happened too fast. One minute I was running, the next minute I was on the ground."

There were more bruises on Noah's chest and along his ribs.

"So, you're out running and someone sneaks up behind you and beats you up?"

"That's about it."

"But you didn't see who it was?"

"Sorry," said Noah.

"They take anything?" Hockney was just going through the motions.

"Didn't have anything to take."

"And this happened where?"

"North side of the river. Near the bridge."

Noah's injuries were real enough, though Thumps had seen worse. Lots of times. He debated telling the sheriff about Grover Many Horses, but there was nothing to suggest that Grover had anything to do with the attack. Then again, this might be the very thing that Grover would do.

"I'll look into it," said the sheriff. "In the meantime, if I were you, I'd stay close to home."

Noah forced his lips into a smile. "Is 'stay close to home' the same as 'don't leave town'?"

"Yeah," said the sheriff, shutting his notebook, "it is."

Behind him, Thumps could hear the faint strains of annoyed voices in the hallway, and he guessed that Cooley was performing his duties with some enthusiasm.

"When you're feeling better," said Hockney, "you and I need to have a little talk."

"Told you everything I know."

"Maybe so," said the sheriff. "But sometimes trauma affects the memory. Always good to double-check."

The voices in the hallway were becoming more insistent. Thumps could hear Spencer Asah explaining that he was an FBI agent and Milo Tashkent beginning a lecture on freedom of the press.

"You mind if I stick around?"

Hockney looked at Thumps. "Going to catch up on old times?"

"Something like that."

"Just remember who's paying you."

Hockney lumbered out into the hallway. The sheriff wasn't as large or as strong as Cooley, but Duke's low tolerance for nonsense gave him the edge.

"They're going to try to hang this on me, you know." Noah slowly sat up. "You see my pants?"

"You leaving?"

"Sure as hell not going to spend the rest of the day in here." Noah held on to the side of the table and waited for the pain to subside. "I didn't kill him."

"Who?"

"You been hanging around with that hick sheriff too long." Noah straightened up, keeping his elbow against his side. "Where's my shirt?"

"Can't blame him. Too much of a coincidence," said Thumps, "you and Mitchell Street showing up in the same town."

"It's a free country."

"Even the hick sheriff isn't going to buy that one."

"I haven't seen Street since Salt Lake City."

"Lucy Kettle?"

"Before that, even." Noah leaned back. "Street was

in charge of the Salt Lake City field office. He'd been coming at me for years. When Lucy disappeared, he turned the investigation into a holy war."

"He thought you killed her?"

"Why not? He figured I had found out that Lucy was an FBI mole."

"Was she?"

"Help me on with my shirt."

Thumps had to hold the sweatshirt while Noah eased himself into it. The bruises looked worse up close.

"What about Lucy?"

"Yeah." Noah took slow, deep breaths to ease the pain. "She was working for the FBI."

There was regret in Noah's voice now, and for a moment Thumps almost believed him.

"It's in my book," said Noah. "If you want to know what happened to Lucy, ask the FBI."

COOLEY WAS STANDING GUARD in the hall, keeping Asah and Tashkent at bay.

"So, can I go in now?" said Asah.

"You bet," said Cooley.

"What about me?" said Tashkent. "I'm press."

"Law enforcement personnel," said Cooley.

Thumps patted Cooley's shoulder and had that mild stinging sensation that you get from slapping stone. "You're doing a great job."

"Yeah," said Cooley. "Sheriff said pretty much the same thing."

Asah pulled Thumps off to one side. "He tell you anything?"

"He thinks the FBI had something to do with Lucy Kettle's disappearance." Thumps watched Asah's face to see if he had been filled in on Salt Lake City. Evidently he had.

"Did he say who beat him up?"

"Says he didn't see who did it."

"Bullshit."

Yes, Thumps thought to himself, it was. "You going to arrest him?"

"If someone's getting arrested," said Tashkent, who had pushed himself up against Cooley, "I want to know about it."

The sun was bright and the air was still. Thumps watched his breath flow out of his mouth and freeze in mid-air. Asah wasn't going to arrest Noah just yet. Maybe later, but not now. Or maybe not at all. So far as Thumps could see, this case, if you could call it that, was a mess. Too many questions. Too few answers.

And then there was Dakota After all these years, the sorrow was still as strong as the day he put her on the train to Albuquerque. Mitchell Street, Noah Ridge, Dakota Miles, Grover Many Horses. And Lucy Kettle. Somehow or other, everything seemed to lead back to Lucy.

Maybe that's where the answers lay, not in the present but in the past.

FIFTEEN

Archie was where Thumps figured Archie would be. Sitting at the counter in Al's, complaining about North American coffee.

"Thumps!"

"Hi, Archie."

"Did you hear the news?"

"I've already been to the hospital."

"Did you get any pictures?" Archie dragged his spoon through the coffee. "You know, she never makes it strong enough."

Thumps wondered if Archie had ever attempted the sheriff's coffee.

"You think she does this just to annoy me?"

"Did you get a chance to make those calls?"

"Sure. I made the calls. That's the nice thing about living out here."

Thumps was too tired to ask.

"Everything's later back east. You can call someone at six o'clock in the morning and it's really nine o'clock in New York. So you don't have to wait to get your day started."

"Archie . . ."

Archie took a sip of his coffee and made a face. "So, I called the publishing house and guess what?"

Al came out of the backroom with the coffee pot and set it down in front of Thumps. "You don't look any better."

"My cat kept me awake."

"That's the nice thing about animals and kids," said Al as she poured coffee into a cup. "You can blame them for all sorts of things."

"So, I called the publishing house," said Archie, "and guess what?"

"You still complaining about my coffee?"

"Your coffee's fine," said Archie. "It's just not thick enough. You got to use more beans."

Al pointed the coffee pot at Archie and looked at

Thumps. "You know, I only let him stay because he's your friend."

"Now the food," said Archie quickly, "your food is good enough to be Greek."

Al considered this for a moment and then filled Archie's cup. "You two want breakfast?"

"I do," said Thumps.

"I'm fine," said Archie.

"You know he's going to eat part of your breakfast," said Al.

"Yeah," said Thumps, resting his head in his hands, "I know."

Al strolled over to the grill and began to work her magic. Having breakfast made for you was one of life's great pleasures. You woke up, unable to care for yourself, you sat down at a table, and someone brought you food. Warm, delicious food. Thumps suspected that having someone feed you might just be better than sex.

"So, I called the publishing house," said Archie for the third time, "and guess what?"

"What?"

"They were surprised."

"About what?"

"That Ridge is on tour."

Thumps could feel the hint of adrenalin creep into his system. "They didn't know about the tour?"

"Nope."

"You got the right publishing house?"

"Please," said Archie, rolling his eyes. "Books and publishing houses I know."

"That doesn't make any sense."

"Maybe they want to keep it a secret."

Thumps didn't know the industry as well as Archie, but he was quite sure that a publishing house would not keep a book tour secret. In fact, Thumps suspected that the literary folk in New York would go out of their way to tell anyone who would listen about one of their tours.

"That doesn't make much sense."

"Nope," said Archie, "it doesn't."

Al wandered over from the grill and slid the plate in front of Thumps. "I put an extra sausage on for your friend."

"Thanks."

"Tell him to make his own coffee, if he doesn't like mine."

Thumps sat at the counter and put the pieces in place. He couldn't see the overall shape of the puzzle yet, but one of the corners was slowly coming into focus.

Archie was busy raiding Thumps's plate. "You think he's going to be able to do the reading tonight?"

"Probably."

"'Cause he wasn't feeling too good last night."

"Last night?"

"Some kind of stomach problem."

"He didn't go to Shadow Ranch?"

"Sure, he went," said Archie. "But he didn't eat."

"He came back to town?"

"Everyone was disappointed." Archie helped himself to a piece of toast. "But you know what? He was lucky. The food wasn't that good."

Actually, so far as Thumps could see, Noah wasn't having much luck at all. Someone threatens to kill him. He gets assaulted on a morning jog. And he winds up a suspect in a murder case.

"Kind of an exciting life." Archie put a thick layer of jam on the toast.

Thumps had eaten at Shadow Ranch. Getting sick

before dinner might have been the only silver lining in Noah's short stay in Chinook.

"Could almost make a movie out of it."

Yes, thought Thumps, you almost could.

Archie licked his fingers and finished his coffee. "Tonight," he said, patting Thumps on the back. "Tonight, wear something nice."

CHINOOK HAD A great many garages, but if you knew enough to eat at Al's, you knew enough to take your car to Chinook Motors and Moe Alvarez. Moe had worked on the Volvo countless times, knew the car better than Thumps did, and, to the man's credit, had never once suggested that Thumps get rid of it and buy something else. And why should he? The car was a mechanic's gold mine. On more than one occasion, Thumps thought it might be cheaper just to pay Moe a monthly fee for service and be done with it.

"Let me guess," said Moe as soon as he saw Thumps. "It won't start."

"I was thinking that it might be the battery."

"We changed the battery last year."

"So, it's not the battery?"

"Could be," said Moe. "But now that the sun is shining, I'd try to start it again."

"And if it starts?"

"Then," said Moe, "it's not the battery."

The Volvo was waiting for him where he left it. In front of the old Land Titles building. There was a parking ticket frozen to the windshield. The sheriff could take care of this one, thought Thumps, as he peeled the paper away from the glass. If he was a deputy, then it stood to reason that the Volvo, appearances aside, was an official police car.

As Thumps put the key in the ignition, he wasn't sure what he was hoping would happen. The car was way past its prime. A new car or at least a good used car might make him feel better about himself. He had read somewhere that middle-aged men liked to buy fast cars as a way of recapturing their youth. Thumps supposed he was willing to put up with middle age, if he could have a vehicle that was simply dependable and didn't complain every time the temperature dropped below freezing.

The engine turned over the first time. If the car had a sense of humour, Thumps didn't share it.

***

When Thumps got to the Tucker, he didn't call from the lobby. He went straight to Dakota's room.

"Thumps."

Dakota didn't seem surprised to see him, but Thumps hoped that she hadn't been expecting him. He had questions and wanted straight answers. Not like last night when she had been able to anticipate what he was going to ask, when she had been able to control the conversation.

"Come on in." Dakota turned and walked back into the room. "You want anything to drink?"

Thumps tried to think of an easy way to begin. "I saw Noah at the hospital."

"He said you stopped by."

"We talked about Salt Lake."

"Ah," said Dakota, her voice holding the line between sarcasm and sadness, "the good old days."

"He said that Lucy was a mole working for the FBI."

"Did he?" Now there was only sorrow in her voice. "I suppose your next question is going to be about Mitchell Street."

"Someone shot him."

"That's what Noah said." Dakota walked to the window. The winter sun was bright and strong, and it flooded the room with light and the illusion of heat. "You know what I want to do? I want to go for a walk. I want to go for a walk by a river."

"We should talk."

"Sure," said Dakota, turning back to Thumps, "let's walk and talk."

Thumps would have preferred talking to Dakota in her room or in the lobby of the hotel or in a restaurant. Someplace where you couldn't see your breath. A few years back, Thumps had tried his hand at some winter photography. He had spent several days walking the river, looking for just the right image, but the grim spectre of cold trees and frozen water had depressed him more than he had expected, and he went home without ever taking a shot.

There was a sharp wind waiting for them when they came out of the hotel. Thumps pulled his head down into the collar of the jacket and shoved his hands into his pockets.

"That's better," said Dakota. "The hotel gets stuffy."

"I like stuffy."

"Come on," she said. "I want to see your world."

It's not my world, Thumps thought to himself as they headed for the river bottom. If it was my world, it would have forced-air heating.

In Thumps's experience, cold weather generally limited movement and conversations. But the temperature didn't bother Dakota. Once outside, she seemed to come alive.

"Did you know my mother was a doctor? My father was an artist. Both very successful. 'Credits to their race' was how people liked to describe them. My two younger brothers are successful. One's a lawyer, and one teaches university."

"Great."

"And then there's me."

There were patches of snow under the evergreens, but the path along the river was open. As he walked along, Thumps could feel his nose turning red and his toes turning blue.

"They wanted me to be an artist. Like my father. Instead I became . . ."

"An activist?"

Dakota turned and smiled. "That's not what my mother called it."

No, thought Thumps, mothers would want other things for their daughters. "They disown you?"

"God, no," said Dakota. "They loved me. They just wanted me to be more like them."

"That's parents."

Dakota stopped and looked at the river. "I wanted to be more like Lucy."

There it was. The signal to begin the questions. Only now, Thumps wasn't at all sure he wanted any part of this.

"Noah didn't kill Street."

"Sheriff and the FBI aren't so sure about that."

"And Lucy wasn't a mole."

Thumps hoped Dakota would start walking again.

"But there was an informant. Do you know who Massasoit was?"

"The Indian who helped the early English settlements in New England."

"At first we thought the FBI and the Salt Lake police were just getting lucky," said Dakota, "but after a while, it was pretty clear that someone was tipping them off to our plans."

"Massasoit."

"Yeah. If we were going to go to Temple Square to

protest the Mormon Placement Program, the police would be waiting for us. If we arranged a secret strategy meeting with AIM, the police would come in and break it up."

"Any idea who Massasoit was?"

"No. That was the frustrating part. But Noah figured that it had to be someone high up in RPM or AIM. Especially after Clinton Buckhorn."

At first the name didn't register. And then Thumps remembered. "The raid in Salt Lake."

"Buckhorn and two other guys kidnapped the CEO of Morgan Energy and broke into corporate headquarters." Dakota bent down and picked up a stone. "They made it as far as Salt Lake. Only a few people knew where Buckhorn was hiding."

"At his cousin's house. Reuben Justice."

"One of the guys was wounded. Reuben tried to help him, but he was in a bad way."

"Who knew?" Thumps tried to remember the events. "Noah and Lucy?"

"Probably."

"Did you know?"

"No. I wasn't part of the inner circle. I was a . . . my

mother called me a groupie once."

"That's just mothers."

"She wasn't completely wrong. I had this romantic idea of what the movement was going to accomplish."

"Everybody had the same idea."

"Anyway, someone tipped the FBI."

"And they raided Justice's house."

"Buckhorn and the other two guys were killed." Dakota picked up another stone. "So were a couple of FBI agents."

"And Lucy?"

"Noah figured that the FBI pulled her and put her in one of those witness protection programs."

Thumps could see the logic, even if it didn't make any sense. "If Lucy was Massasoit, and she tipped the FBI, then they should have known what they were walking into."

"I guess."

"Which means that either the FBI botched the raid, or Massasoit set them up."

"After the raid, Lucy disappeared. And so did Massasoit."

"Which made it look as though Lucy was the

informant." Thumps knew the answer to the next question, but he asked it anyway. "But you didn't believe it?"

"I knew her," said Dakota simply and without emotion. "She wouldn't have done that."

The wind had picked up. Dakota stepped into him, almost touching.

"We should go back."

Thumps wanted to hold Dakota, as he had when he took her to the train all those years ago. It had seemed a comfort for her at the time. Perhaps it would be a comfort for her now.

"Why do you think Mitchell Street came to Chinook?"

"I don't know." Dakota took another step forward and brushed Thumps's cheek with her scarf. "Noah thinks it was Street who sent the death threat."

Thumps took his hands out of his pockets and put his arms around Dakota. "I'm cold."

Dakota settled in against him and laid her face against his. "Are you going to try to save me again?"

"From what?"

"From Noah." Dakota smiled. "From myself."

"You could walk away," said Thumps. "Start over.

Take up art, the way your folks wanted."

"I've come too far." Dakota looked back at the low skyline of the town in the distance. "I wouldn't know how to get back."

"What are you doing after the reading?"

"This another date?"

"If you like."

The wind and the cold were behind them as they walked back to town. Neither of them spoke, as though they had run out of things to say. But Thumps had more questions, some he had intended to ask, some that had appeared on their own. For now, they could wait. If Street had meant to kill Noah, then Noah was safe, and the sheriff would have to try to find out who had killed Street. And why. But if Street had been killed by the same person who wanted Noah dead, then the business of murder had only begun.

SIXTEEN

Thumps left the Volvo in the hotel garage and walked to the sheriff's office. He would have preferred to spend the rest of the day with Dakota, and she might have said yes, but Thumps knew Hockney would want to see him before the evening's activities began.

"About time."

Asah was sitting in the spare chair next to the coffee pot.

"Did I miss anything?"

"Nothing much," said Duke, working his mouth from side to side in his peculiar way that always reminded Thumps of oatmeal on the boil. "Special Agent Asah and I have been catching up on old times."

Duke and Asah didn't know each other well enough to have old times. So, if Thumps had to guess, his money was on "old times" being Noah Ridge.

"Special Agent Asah here has been telling me all about Salt Lake City, and guess what?"

Thumps had all sorts of answers for "guess what" questions. "You guys know who killed Mitchell Street?"

Asah did something with his face that was somewhere between a sneer and a smile. "I took a look at Street's old case files."

"Evidently," said Duke, "the FBI can send that sort of stuff over the internet just by pushing a button, and guess what Special Agent Asah found?"

There was that "guess-what" question again.

"You know who Massasoit was."

This time it was the sheriff's turn to look amused. "Evidently, Street thought it was Lucy Kettle."

"So, there actually was a Massasoit. There really was a mole in RPM."

Asah reached over and poured himself a cup of

coffee. Thumps thought about warning him, but he didn't want to stop the conversation and then have to start it again.

Besides, drinking the sheriff's brew was probably good field experience.

"Oh, Massasoit was real enough. And well paid." Asah watched the coffee slip out of the pot like cold syrup. "Over a period of five years, the bureau paid Massasoit in excess of three hundred thousand dollars."

"And Street was Massasoit's contact?"

Hockney leaned back in the chair and stretched his legs. "Tell him the interesting part."

"Lucy Kettle was from around here." Asah put the cup on the table and stepped away. The man was a quick learner.

Thumps concentrated on sounding surprised. "You're kidding."

"Tell him the rest."

"Kettle had a brother. Man by the name of Grover Many Horses."

Hockney pulled his legs in and rolled the chair forward. "You ever meet Grover?"

"Nope," said Thumps, and this time he didn't have to pretend.

"Here you go," said Duke, holding up a piece of paper. "You and Asah get Grover. I get the television stations."

"Television stations?"

"As soon as Milo put his damn story on the wire, every network west of Newfoundland began calling me." The sheriff went to the table and poured himself a cup of coffee. Thumps wondered if Hockney's coffee could stay in liquid form at room temperature. "So, which of you puppies told Milo about Street being FBI?"

Thumps looked at Asah.

Asah smiled and shook his head. "Not guilty."

"That's what they all say," said the sheriff, without the hint of humour in his voice.

"No reason to give the press something to feed on," said Asah. "Just makes our work harder."

Hockney grunted and turned to Thumps.

"Don't look at me."

"Well," said the sheriff, "someone did, and the big three are sending crews to cover the reading and to

196

interview anyone who was within shouting distance of Ridge or Street."

"What about the coroner?" said Asah.

"Beth?" Thumps smiled and turned to see if Hockney was smiling. "It wasn't her."

Asah shrugged. "Nobody else knew."

Not exactly right, thought Thumps.

"Sonofabitch!" Hockney gave the desk a friendly punch. "Don't suppose I have to guess why he would do something like that."

"Ridge?" Asah seemed surprised by the answer.

"Makes sense," said Thumps. "The publicity would help book sales."

Hockney turned on Thumps. "I'm getting real annoyed with your buddy."

"He's not my buddy." Thumps could see that there was no more fun to be had at this gathering. "I'm just taking his picture."

"Not anymore," said Hockney. "You've been fired."

"Fired?"

"Yep," said Hockney. "Archie came by to ask me to tell you that, with the big boys covering the story, the library committee wouldn't be needing you."

"Great."

"I told him to tell you himself." Hockney put the coffee cup down and checked his tie in the mirror. "Sure as hell not a messenger service."

So far as Thumps could tell, Asah hadn't touched his coffee. Watching it come out of the pot had been enough to make him think twice about the wisdom of trying to drink it.

Asah got his parka. "I'll drive."

"Where we going?"

"Grover lives in some town called Glory," said Asah.

"We're going to drive up there and ask him if he beat up Noah Ridge and killed an FBI agent?"

"That'll do for starters," said the sheriff. "And if you don't like the answers you get, arrest him. It'll save me a trip. We can sort out the pieces later."

GLORY WAS AN old gold-mining town that had been saved from oblivion by Hollywood, though Thumps found it hard to believe that Hollywood could save much of anything. The town was down to its last few inhabitants when a film crew happened upon it, and the director pronounced the main street with its run-down but authentic turn-of-the-century storefronts perfect for the big battle scene, where the town itself would be blown to smithereens. On cue.

The only problem with the plan was the female lead, a woman whose name Thumps could not remember, who took a liking to the town and the surround-ing mountains. Before the director could plant the charges, his leading lady rounded up a flock of her friends from Los Angeles, who bought most of the land and declared Glory to be the next Palm Springs or Lake Tahoe or Carmel. The script was rewritten, and the town in the film and the town in real life were saved in the nick of time.

Thumps couldn't recall if the movie had been a success. Glory certainly had been. Almost overnight, townhouses and condominiums sprang up in the foot-hills around the town, and the wonderful old build-ings on Main Street were bulldozed and replaced with wonderful new buildings that were exact replicas of the originals.

"You know how to get there?"

Glory wasn't on the main road. And it wasn't on

the map. Word that the town had been saved evidently hadn't reached the road-map makers in time, and current editions of the various travel atlases had a blank space where the town should be. Not that this omission bothered any of the residents. Thumps suspected that the rich did not mind the anonymity of not being on a map, that, for them, living in a non-existent place had a certain cachet.

"You sure you know how to get there?"

Asah was right to be concerned. The road Thumps told him to turn onto didn't look at all promising.

"Don't worry. We hit pavement in about two miles."

The road to Glory had always been a dirt track, but with the advent of film and fame, all of that changed, and plans were drawn up for a four-lane boulevard accented by a raised interlocking-brick centre divide. With aspens set in iron gratework every forty feet.

But as the landscape architects and the bulldozers and the pavers had moved out of town on their way to the main road, a dispute arose over part of the right of way, and the folks in Glory and the rancher who owned the land adjacent to the road, who had no appreciation for celebrities or tree-lined boulevards, all wound up in court. So far as Thumps knew, the case was still there, and the first mile and a half of the road remained in the same natural state in which the film crew had found it.

"We on the reservation?"

But once you got to the top of the first rise, the new road took over, and all the way down into the narrow valley, you could watch the buildings flash in the light and marvel at the magical powers of money.

"Jesus," said Asah. "Grover Many Horses lives here?"

Actually, no one lived in Glory. Not year-round, that is. People with money, Thumps had observed, didn't stay in one spot. They were nomadic, moving with the seasons. Migratory. And skiing vacations at St. Moritz and Banff aside, rich people tended to follow the sun.

As they drove along the main street, Thumps had to remind himself that success should not be measured in terms of real-estate acquisitions and disposable income. Though from what he could see, no one in Glory believed this.

"Look for the video store."

The Glory Video Emporium was not hard to find. It was on the main street, and it was one of the few storefronts that was still open. Grover Many Horses was standing behind the counter checking DVDs into the computer.

"I'm looking for Grover Many Horses," said Asah, making his voice sound as official as possible.

"You found him."

Grover was a short, thin man with large hands that bore a striking resemblance to Vise-Grips. His hair and face were cut at angles, and when Thumps looked at Grover from the side, the man reminded him of Cherokee actor Wes Studi.

Asah took his identification out of his jacket pocket and held it up so Grover could see it.

"You guys actors?"

"No, he's really FBI," said Thumps. "I'm a photographer."

"DreadfulWater," said Grover. "Right?"

"That's right."

"I've been expecting you."

Asah looked at Thumps as if he had somehow broken the law.

"Yeah, old man Blood said you'd probably stop by."

"Moses?"

"He's my mother's uncle. He said you'd want to ask me questions about Lucy."

Asah didn't like being cut out of the conversation. "Actually," he said, "I get to ask the questions."

Grover turned back to Asah. "You're not Blackfeet." It wasn't a question, and it wasn't a complaint.

"He's Kiowa," said Thumps. "But he's okay."

Grover put the DVDs to one side. "Yeah," he said, "well, make it quick, unless you want to pay me for my time."

Thumps could feel Asah bristle.

"Mr. Many Horses," he said, pitching his voice in the way that cops did when they wanted to make things sound official and serious, "you really want to piss me off?"

"What the fuck is your problem?"

Asah leaned on the counter. "Do you?"

Grover glanced at Thumps. Thumps shrugged and shook his head.

"So, ask your damn questions."

Asah didn't sneak up on the questions the way

Hockney liked to do, and Grover didn't try to slip around the edges as Thumps thought he would, and the interview was over in no time at all.

Do you know a man named Mitchell Street?

No.

Do you know Noah Ridge?

My sister worked with him in Salt Lake City.

Do you have any reason to believe Mr. Ridge was responsible for your sister's disappearance?

Lucy said he was an asshole.

Where were you evening before last?

Here at the store.

Where were you this morning?

Home.

Can you prove it?

Nope.

Nice clean questions. Nice clean answers. Asah rattled them off as if he had each one written on his cuff. Grover answered each one as though he were reading them off a teleprompter.

Thumps waited until Asah had finished. "You got any good deals on movies?" he asked.

Grover took a deep breath and unclenched his fists. "DVD or tape?"

"DVD."

"Not too much left. The kids always clean me out just before they go back to school."

"Pretty good business?"

"Little slow right now, but summer is great."

"You going to close it down over the winter?"

"I just close early," said Grover. "Summertime I stay open till one. After the long weekend, I generally lock it up around five."

"So, who told you Ridge was coming to town?"

Grover picked up the stack of DVDs. "No one," he said. "Saw it in the papers."

"You going to the reading?"

"Maybe." Grover lowered his eyes. "Why?"

"Just curious," said Thumps. "If Lucy was my sister, I'd want to meet him."

"Maybe I'm not you."

Yes, thought Thumps, that's true. And then again, maybe you are.

* * *

"THAT WAS SLICK," said Asah as they drove out of town. "How old do you think he was when his sister disappeared?"

"You've seen the file."

"Eight," said Asah. "Grover was eight?"

"I can't remember a thing from when I was eight," said Thumps. "How about you?"

"You think he assaulted Ridge."

The cuts and bruises on Grover's knuckles were fresh. Thumps had seen them. So had Asah.

"Maybe," said Thumps. "But that's not the problem."

Asah nodded. "Yeah. No way Ridge didn't see the guy."

Hockney wouldn't have missed that either. All of Noah's injuries had been to his face and chest. Whoever had attacked Noah had come at him from the front, not behind.

"So, why would he lie?"

That, thought Thumps, was one of the better questions. "Maybe he's protecting someone."

"That would have to have been a very special

someone. You know anyone he cares about that much?" Asah looked across at Thumps and grinned. "Besides himself?"

Thumps settled in against the door. Nice to meet an FBI agent with a sense of humour.

"Sheriff says you used to be a cop," said Asah.

The hand-hewn log homes on five-acre lots and the glistening stone and glass condominiums slid across the windshield. On the near ridge, a herd of deer was making its way into the valley. "Why'd you quit?"

"Is that an official question?"

"No," said Asah. "I was just curious. You can tell me it's none of my own business."

Thumps wondered how the deer might have felt about the film company's plan to blow up Glory and leave the valley to the seasons. He suspected that they would have been in favour of it.

"Okay," said Thumps, closing his eyes. "It's none of your business."

SEVENTEEN

While they were gone, the circus had come to town. Thumps had no idea how it had got there so fast, but there it was. CBS, NBC, ABC, all the alphabet networks with their trucks and their cameras, with their elephants and their clowns. As Asah and Thumps drove down the street, Thumps could see that it was going to be a very long evening. No doubt he'd be able to watch everything on the evening news—the interviews, the background, the analysis—all reduced to a series of inane but provocative sound bites.

"I don't think the sheriff is going to like this," said

Asah as they passed the television trucks jammed together in front of the Tucker.

"Not a whole lot to like."

"You want to tell the sheriff, or do you want me to do it?"

"About Grover? Not a whole lot to tell."

"What about Grover lying to us?"

"He could have been telling the truth."

Asah pulled over to the curb. "Grover's sister disappears when he's eight."

"Witness protection works for me."

Asah grinned. "Not a chance."

"You sure?"

"Yeah," said Asah, "I'm sure. Which leaves us with only two possibilities. One, Kettle was killed and we've never found her body. Or two, she's still alive and has been in hiding for more than twenty years."

"Twenty-five."

"Which one do you like?"

"Maybe Lucy Kettle killed Street."

"Which one you think Grover likes?" Asah paused to see if Thumps had anything else clever to say. "Now after all this time, the man she was working with and who would have been a prime suspect if Lucy's body had ever been found shows up flogging a new book about those years. What do you do?"

Thumps opened the door and stepped out. "I go home and take a shower."

"You want me to drop you off?"

Thumps shook his head. "I have to pick up my car."

"You know, she may be involved." Asah waited to let this sink in. "According to Street's field notes, Ridge and Miles were close."

"That was in the past."

"Sure, but she's still with Ridge. Has to make you wonder."

"You think Dakota killed Street to protect Noah?" Thumps didn't even try to keep the incredulity out of his voice.

Asah shrugged. "Street led the raid in Salt Lake. It blew up in his face. The bureau quietly shipped him off to Nebraska, and that was the end of his career."

"I see they're still trying to teach logic at the bureau."

"Street blamed Ridge for what happened. At the review board, his defence was that Ridge had found out about the raid and tipped Buckhorn. Ridge and

Street hated each other. Have you read Ridge's book? You can bet Street did."

Thumps wasn't sure whether to laugh or just smile. "So, when Street finds out about Noah's reading, he drives to town with murder on his mind, only Dakota finds out and kills him to protect Ridge. Is that your theory?"

"You're not exactly impartial."

"I'm not exactly brain-dead either," said Thumps, surprised by the anger that had got loose.

"Street's death wasn't a suicide, and he wasn't killed by a tourist in town for the weekend."

"Noah's a better suspect."

"That he is," said Asah. "But if you watch enough television, you know that the murderer is never the obvious choice."

THE VOLVO COMPLAINED and moaned, but it made the trip home without stalling or playing dead. So, Asah wasn't just another pretty face with a badge. He had found something in Street's field notes. And he wasn't going to share. At least not yet. What had he seen that would make Dakota a suspect? Asah hadn't thrown that scenario out just for fun.

The light on the phone was blinking. Thumps wasn't sure that buying an answering machine had been a wise move. If someone called and you weren't home, then you never knew they called, and you didn't have to feel guilty about not being available. With an answering machine, while you didn't miss anything, you still felt responsible for not being home and were now burdened with the obligation of calling the person back.

The first message was from Archie, brief and to the point, as if he had to pay for it by the word. Don't worry about tonight, he said. Getting pictures from the networks.

The second message was from Claire. It was even shorter than Archie's. Coming to the reading, she said, her voice soft and encouraging, how about dinner afterwards?

The third message was a hang-up. So was the fourth.

Great, thought Thumps, as he headed for the shower. It would be nice to see Claire. Maybe even spend some time together. Her voice had had the hint of intimacy, something he hadn't heard in a long time.

He had just finished rinsing his hair when he remembered Dakota.

"Shit!"

He stood under the shower and let the water hit him in the face.

"Shit! Shit! Shit!" Somehow he had wound up with two women at the same time. And it wasn't even his fault. He rested his head on the wall and quietly banged it against the tile.

Freeway wandered into the bathroom to see what all the noise was about and to complain about not being fed on time.

"Forget it," Thumps growled at the cat as she tried to pull the bath towel off the rod so she would have something to lie on. "I've got my own problems."

At least he didn't have to take the photographs. He had never been keen about that, about wasting good film on Noah, about having to endure his smiling face on the easel, negative after negative.

And yet here was his salvation. And he grabbed it. If he was taking official photographs of Noah and the reading—the "historical moment," as Archie called it—he couldn't really have dinner with Dakota or

Claire or spend any time with either woman. And neither would feel slighted.

The network folk would never take the kinds of photographs Archie would want anyway, photographs of Noah signing books with Archie by his side, photographs of Noah talking to Archie, photographs of Archie and Noah standing together, their arms around each other's shoulders.

Thumps pulled the towel from under Freeway and began humming to himself as he rubbed shaving cream on his face.

With any luck, the reading would go off without a hitch, and tomorrow Noah would be on his way to Portland or Seattle or wherever the next stop on the tour that Ridge had invented for himself was supposed to take him. Maybe he could talk Dakota into staying for a few days or maybe Claire would suggest that the two of them take a week off and go someplace warm. As he stood in front of the mirror, scraping his face, Thumps had an absurd picture flash through his mind of Claire lying naked on a white sand beach under a palm tree, while he took pictures of Indians in multi-coloured shirts wrestling alligators.

Of course, Noah's leaving town wouldn't settle anything. Hockney and Asah would still have a dead body
on their hands, though, to be honest, Thumps was
more than happy to walk away from that mess. But
he was curious. Street had come to town for a reason.

Thumps stopped shaving and looked at his reflection. Surely the sheriff or Asah would have thought of
that. Then again, maybe they hadn't. Thumps hadn't,
until just now. He checked the clock. More than
enough time to pack his gear and make a quick stop.

BETH AND ORA MAE were just coming out the door
of the old Land Titles building when Thumps pulled
up in the Volvo.

"We appreciate the thought," said Ora Mae, her
eyes dancing at the prospect of having someone to pick
on, "but we have our reputations to consider."

"What?"

"She doesn't want to ride in your car," said Beth.

"I need a favour."

Beth looked at him hard. "Is this one of those 'I
need to look at the body again' favours?"

"Not exactly."

"Do we look like we got dressed up to go play in a morgue?" Ora Mae was a big, fierce woman, and most times Thumps liked her and she liked him.

"It's important."

"It better be," said Ora Mae, "or we're going to tie you to a table and leave you there."

Thumps knew that Ora Mae was kidding, but just the threat of being left alone in the morgue in the dark with all those nasty smells made his entire body cramp up. And as Beth unlocked the door to the basement and they made their way into the bowels of the building, Thumps regretted having come here at all.

"Okay," said Beth, "what do you want?"

"You still got all his effects?"

"Right here." Beth opened a drawer and took out two large, clear plastic sacks. Street's wallet and the book were in the second bag.

Thumps sat down on a stool and turned the book over. Then he opened it and checked the inside of the jacket.

"You going to read us a passage?" said Ora Mae.

Thumps flipped through the pages. "Was there a bookmark?"

"What you see is what you get," said Beth.

Some people used bookmarks to mark their place. Archie, for instance. And some people liked to fold down corners. Thumps was hoping that Street was one of the latter.

"What are we looking for?" Ora Mae was losing her sense of humour and adventure.

"Evidence," said Thumps.

"Get the straps," said Ora Mae. "I'll hold him down."

Thumps laid the book on the table and went through each page individually until he found what he was looking for. A page that had been turned down at the corner and then straightened. Thumps ran a finger across the paper. This hadn't been an accident. The crease was clean and symmetrical.

"That's no way to treat a book," said Beth.

Chapter Six. "Murder in Zion." Street had marked this page for a reason.

"Are we done?" asked Ora Mae. "'Cause you don't want to make us late."

"We're done," said Thumps.

"Did we solve the murder?" Beth turned off the lights and locked the door.

Not yet, Thumps thought to himself, but now he could see that if he was going to solve the crime in Chinook, he was going to have to figure out what had happened in Salt Lake. At the same time.

Moses had been right, as he generally was. Understanding the past was the only hope for understanding the present.

EIGHTEEN

The church was packed. The networks had taken up the front rows, and the town's dignitaries, who were all in attendance, had had to squeeze themselves in between large men with video cameras and large men with computers. Archie was standing at the back, watching the crowd adjust itself.

"Thumps."

Thumps could feel Archie's eyes on his camera bag and tripod. For a moment, he thought about having a little fun.

"Didn't you get my message?" asked Archie.

"What message?"

Thumps watched Archie twist. "Oh, you mean about being fired?"

"Fired?" said Archie. "I never said fired."

"It's okay," said Thumps. "I figured I'd take shots on my own. As you said, the guys who shot the Beatles and Elvis are all rich and famous."

"Sure," said Archie. "Just don't get in the way of the professionals."

When Claire arrived, she had Stick with her. Thumps couldn't imagine him coming to a reading, even if his mother had insisted.

"Hi."

Claire was wearing a dress, which was always a good sign. It meant that she had left work at work and was making a conscious effort to enjoy herself. Thumps tried to swing the camera bag behind him out of sight with the least amount of motion.

"You're taking pictures?" Claire's tone was matter of fact, but he could see the disappointment in her eyes.

"Library committee hired me." Which wasn't completely untrue. "I would have called, but I didn't get in till late."

Stick came riding to his mother's rescue with his

teeth showing. "You're standing my mother up?"

"He's not standing me up." Claire was not about to have her son rescue her from anything. "He has to work."

But Stick had already lost interest in the conversation. "Whatever," he said and wandered off to find someone who wanted to listen to him talk about himself.

"His eye looks better."

"He said you talked to him."

"A little."

"Did he tell you anything?"

Claire was a fine figure of a woman. Even hidden away in blue jeans and a flannel shirt. Which is what she normally wore. But when she put on a dress, she was stunning. For one thing, you could see her legs, particularly her calves.

"Didn't know Stick was the literary type."

"Stanley," said Claire, "and he wanted to come."

"You're kidding."

Men tended to divide women up into pieces and judge each piece separately. Face, breasts, butt, legs. Thumps liked legs, especially Claire's legs. They were long with well-formed muscular calves and thin ankles. When he was a cop on the Northern California coast,

Sharon Doyle had loaned him one of her romances in which the heroine had long, tawny legs.

That was Claire. Long and tawny.

The heroine in the novel also had alabaster thighs, which didn't make much sense since Thumps didn't think you could have tawny legs and alabaster thighs on the same body, unless you spent most of your time sunbathing in long shorts.

"Stanley wanted to come to this?"

Claire's face hardened slightly. "What did he say about the eye?"

Thumps shook his head. "If he's not going to tell you, he's not going to tell me."

"Did you try?"

Thumps looked over at the book table. Stick was talking with Judy Ferraro, and unless Thumps was reading the signs wrong, Stick was bragging about something, trying to impress the young woman.

At least he was out of trouble and out of Thumps's hair. For the moment.

"You look great. I like the dress."

Claire blushed, but her defences didn't come down. "It's the only dress I own."

"I know."

"So, it wasn't really a compliment."

Things had started off well enough, Thumps thought to himself, even promising. But now it was time to disappear and take some pictures.

Noah hadn't arrived yet. Or he was in one of the backrooms waiting to be announced, waiting for that moment when all eyes would be on him. Or perhaps he was just being fashionably late, allowing the suspense to build. Thumps wondered if Noah would read from the chapter that Street had dog-eared, or if he would do as he had done in the old days and just haul out the sound and fury. With the television crews in attendance, Thumps was betting on performance over substance.

After all, reasonable Indians intelligently debating important issues didn't get on the evening news.

Ten after eight. Archie had disappeared, probably to tell Noah that he had a full house. Thumps looked around the audience and realized that this could well be the social event of the year. Everyone was here. Doctors, lawyers, Indian chiefs. But he would have missed Hockney completely if he hadn't seen Duke's wife, Macy, sitting next to a large man in a brown suit. Thumps tried to remember the last time he had seen the sheriff in a suit. He had been with his wife that time too.

Thumps waited for Hockney to look his way, but Duke was keeping his eyes straight ahead, hoping, Thumps supposed, that if he couldn't see anyone, no one could see him.

"Thumps!"

Archie was standing in the shadows motioning to him. He didn't look particularly happy.

"Full house. Pretty good."

"You seen him?"

"The sheriff?" Thumps chuckled. "Yeah. Looks like a dog on a leash."

"No," said Archie. "Noah Ridge."

"He's not here?"

"Not yet." Archie scratched his head. "Does he like being late?"

"Did you call the hotel?"

"Sure."

"And?"

"No answer."

Thumps looked at all the cameras at the ready. "He'll be here."

At eight-thirty, everyone began to get restless, especially the news teams who Thumps suspected were on a schedule. At a quarter to nine, the networks pinned Archie and demanded, in their noisy, unctuous way, to know what was happening. Archie smiled and assured them that everything was running a little late.

Thumps found Dakota in the balcony.

"He's supposed to be here," said Dakota, answering the question before Thumps could ask it.

"Didn't he come with you?"

Dakota shook her head. "He wanted to rest. Said he'd meet me here."

"Trouble?" Hockney was standing by the staircase.

"He's a little late," said Thumps.

"What you mean," said the sheriff, "is that he's not here."

Dakota began pulling at the skin around her fingers. "This is wrong."

Hockney was shifting from one foot to the other and leaning in the general direction of the front door.

"We'll check it out," Thumps told Dakota.

"I want to come."

Thumps shook his head. "No," he said. "Stay here. In case he shows and all this is just part of the game."

THE JOG FROM the church to the Tucker was cold and brisk. Thumps always made the mistake of thinking that because Hockney was big and old and out of shape, the man couldn't move. The chances were good that Noah was fine. The beating might have been worse than it looked, but more than likely he had simply fallen asleep and slept through the reading.

The sheriff didn't waste any effort. He showed the desk clerk his badge, and two minutes later, Hockney was sliding the card key into the lock and pushing his way into the room without so much as a hello.

"Shit!" Duke loosened his tie and broke his neck out of jail. "Nobody touch anything."

Noah had not fallen asleep. From the looks of the room, nobody had got any sleep. Several chairs had been overturned. The sofa had been shoved to one side, taking the rug with it. The smell of blood was everywhere, along with the lingering scent of gunfire.

Thumps stood by the doorway and watched Hockney move through the living room slowly, like a bear stalking game.

"Just great."

"We got a problem?" Special Agent Asah had magically appeared at Thumps's shoulder.

Thumps shrugged. "You guys are the professionals."

Hockney turned to Asah. "Thumps used to be a cop. Did I tell you that?"

"Thought you hired him as a deputy."

"That I did," said Hockney.

"Where's the body?" Asah squatted down next to a large dark stain. "Nobody loses this much blood and walks away."

"That's not much help," said the sheriff, letting the frustration of having to wear a suit and tie show. "Andy could have figured out that much."

Maybe so, thought Thumps, but if the parking lot at the Holiday Inn had been any larger, Andy might still be walking around in the snow, looking for Street's car.

"So, what do you two geniuses make of this?"

It was a rhetorical question, and Thumps knew better than to offer an opinion.

"Hard to tell," said Asah.

Smart, thought Thumps. Let Hockney do all the work and save your head from being taken off at the shoulders.

"They teach you that at FBI school?" Hockney jerked his cellphone off his belt. "This is Sheriff Hockney," he barked. "Put me through to Emergency."

"Okay." Asah turned to Thumps. "Ridge is in the room alone, and someone knocks on the door."

"Someone he knows."

"Maybe," said Asah. "The two of them come into the room, and for whatever reason, Ridge gets shot."

"Then where is he?"

"He gets up," said Asah, trying to pretend that he believed this scenario. "And then he leaves."

"And goes where?"

"Well, not to the hospital," said Hockney, joining the conversation. "Nobody has checked in there all evening. And that little piece of fiction you two were working up doesn't explain the drag marks."

"Nope," agreed Asah. "It doesn't."

"Okay," said Thumps, "someone comes in and shoots Ridge and then drags him away."

"You're beginning to piss me off, DreadfulWater."

"But that's not what happened." Thumps was surprised to hear his voice saying what his mind was thinking.

"No, it's not," said the sheriff. "Maybe Mr. Ridge had company. Maybe he got shot. But there weren't two people in this room. There were three."

Asah looked at Hockney.

"He's right," said Thumps. "There are three sets of footprints."

The sheriff gestured to the blood near the sofa. "One set there and one set by the rug. But this set by the door. These prints are different from the first two."

Asah walked the room. "So, you think that Mr. A shot Mr. B and then was carried off by Mr. C."

Crude, thought Thumps, but accurate.

Everyone was getting ready for round two when Hockney suddenly stopped and raised a hand. "What's that?"

Asah moved to the arched window and looked out. "Oh, you're going to love this," he said.

The network people with their cameras and tape recorders had evidently got tired of waiting and were coming down the street toward the Tucker like a herd on the run. Somehow they had smelled the blood in the air.

"Great." Duke flipped his phone open and tried to destroy the tiny keypad with his finger. "Andy," he bellowed into the phone, "haul your butt over to the Tucker. Seal the place off, and shoot any reporter who gets in your way."

Asah was smiling and shaking his head, but then Chinook wasn't his town. It was going to take Hockney a very long time to dig himself out of this mess, and Thumps suspected that if the sheriff found Noah Ridge alive, he'd probably shoot the man himself.

"Talk to your lady friend," said Hockney, his voice low and controlled. "She knows more than she's telling."

"Where you going to be?"

"After the reading," said the sheriff, "my wife and I were going to go out to dinner. At that fancy Italian place south of town. But instead, Andy and I are going to fingerprint this room, search for clues, and talk with our good friends in the press."

"Can I watch?"

"What'd I say about pissing me off?"

Thumps looked at the lamp on the floor and the blood stains on the shade. "You think someone grabbed him?"

"Then why shoot him?" said the sheriff. "Besides, you know anyone who would pay his ransom?"

As he walked down the hall to the elevators, Thumps reasoned that there were any number of people whom Noah had annoyed over the years who might like to see him inconvenienced, even dead, but he couldn't think of many who would go to the effort of kidnapping the man, and he couldn't think of anyone who would pay the ransom.

NINETEEN

Thumps caught Dakota as she was stepping off the elevator.

"Where's Noah?"

"The press is right behind you." Thumps hurried Dakota down the hall toward the red Exit sign. "You want to talk to them?"

"No."

"Then let's get out of here."

"What about Noah?"

By now the hotel would be filling up with news people waiting for the elevators to take them to Noah's room and Sheriff Duke Hockney. Thumps knew that if he tried to take Dakota through the lobby, she would be swarmed. The only hope was if the stairs went all the way to the parking garage.

They did.

The Volvo actually seemed happy to see him, or maybe it was just happy to have been parked somewhere under a roof.

"Damn it! Where's Noah?"

Thumps eased the car past the television trucks, slipping and sliding on the ice like a frozen turkey on a hockey rink. Tomorrow, he promised himself, he would change the tires.

FREEWAY COULD SMELL COMPANY a mile down the road and was waiting for Dakota at the front door.

"Is she yours?"

Thumps put the water on before he took off his jacket. "No," he said, "she just lets me live here."

Freeway led Dakota to the sofa and settled in her lap.

"She's friendly."

"No, she's not."

As Thumps waited for the water to boil, he tried to make sense of how the day had gone so far. Noah is attacked on his morning jog and winds up in the hospital. He goes back to the hotel, lies down to rest, and disappears.

"Noah's room had been roughed up." Thumps took a deep breath. "And there was blood."

Dakota stopped petting the cat. "Noah?"

"No sign of him." The tea kettle began to whistle. Thumps dropped the tea bags into the pot and poured the boiling water over them. "Would he run?"

"From what?" said Dakota. "With all that publicity waiting for him at the church?"

"The book wasn't doing so well."

"It was just slow." Dakota wasn't going to give up easily. "But it was catching on."

"Publishing house didn't think so," said Thumps. "They didn't send Noah on this tour. He sent himself. His idea. RPM money."

Freeway rolled over on Dakota's lap and stretched. She was willing to put up with boring conversations so long as someone continued to pet her.

"RPM doesn't have any money." Dakota ran a hand

along Freeway's belly. "Noah couldn't send himself anywhere."

"Then who's paying for the tour?"

"Look around," said Dakota. "Who else is there?"

The only tea Thumps had left was an organic white tea that he had bought in Alberta. It was supposed to be high in antioxidants. He wasn't exactly sure what antioxidants were or what they did, but right now he could use something that made him smarter.

"You?"

"My parents. They weren't wealthy, but they made good investments."

"And you've been giving their money to Noah?"

"Not to Noah," snapped Dakota. "To the movement. To the cause."

"You think he's worth it."

Dakota came off the sofa in a flash, sending Freeway sprawling. "What the hell would you know about worth?"

Thumps was sorry he had started this, but now that he had, he wasn't about to retreat. "He's an egotistical asshole."

"Yeah," said Dakota, "he is. He also puts his

egotistical asshole on the line. Remember when the army wanted to build a test facility for nuclear-waste storage on the Ute reservation? That was Noah who stood in front of the bulldozers, and it was Noah who went to jail."

Thumps did remember the blockade. RPM had organized the protest, and Noah had stood in front of the dozers. Along with about a hundred other people. And he had gone to jail. But he was bailed out almost immediately. The other people hadn't been so lucky. They stayed in jail until the case was thrown out of court.

"And the survival schools? Noah set those up for our kids, who thought being Indian was the same thing as being shit."

Noah had raised the money, all right. Foundations, government agencies, corporations, private individuals. He had criss-crossed the country, shaking hands, flattering egos, making speeches. But he hadn't run the schools. He hadn't taught the kids. He hadn't sat down and helped the families deal with the joys of poverty.

Thumps could feel the anger rising. "He wasn't the only one. There were other people who did the real work."

"That's right," said Dakota, her voice hard. "He only made it all happen. What the hell did you do?"

"This isn't about me."

"No," said Dakota. "It's not."

The tea was ready now, but Thumps was pretty sure it was going to stay in the pot.

"Nobody cares anymore. Nobody remembers. Most of those programs we started are gone now. Most of the gains we made have been lost. You know what it means to spend your life trying to make a difference, only to discover no one cares?"

"I'll find Noah if I can."

"Why?"

"Because you believe in him."

"But you don't."

No, thought Thumps, I don't. But Dakota was right. He hadn't done much. A couple of marches. A sit-in or two. Lots of indignation. Not much action. Always in the shadows. Always out of harm's way.

"I need to know something."

"What?"

"I need to know who chose the towns."

"Why?"

"Jesus, Dakota, you want my help or not?"

"Noah." The flash was gone from Dakota's eyes, but the anger remained in her voice. "Noah chose the towns."

"So, why Chinook?"

"Lucy was from here." Dakota sat in the chair, her hands in her lap. "At the reading, Noah was going to announce the creation of a scholarship in her name."

There was value in that, Thumps supposed. Noah Ridge coming to Chinook to make peace with the past, to bury the ghosts. But it didn't sound like the Noah Ridge that Thumps knew. That Noah was an Old Testament god. If Lucy had been an FBI informant, why, after all these years, would he honour her memory? Especially in such a public way.

"What about Lucy and the FBI?"

"Noah's wrong about that," said Dakota quickly. "He's always been wrong about that."

Thumps was getting slow. He should have seen it sooner.

"It wasn't Noah's idea. It was yours."

"What difference does it make?"

"And your money."

"No," said Dakota, "that's gone. There's nothing left but the book. The book was going to pay for everything."

"But without Noah?" Thumps let the question hang in the air.

Dakota didn't have to answer that question. Without Noah to give it a face, the book had little chance of garnering a national audience, the kind of audience it would need to bring in enough money and attention for RPM to survive. That's what the book tour was about. Survival.

And in that regard, Thumps suddenly realized, a dead Noah might just be more valuable than a live Noah. The media loved blood and mystery, mayhem and intrigue. A second murder would send them into a feeding frenzy.

"I want to go back to the hotel." Dakota put her coat on. "You haven't told me everything, have you?"

"For what it's worth," said Thumps, "I don't think he's dead."

"But you don't care."

"I care about you."

"You don't know me." Dakota pulled her coat around herself and turned up the collar. "You just know who you'd like me to be."

THE LOBBY OF the Tucker was alive with activity. Through the windows, Thumps could see correspondents milling around, talking to each other and to their cameras. He was sure that Hockney was, somewhere in the middle of the herd, grumpy about all the nonsense, grumpy that he had had to button his collar and fix his tie.

Dakota didn't get out right away. "No point in coming in."

"If you need me to, I will."

"I need you to find Noah."

The windows of the Tucker were ablaze with lights. Outside, by the network vans, people were running back and forth, shouting to each other, their breath pouring out of their mouths like smoke, and for a moment, as Dakota ascended the stairs to the main entrance, it looked as though she was walking into a house on fire.

TWENTY

Thumps never expected the nightmares, but that didn't keep them from coming. After all these years, he would have thought that they would have lost some of their power. But this was not the case. And when they did arrive, they arrived in force. Always the same. Always terrifying. Always with Anna and Callie lying on the beach. On those nights, he would wake up shouting and come up from the depths of sleep swinging. And in the morning, the sheets would be soaked in sweat and his muscles cramped and aching.

When Thumps woke, he imagined that the phone

was ringing or that someone was knocking on the door. But the house was silent. Thumps looked at the clock. Nine. Much too late to be in bed. Dakota probably hadn't got any sleep. The sheriff would certainly be up by now. So would Asah.

And the television folk? They might be up, but somehow Thumps doubted it.

Last night should have been the end of it. Ridge should have given his reading and left town. Thumps and Dakota should have had a quiet dinner, talked about old times, and left it at that. Or he and Claire should have had a quiet dinner, talked about anything but Stick, and left it at that.

All those "shoulds." Any one of them would have done just fine. Instead, Ridge disappears, Dakota sends him packing, and Claire . . . what had happened to Claire? Thumps pulled himself up to a sitting position and found the phone.

"Sheriff's office."

Hockney sounded murderous. For a moment, Thumps thought about just hanging up and going back to bed.

"Any luck?"

"Where are you?"

"In bed."

"I'm not paying you to be in bed."

"So, I'm still a cop."

"You are, until I say you're not."

Thumps was thinking of something clever to say when he realized that, once again, the sheriff had hung up on him. So, nothing new had happened overnight. Street was still dead, Ridge was still missing, and Hockney still needed a suit that fit.

Thumps wondered if Asah had developed a flow chart yet that listed the various characters and their relationships to each other, along with the appropriate dates and times. And a map with pins in it. It was something that the FBI were fond of doing. They had done that in Northern California for the Obsidian Murders, had even developed a series of profiles, psychological fictions that tried to imagine aspects of the killer—age, race, class, education. Thumps still had all of it, the charts, the maps, the profiles, all packed away in boxes in the basement. He should have thrown them out long ago, but the cop in him couldn't do it.

There was nothing wrong in all of this plotting and

guessing. The database that the bureau had amassed over the years had turned guessing into a science of sorts. But in California, it hadn't helped. Even though each murder had been a meticulously constructed diorama, the bodies left on a beach, arranged in the sand just beyond the high-tide mark, neither the FBI nor the state police could find a common link, a common thread. The victims had been both men and women, young and old. A few had been from the area. Most of them were tourists or had come up from the city to visit friends. Ten victims in all, each with a small piece of obsidian in their mouths.

And there it was. The nightmare come back, leaning across the table, whispering, telling the story of that summer, reminding him of how he had failed to protect the people he loved, chiding him for his inability to find their killer. And always in the background, behind the sound of the surf breaking on the sand, was the vague hint of laughter.

Thumps stood under the shower until he had washed the memories out of his blood. Freeway, who had little patience with regret or depression, stuck her head under the shower curtain several times to tell him that it was her turn. The cat loved jumping in the tub after Thumps had used it so she could lick at the water that pooled up next to the drain.

She also liked to stick her head in the toilet.

As he stood in front of the small mirror, drying himself and trying to find a good angle in the glass that would firm up the slope of his stomach, he wondered what Street had done in town for the days before he was murdered. If he had just wanted to come to Ridge's reading, either to embarrass him or to kill him, he could have come in the night before and saved himself the cost of a motel. Maybe he had other business to take care of, other people to visit, other arrangements to make before Noah arrived.

THE CERAMIC LOG FIRE at the Holiday Inn was still burning brightly, and the woman at the front desk was the same woman who had tried to talk him into going down to a dead man's room. Jill. No last name.

"Good morning," said Jill. "How can I help you."

"I was here the other day."

"That's right," she said. "With the sheriff."

"You have a good memory."

"That was an interesting day," she said. "In a bad way, of course."

That's the way a great many people saw death in general and murder in particular. Interesting. In a bad way. Thumps hoped that Jill's memory for details was as good as her memory for faces.

"The sheriff asked me to stop by and check a few things."

"Sure." Jill turned to her computer and began pressing keys. Computers were a mystery to Thumps, so he was glad that there were some people in the world who knew what they were doing.

"I suppose the sheriff asked you about any visitors, or if Mr. Street made any phone calls."

"Yes," said Jill, "he did."

"And?"

Jill looked almost suspicious.

"It's what we do in police work," said Thumps quickly. "We ask the same questions several times in an investigation. Sometimes people remember something later that they forgot about the first time."

"That's interesting."

"So, did he have any visitors?"

"As I told the sheriff, he might have. You have to come through the lobby to get to the rooms, but we don't keep track of people as they come and go."

"Phone calls?"

Jill went back to the computer. "I gave the sheriff a printout."

"I don't need a printout. But maybe you could tell me whom he called."

"Do you have to have a warrant or something?"

"No." Thumps didn't like lying. "The guy's dead, so it doesn't matter."

"Sure," said Jill. "He made two phone calls. One local and one long distance."

"To where?"

"Don't know," said Jill. "It was a credit-card call."

"And the local?"

"Sometimes when we're full, we send people there," said Jill. "But it's more expensive, and it doesn't have a pool."

"The Tucker?"

"I hear it's a little overpriced."

So, Hockney wasn't sharing with all the children.

Thumps wondered if Asah knew about the phone calls.

"You never know about people," said Jill. "I thought he was a tourist."

Thumps was almost to the door before he heard the question. He walked back to the front desk slowly, turning things over in his mind.

"Why did you say that?"

"What?"

"That you thought he was a tourist."

"Oh, that," said Jill. "It's the first thing that tourists ask for."

"And that is?"

"Directions to Glory."

THUMPS WAS ANNOYED as he pulled out of the Holiday Inn parking lot and headed back to town. By the time he got to the sheriff's office, he was angry. Hockney was sitting behind his desk with a pad of paper, looking the worse for wear after last evening's activities, but Thumps was not in the mood to cut the man any slack.

"I quit."

Duke tossed the pad on the desk.

"I was just at the Holiday Inn."

"I know," said the sheriff. "Smart young girl at the front desk called to ask if she should be talking to you."

Thumps sat down in the chair and waited.

"I said it was okay."

"Why didn't you tell me about the phone call?"

"There were only two."

"You know whom Street called?"

"Nope," said Hockney. "I'm waiting for Street's long-distance company to send me a list of the calls he made in the last week. The local one we can only follow as far as the front desk."

"So, he called Noah."

"Or your girlfriend."

"Does that make any sense?"

"Don't think he called for dinner reservations."

The chance of that, Thumps had to admit, was slim. If Street had called the Tucker, Noah and Dakota were the two best choices.

"You didn't trust me."

"Don't be a baby," said the sheriff.

"And when were you going to mention Glory?"

The sheriff put his pen down. "Might have been nothing."

"But you didn't mind sending Asah and me up there to rattle Grover's cage."

Hockney shrugged. "Never know what might happen."

"I quit."

"Jesus H. Christ," said Hockney. "Keep your shirt on."

"Does Asah know?"

"Of course not. If I'm not going to tell you, I'm sure as hell not going to tell him."

For some reason, that made Thumps feel a little better. "I still quit."

"You want some coffee? Made it this morning."

"No."

"You are one mean-tempered son of a buck."

"You lied to me."

"No, I didn't. I just didn't share."

"Same thing."

"Anyway," said the sheriff, "I can't let you quit."

"Why not?"

"Because I need you."

Thumps helped himself to a cup of coffee. It didn't look as black or feel as thick as he remembered. It wasn't as good as Al's, but it was potable.

"So," said the sheriff, "what would you have done?"

Thumps had to admit he probably would have done the same thing. After all, he had known Noah and Dakota in Salt Lake City. For all the sheriff knew, he might have been romantically involved with Dakota during those years. For that matter, Hockney had no reason to think he wasn't involved with her now.

The phone began ringing. Hockney stared at it the way a hawk might eye a groundhog. "It's been doing that all morning," he said. "Thought about shooting it."

"Press?"

"You name it, they've called. Press, television, movie producers, publishing houses, publicists, talk shows. Every damn rat in the woodpile, including two psychics who said they could find Ridge."

"Good thing you've got an answering machine."

"It's already full. Hell, if someone robs a bank, it'll be a week before we know it."

"Is it safe to go to the Tucker?"

"Sure, as long as you take a knife and a rifle."

Eureka and Arcata had been like that. Towns under siege. After the fifth of the Obsidian Murders, after the police figured out that they had a serial killer on their hands, the media moved in. They took over hotels, camped out at restaurants, dragged their cameras up and down the beaches destroying crime scenes. They interviewed anyone who had a theory, no matter how absurd, and turned the victims into sideshow attractions.

"You got any ideas?"

"Hell," said the sheriff, "if I had any ideas, I wouldn't be sitting here talking to you and listening to the phone ring."

Thumps took another sip of coffee. He had been wrong. It wasn't potable after all.

"Don't suppose you were friends with Reuben Justice."

There it was. The past come around again. The sheriff hadn't got that name out of a cereal box. He had been busy.

"You actually read Noah's book?"

"They say reading is broadening," said Hockney.

Thumps had known Reuben only from a distance, but what he had seen, he had liked. The man was one of those rare individuals who was able to manage the intricacies and dangers of living in two worlds. He was a traditional singer, organized the community sweats and ceremonies, and he worked at the university hospital as a paramedic.

"I knew him."

"How about Clinton Buckhorn?"

Thumps could see that he was going to have to read Noah's book too. "You've been talking to the FBI."

"Are you kidding?" said the sheriff. "Those boys wouldn't tell you which way the wind was blowing."

"Where'd you get all this?"

"Friends," said Hockney. "I've got friends here and there. You know how much Buckhorn and his crew stole from Morgan Energy?"

Thumps tried to remember if he had ever heard a figure.

"Around eighty thousand dollars," said the sheriff. "Given the cost of real estate, it wasn't enough to split three ways and buy a vacant lot. You see my problem."

"It was a protest thing," said Thumps. "They weren't after the money."

"Matthew Colburne, CEO of Morgan, gets shot.

Wallace Begay gets shot. That's one hell of a protest."

"You had to have been there."

"I was," said the sheriff. "So, why do you think Justice let them stay at his house?"

Thumps wasn't sure Reuben had had much of a choice. Begay had been wounded in Denver. Clinton needed a place to hide until things calmed down. The two men were cousins. Reuben may not have liked what Clinton had been up to, but he wasn't the kind of man who was going to turn relatives away, and he wasn't the kind of man who would turn them in.

"What's this got to do with anything?"

"From what I hear, this Justice fellow was an upstanding citizen."

"He was."

Hockney looked at the pad of paper on his desk. "You want to guess who led the raid?"

"Mitchell Street."

"Good guess."

"It wasn't a guess."

"Rumour has it that the feds got a tip on where they could find Buckhorn." Hockney rubbed the back of his neck. "It should have been an easy bust. The bureau went in at three in the morning, when everyone was supposed to be asleep."

"But they weren't."

"To hear tell, Buckhorn and his buddies were waiting for the feds. Whole place turned into a war zone. Bureau lost two agents in that raid."

"Buckhorn, Scout, and Begay were killed too."

"Yeah," said the sheriff, "but they're the bad guys. They're supposed to be dead."

The only one left standing had been Rueben Justice. He wasn't in the house at the time of the raid, was at the hospital working when his place was turned into a shooting gallery. But it was his house, and he was arrested as an accessory and co-conspirator. Nobody really believed that Justice had anything to do with the robbery, but after such a public disaster, the FBI went looking for blood, and Justice was the only one left who could bleed.

"The same day Lucy Kettle disappears." It was a good story, and Hockney was taking a great deal of pleasure in telling it. "Street is quietly shipped off to Nebraska. Justice goes to prison for life. And the rest is history."

"Reuben was a scapegoat."

"Maybe we should ask him about that," said Hockney.

"Who?"

"Reuben Justice," said the sheriff. "Seems he's out of prison."

Justice hadn't taken part in the robbery, but given the circumstances and the dead federal agents, there was no way he would have been paroled.

"Pardoned?"

"Nope," said Hockney. "Found himself one of those eager civil-liberty lawyers. The smart variety. Conviction was overturned on a technicality."

"When?"

"A month ago," said the sheriff. "Reuben Justice got out of jail a month ago."

"You think Asah knows about any of this?"

Hockney rubbed his forehead as though his brain hurt. "What do you think?"

"But he didn't tell us."

"Maybe you should ask him about that," said Hockney just as the phone began to ring again. "Let me know what he says."

TWENTY-ONE

Things were getting out of hand. Mitchell Street, Noah Ridge, Dakota Miles, Grover Many Horses, Lucy Kettle, and now Reuben Justice. What had started off as a short story was fast becoming a Russian novel. If things got any more out of hand, Thumps was going to have to make up a chart himself. Or a scorecard.

So far as Thumps could tell, all the sheriff had was a bunch of pieces. Mitchell Street comes to Chinook three days ahead of Noah. Maybe he goes to Glory. Maybe he doesn't. Maybe he sees Grover Many Horses. Maybe he doesn't. After Noah and Dakota arrive in town, Street does make a phone call to the Tucker. Whom does he talk to and about what?

And then someone kills him.

Noah Ridge writes a book that goes nowhere, so he invents a book tour in the hopes of drumming up business. And one of the stops just happens to be Lucy Kettle's hometown. He's threatened, beaten up, and then, rather dramatically, disappears.

Wonderful.

THUMPS SAT IN HIS CAR and started at the beginning. The Red Power Movement comes to Salt Lake City and opens shop. With Noah Ridge leading the way, RPM is successful in bringing national attention to the problems facing Native people. RPM leads demonstrations, opens survival schools, funds after-school programs. Most of all, it annoys the FBI and local law enforcement, which would like nothing better than to close the organization down and toss Noah's sorry ass in jail.

Then Clinton Buckhorn comes along and everything changes. Buckhorn and Wilson Scout and

Wallace Begay kidnap Matthew Colburne and force him to open the company safe. Colburne plays hero and shoots Begay, and Buckhorn shoots Colburne. Buckhorn et al. disappear with a bag of cash and head for Salt Lake, where Buckhorn imposes on his cousin.

Thumps wondered if Buckhorn had taken more than just cash from Morgan Energy. The copy of the $50,000 bond had to have come from somewhere. If Hockney knew, he wasn't telling. If he didn't know, he must have had his suspicions. It wasn't something that every former FBI agent would carry around.

In the meantime, the FBI runs all over the country trying to find the three men until they get a tip from a mysterious informant named Massasoit. The bureau raids Justice's house, but Buckhorn is waiting for them, and the ensuing battle leaves five people dead.

That same night Lucy Kettle disappears. Reuben Justice goes to jail for life, and Mitchell Street is summarily shipped off to Nebraska.

Just trying to keep everything straight made Thumps's head hurt. In the activist/terrorist game, Ridge was a lightweight contender. So why, after all these years, send an agent to shadow him? Noah's book might have annoyed the boys in Washington, but the FBI must certainly have better things to do than chase around the countryside after one medium-naughty Indian. Then again, the bureau was famous for withholding information. Maybe there was more to this than Thumps could see.

Not that he wanted to look.

Thumps picked up Noah's book and flipped through the pages, in case a clue wanted to fall into his lap. It would be nice if the book were the key to the past and to the present. Then all he'd have to do is read it and arrest the bad guys. It certainly seemed to be a catalyst of sorts. Salt Lake City and Lucy Kettle had been forgotten and buried for years. Then Noah writes a book, and the past rises out of its grave and walks the land.

Night of the Living Dead Indians.

Thumps tossed the book onto the back seat. He'd look at it later, when he had more time. When he was in the mood.

He turned the key in the ignition. Nothing. He tried again. Nothing, nothing, nothing. There were Volvos in the world, he was sure, who looked forward to winter, who found summer hot and unbearable. Of course, you couldn't tell just by looking. His Volvo had appeared perfectly normal when he bought it.

THE LOBBY OF the Tucker was quiet, the media having retreated to regroup and recharge their cameras.

"Hey, Thumps."

There were any number of people that Thumps might have expected to see in the lobby of the Tucker. Cooley Small Elk was not one of them.

"Hi, Cooley."

Cooley was sitting in one of the wingback chairs at the far side of the lobby, a notebook on his lap. It was a large chair with a heavy floral brocade, and Cooley filled it completely. He was dressed all in black, black pants, black jacket, black toque. Against the chair he looked like a large shadow in a small forest.

"You looking for Ridge's woman?"

Thumps was sure he would not have described Dakota in that fashion.

"'Cause she's not here." Cooley wrote something in the notebook. "She went out with some of those television guys. They wanted to interview me, but when you're working security, you want to stay as anonymous as possible, so I said no."

Thumps couldn't imagine Cooley as anonymous under any circumstances. "What about Buffalo Mountain?"

"They got that new arm," said Cooley. "So they laid me off. Now I'm working for the hotel."

"Thought you were working for Noah Ridge."

"Kind of hard to protect someone when you don't know where he is."

Thumps couldn't disagree with that logic.

"It's okay," said Cooley. "This job's not full-time."

"Cooley," said Thumps, "this is a pretty serious case."

"You bet," said Cooley. "That's why you need good security."

Thumps wasn't sure he wanted to spend the day debating security with Cooley, but as he thought about his options, he couldn't think of anything he had to do that was any better.

"Maybe we should team up," said Cooley. "You used to be a cop, and I've just finished the advanced KGB training course."

Thumps promised himself not to ask.

Cooley held up the notebook. "That's what I'm doing."

Cooley had divided a page in the notebook into two columns. At the top of one column, he had written *Normal*. At the top of the other, he had written *Unusual*.

Below each heading was a list of items.

"If you want to solve a mystery, you have to break everything down into normal occurrences and abnormal occurrences, so you can see things clearly."

"Did you notice what time Dakota left with the television people?"

"Under Normal, you put things such as Billy Owens getting drunk and winding up in the tank. And under Unusual, you put that dead guy at the motel."

Cooley waited for Thumps to react.

"That's great."

"And when you get everything on the two lists, you look at everything under Unusual and ask yourself why these things happened and what relevance they might have to the mystery you're trying to solve. Pretty good, eh?"

"Terrific."

Cooley wrote a couple of sentences under the Unusual column. "If I do it right, there's a good chance that I'll be able to find out what happened to Mr. Ridge."

"Well," said Thumps, "we've certainly had more than our share of abnormal occurrences."

"Not that many," said Cooley, and he consulted his notebook. "Since the day when Mr. Ridge arrived, we've had only three."

There was a certain determination to Cooley that Thumps liked. "The guy at the motel?"

"Yeah," said Cooley. "That's number one."

"And Ridge disappearing."

"That's two."

Thumps tried to think of a third and came up empty. But the first two were enough to fill several notebooks.

"And number three is the fight at the Mustang a couple nights ago."

The Mustang was a country-and-western biker bar at the edge of town. It had a reputation for being rough, and finding a fight at the Mustang would be no more unusual than finding french fries at McDonald's.

"Normally, a fight at the Mustang would go under Normal," said Cooley.

"That's probably where I'd put it," said Thumps.

"But Big Fish Patek said this one was unusual."

"Big Fish Patek?"

"Yeah," said Cooley. "He's tending bar at the Mustang."

According to local lore, which, so far as Thumps could tell, the man had helped to create, Big Fish was either French Canadian from Manitoba or Swiss German from upstate New York. Why he settled in Chinook was equally clear. One version had him running out of gas and money as he got to the outskirts of town. Another had him coming west because he had seen the Rockies in a vision.

Thumps tried to imagine Big Fish tending bar at the Mustang. The man did not like steady employment in any form, preferred to work on the road out of his van selling anything that he could lay his hands on and turn around quickly. More to the point, Big Fish and the Mustang were, to Thumps's way of thinking, incompatible. Big Fish was built like a match, but he had a blowtorch for a mouth. At the Mustang, you had to be able either to fight or to talk your way out of trouble. Big Fish couldn't do either.

"He's one of my associates."

"Associates?"

"Sure," said Cooley. "In my business, you have to have a steady source of information. You have to know what's happening around you. That's one of the first principles of security."

Thumps glanced at the front doors. "So, there was a fight at the Mustang."

"Right," said Cooley. "Old guy comes in, orders a coffee, and then proceeds to pick a fight."

"Coffee?"

"Told you it was unusual."

"That's it?"

"Big Fish said he was wearing an expensive watch."

If Big Fish Patek had a passion, it was watches. At any time he had at least a hundred watches with him, and if he couldn't sell you anything else, he'd try to sell you a watch.

"Big Fish say who the guy was?" Thumps was half-hoping that Dakota was going to walk through the doors and save him from what he was thinking of doing.

"Nope," said Cooley. "Said he'd never seen him before."

COOLEY'S CHEVY WASN'T nearly as spacious as Thumps's Volvo. American car companies liked to build large, bulky cars, but they couldn't seem to design them with any legroom or headroom, while the Europeans, who made decidedly smaller cars, could.

Thumps pushed the seat all the way back, but he was still left sitting upright, his knees against the dash, his head touching the roof.

"My girlfriend thinks I should get a uniform."

At least the Chevy had a heater that worked.

"Personally, I think a T-shirt with a nice logo would be just as good. Black on black. So people will take you serious."

THE MUSTANG WAS the latest in western high tech, a red prefab aluminum building with a herd of wild horses painted across the front and a satellite-receiver array on the roof. You could drink beer with your buddies, watch any sporting event in the country, enjoy semi-clad dancing girls, or catch up on your email.

Lorraine Chubby, who owned the Mustang, was of the opinion that even cowboys and bikers deserved consideration and would appreciate a modern facility with all the latest amenities. And she had only three rules. If you wanted to fight, do it outside where Lorraine had thrown up a rope ring around a sand pit. With lights. And a spectator area. You could get at least eight reasonably large men in the ring at any one time, and to help ensure that injuries could be dealt with immediately, Lorraine had set up an outdoor sink with a remarkably well-stocked first-aid station.

Lorraine's second rule was no puking in the bar. All the bathrooms had a corrugated metal trough along one wall that, in the case of the men, doubled as a urinal. Anybody who was feeling under the weather was expected to make it to one of the bathrooms and use the facilities. If you threw up on the floor, you were thrown out.

Her last rule was fairly simple and straightforward. No excessive noise or interruptions when she was singing. Not that Lorraine had a great voice. It was okay, but she liked to sing and when she sang, she liked people to listen, and anyone with a modicum of sense knew to shut the hell up.

"Lorraine put in a new sound system," said Cooley as he pulled into the Mustang parking lot.

"What was wrong with the old one?"

"Said it made her sound flat."

BIG FISH PATEK was behind the bar, arranging glasses on a white towel. The last time Thumps had talked with Big Fish, the man tried to sell him a Nikon F80, arguing that all photographers needed an auto-focus camera, in case their eyes went bad. The camera had seen better days, and Thumps had made the mistake of asking the price. It had taken an additional two hours to extract himself from the sales pitch.

"Hey, Cooley."

Big Fish Patek's real name was Patek Carpenaux, but Wutty Youngbeaver had shortened his surname to Carp because he thought the French sounded pretentious. How it got from there to Big Fish, Thumps didn't know, but things like that happened in the West with alarming regularity.

"Thumps!"

"Hi, Big Fish."

"You ever find a camera?"

"Wasn't looking for one."

"Digital," said Big Fish. "That's the way to go. Got just the thing for you."

"We came about the fight," said Cooley.

"Oh, yeah," said Big Fish. "Weird."

Thumps frowned. "Weird?"

"Old guy," said Big Fish. "About your age. Hey, guess what he was wearing?"

Thumps knew Big Fish well enough to keep the questions to a minimum. "Okay, what was he wearing?"

"A Rolex," said Big Fish. "You believe that? A Rolex Daytona."

Cooley nodded. "That's a watch, right?"

Big Fish's eyes lit up. "You don't see many Rolexes out here. Course, they tend to be a little bulky. The new Cellini with the alligator-skin strap and platinum-pronged buckle is more elegant, though if you want elegant, you can't beat the Audemars Piguet, with the hand-engraved face."

"Big Fish—"

"Course, if you ask me, there's nothing like the Girard Perregaux, Vintage 1945 Tourbillon, or maybe a Blancpain minute repeater."

"Big Fish—"

"But if I had to choose, I'd probably go for a Patek Philippe Moonphase with a ten-day power reserve and a hinged half-hunter cover. Now that's a beautiful watch. Did you know my father named me after that watch?"

"Yeah," said Thumps. "You've mentioned it."

"You guys want something to drink?"

"How about a Pepsi," said Cooley.

"We got imported beer."

"I'll take a Pepsi too," said Thumps quickly.

"The German beers are always good, and so are most of the Canadians, but you really should give some of the New Zealand brands a try."

"The old guy with the Rolex?"

"Right," said Big Fish. "He comes in and orders a coffee."

"What time?"

"Eleven-thirty, maybe midnight. Place was pretty empty. The weekdays are a little slow. But you should see it on the weekends. Lorraine likes to get a band in on the weekends."

Thumps wanted to grab Big Fish by the neck and hold him in place. "So, this guy got into a fight?"

"No," said Big Fish. "He started the fight. Lorraine doesn't like the place getting broken up, so I told them to take it outside."

"Did they?"

"Sure," said Big Fish, "and he got the shit kicked out of him."

Thumps could see the watch clearly. Stainless steel with a metal band.

"Man must have had a death wish," said Big Fish. "The stupid sonofabitch picks a fight with Grover Many Horses."

TWENTY-TWO

Thumps and Cooley drank their Pepsis while Big Fish regaled them with suggestions for watches.

"Since you're in the security business now," he told Cooley, "you're going to need a watch that keeps good time, and not one of the slim-line models 'cause they just aren't as tough as the steel-cased watches."

So, Noah had gone to dinner with Chinook's society page, pretended he wasn't feeling good, run out to the Mustang when no one was looking, and staged a beating. For publicity. It was the only explanation that made any sense. Still, to drive to the Mustang and let someone beat on you, then go back to your room in pain and wait until morning so you could claim you were attacked, just to get coverage, was hard for Thumps to imagine.

"Of course, the hot watch right now is the TAG Heuer, but that's just because Tiger Woods is endorsing it."

But it shouldn't have been that hard to believe. Noah's life had been one theatrical performance after another. He had learned the lessons of journalism early. A story had to bleed or blow up or threaten or cry or really piss someone off if it was going to get told. For the celebration of the Columbus quincentennial at the Smithsonian, Noah had cut his forearms and splattered a model of the *Santa Maria* with blood.

"Thumps here is going to need something rugged with an easy-to-use timing system for those long exposures, and now that I think about it, the Fortis Pilot Professional Chronograph would be a good one for the both of you."

"Got a watch," said Cooley, and he held out his wrist.

"Timex?" Big Fish turned his head away. "Sure, it keeps time, but where's the joy?"

Thumps finished his drink and pushed the glass to one side. "Did you see the fight?"

"Nope," said Big Fish. "Had to watch the bar."

"Anybody see it?"

"Yeah, Wutty saw it and so did Reno Johnson." Big Fish stopped for a moment to think. "That was the other funny part. Wutty said the old guy never threw a punch, just kept shooting off his mouth and Grover kept hitting him."

"Sure sounds like the Unusual column to me," said Cooley.

Not as unusual as you might think, thought Thumps.

"So," said Big Fish, "what about those watches?"

On the way back to town, Cooley turned up the radio and sang along with Randy Travis. Just for fun, Thumps gave Cooley's columns a try, but everything wound up in the Unusual column. Noah's coming to Chinook was unusual. So was Street's death. Then Noah disappears. And Dakota still with the man? That was unusual as well. In fact, by the time Thumps had sorted through all of the items, he found he didn't have anything under Normal.

Cooley parked the car in front of the Tucker.

"You think it was him?"

"Don't know," said Thumps.

"It's okay," said Cooley, "I won't tell anyone."

No, thought Thumps, I don't guess you will. "Yeah, I think it was Noah."

"That means nobody beat him up down by the river."

"That's a good bet."

"Makes security tough," said Cooley. "Pretty hard to protect someone who wants to get beat up. Maybe he wanted to disappear too."

That, thought Thumps, was getting to be a very good possibility. "Good thing he's not a client."

"Oh, he's a client," said Cooley. "I gave him a complimentary security package. Got to do what you say you'll do. Otherwise, word could get out that you can't be trusted, and that would be the end of business."

"Don't know that Noah deserves that kind of dedication."

"Not doing it for him."

* * *

By the time Thumps got to Dakota's room, he wasn't in the mood to waste time. "He didn't get attacked by the river."

"What?"

"Noah. He went to a place called the Mustang the other night and let Lucy Kettle's kid brother beat the shit out of him. You want to tell me why?"

"What are you talking about?"

"Publicity," said Thumps. "It was for the publicity."

"You don't know that."

"Did Street call you?"

"What?"

"Mitchell Street. Did you talk to him?"

"No."

Dakota might have been lying, but Thumps didn't think so. There was something in her face, confusion perhaps, maybe anger.

"Street called the Tucker from his room. If he didn't talk to you, then he talked to Noah."

"Why would he call Noah?"

That was one of the questions for which Thumps did not have an answer. Why would Street call Noah? To threaten him? Given the history, it wouldn't have been to catch up on old times. Or maybe it had.

Dakota walked to the door and opened it. "I think you better leave," she said, her voice low and controlled.

"If you don't talk to me," said Thumps, "you'll have to talk to the sheriff and the FBI."

"Then," said Dakota, opening the door wider than necessary, "I'll talk to them."

As THUMPS RODE the elevator to the lobby, he wondered if he could have been any more churlish. It was the weather, of course. That was it. And the prospect of not feeling truly warm again for six months. Maybe seven. Not that Dakota had made things easy. Why he was attracted to women with no give was a mystery. His mother had been flexible. More or less.

The wind was up, and a very cold day had suddenly become frigid. Spencer Asah was waiting at the bottom of the stone steps, his breath steaming out of his mouth.

"We need to talk."

"No, we don't," said Thumps.

"Yes, we do."

Thumps wrapped his coat around his body, pulled his neck into his shoulders as far as he could, and headed down the street at a trot. "Give me your parka and we'll talk."

"No chance," said Asah.

"Then I'm going someplace warm."

"I may know where Ridge is."

Thumps didn't break stride. "Tell it to the sheriff."

"Okay, so I don't know. But we still have to talk."

The sun was out, and the horizon was bright. If it weren't for the wind and the temperature, Thumps might have imagined that it was summer.

"Sure," said Thumps, stopping for a moment and turning back to Asah. "Let's talk about the bonds."

Asah tried to keep his voice cheery, but Thumps could hear the growl. "What bonds?"

"Save it for the cameras." Thumps jammed his hands in his pockets and headed down Main Street. "And while we're at it, we can talk about Reuben Justice too."

* * *

AL'S SERVED BREAKFAST, sometimes into the early afternoon, but it wasn't open at this time of day, so Thumps settled for the closest alternative with heat.

Dumbo's.

Dumbo's sat at the edge of Main Street, a brown clapboard building in the middle of a parking lot. Normally Thumps wouldn't be caught alive in Dumbo's, but the wind pushed him down the street and in through the front door.

"Jesus," said Asah, wrinkling his nose, "you eat here?"

Dumbo's was known for two things, grease and doughnuts. Everything at Dumbo's was fried. Except maybe the coffee, and Thumps wasn't completely confident about that. But it was the smell that caught you first, a damp odour that reminded Thumps of wet clothes left too long in a plastic sack.

"The doughnuts are good." Thumps slid into a booth.

"You're kidding."

The owner/operator of Dumbo's was one Morris Dumbo, a rusty rail of a man who liked to speak his mind. Not that Morris had any mind to speak of.

"Hey, chief, long time no see." Morris eased himself

out of the brown Naugahyde recliner behind the counter. "Who's your friend?"

"FBI," said Thumps.

"No shit," said Morris. "You hear about our asshole mayor?"

Asah looked to see if Thumps was going to help.

"Doesn't want to let Wal-Mart open a store in town." Morris ran a wet rag across the table. "You believe that?"

"Really," said Asah, who could see he was going to be left on his own.

"What about a nice doughnut?" said Morris. "The both of you want doughnuts?"

"Just coffee," said Asah. "We have to talk."

"This look like a fucking chat room?"

"Two doughnuts," said Thumps.

"Damned straight," said Morris. "You want raised or cake?"

Asah waited until Morris had delivered the coffee and doughnuts and had crawled back into his chair behind the counter.

"Okay," said Asah, "so how the hell do you know about the bonds?"

Thumps willed his face to go blank.

"Come on. Don't give me that."

Thumps took a deep breath and let it out all in pieces. "Why is the FBI wasting time and money shadowing Noah?"

Asah was ready for the question. "The book," he said smoothly. "It opened old wounds."

"So, you're not here to protect him."

"Nope."

Thumps took a bite of his doughnut. "You're lying."

"You always so personable?"

"Only when someone lies to me."

Asah tried the doughnut tentatively. "You know," he said, "these aren't half-bad."

Thumps ran through the various scenarios, checking each one for flaws. "Okay," he said. "Let's do it the fun way. I'll guess at the right answers. You sit there and play dumb and eat your doughnut."

"Works for me."

"First, you didn't come because of the book."

Asah leaned back in the chair. "Really."

"If Ridge had anything on the FBI, he would have broadcast it on national television years ago. And if there had been something in the book that might have embarrassed the bureau, you guys would have been all over the publisher before the book ever hit the street."

Asah sat stone-faced. Good, thought Thumps, now I have his attention.

"The Xerox that Street had wasn't a novelty. It was a copy of the real thing." Thumps closed his eyes and tried to find the right rhythm. "How much did they get?"

Asah pursed his lips. "You want another dough-nut?"

"What I want is the truth." Thumps stuck his fork into a piece of doughnut. The outside edge glistened slightly in the light, and he wondered if it was sugar or grease.

"Okay, I'm going to trust you." Asah lowered his voice and made it sound as though his trust was a prize that Thumps had just won. "But nothing to the sheriff."

"I'm not going to lie to Duke."

"Just don't volunteer anything."

Thumps remembered how the bureau always liked to make everything sound more mysterious and more complicated than it was.

"Five million dollars. Pretty good motive, eh?"

Asah had thrown him a bone, but there wasn't much meat on it. "Buckhorn and Scout and Begay weren't bank robbers," said Thumps. "They were activists."

"Activists have to live."

"Why would Morgan have five million dollars in bearer bonds in its safe?"

"You'll have to ask Morgan about that." Asah finished his doughnut and pushed the plate away.

Thumps wondered how Street had felt when he opened the package and found the Xerox neatly tucked into a copy of Noah's new book. That was why he had come to Chinook. He had come to find Massasoit.

"When did Street call Denver?"

"Two weeks ago."

"Kemo-sabe," said Thumps, letting the word roll out of his mouth softly. "That was the authenticating phrase, wasn't it? The way Street knew that the message had come from Massasoit. That it was genuine."

Morris came around with the coffee, filled each cup about halfway, and tucked the bill between the napkin dispenser and the sugar jar. By then Thumps knew the conversation was over. He had told Asah everything he knew, and Asah had told him what Thumps had already known. Like looking in a mirror.

Asah paid the bill and walked with Thumps to the corner. "What are you going to do now?"

"Think I'll read Noah's book," he said.

"There's nothing in it," said Asah. "Already looked."

Thumps glanced at the sky. He had hopes that the sun would still be loose. But it was gone now, swept away by a flood of gun-metal grey ice. Street had come to Chinook to catch Massasoit. And maybe he had found him. Or her. Maybe that's why he was dead. Now it was Thumps's turn.

TWENTY-THREE

Asah got his car and dropped Thumps off in front of his house. It was a small kindness, but one that Thumps appreciated, though it made him feel a little ashamed of having given the man a hard time at Dumbo's. Well, maybe not ashamed. Apologetic perhaps. After all, Asah was only doing his job, and his job did not include sharing the particulars of a case with a photographer.

As Thumps hurried into the house, his neck buried in his shoulders, that's what he reminded himself that he was. A photographer. Nothing less and certainly nothing more. A photographer who had a darkroom filled with negatives just waiting to be printed.

Freeway was nowhere to be seen, which was just fine. Thumps was in no mood for a loving cat, much less a surly one. But as he made his way to the basement, he could feel his shoulders begin to relax. The darkroom was his sanctuary, a place where he could hide for hours, for days, and never miss anything or anyone. Sometimes he would turn the phone over on its back, so all anyone calling would get was a busy signal. The phone didn't like this, made a nasty siren-like sound for about thirty seconds, but then it would shut up, and all would be still.

Some photographers enjoyed listening to music while they printed, and on occasion Thumps would slide a powwow tape into the player or find some soft jazz on the radio. But for the most part, he kept the darkroom dead silent, which, as it turned out, was the wrong metaphor, for as soon as he thought "dead silent," he immediately saw Beth's morgue and, worse, wondered if her basement was as quiet as his, at which point he was sorry he had entertained the thought at all.

So, instead of going into the darkroom, Thumps settled in the overstuffed chair in the corner of his studio and began cleaning his lenses. It was a ritual he enjoyed, taking each lens out of the bag and holding it up against the light like a diamond or a glass of wine. He'd check each lens for clarity, brush the dust away, rub off any fingerprints or smears with a soft cloth and a gentle, circular action. And after that, he would sit and test-fire each lens at each aperture, at each speed, to make sure that the intervals were even, so he could hear the blades of the shutter slide across each other with a smooth hiss.

All the puzzle pieces were there in the puzzle box. Noah, Street, Dakota, Grover, Reuben. Along with Clinton Buckhorn, Wilson Scout, Wallace Begay. And always, always, Lucy Kettle. The living and the dead. Not that either group was saying much. Not that any of it made much sense. The more Thumps looked, the more he felt he was missing something. A large piece. A piece that would help the other fragments organize themselves into a shape.

That was the moment Thumps most liked in photography. When all the shapes came together on the ground glass, when the variations of light organized themselves in a pleasing, sometimes astonishing pattern. That moment when everything was clean and perfect. Maybe that's what he had liked about police work.

Thumps held the gold-ring Goerz Dagor and checked it for any signs of mould. It was a lovely lens, 8 1/4 in a No. 1 Copal shutter, small and compact with a wonderful signature that was particularly valuable in portraiture, a lens sharp enough to catch the brilliance of eyes but with a soft, rounding effect that gave dimension to a face and didn't flatten out features the way the newer Nikons and Fujis did.

It took him less than an hour to clean and test all the lenses, and because there was nothing but trouble and sorrow waiting for him upstairs, he took the field camera apart and cleaned the bellows, checked it for light leaks, and inspected the gear drive and the rails for any signs of misalignment and wear.

Then he cleaned the camera bags, rearranged the photo storage folders, wiped down the light box, vacuumed the floor, and stacked the containers of slides in groups of four rather than three.

At seven o'clock, Thumps turned the phone over and called Claire. "I'm sorry about the other night."

"I hear it got rather exciting."

"You doing anything?"

"I'm going to bed."

"Can I come by?" Thumps tried to think of the right thing to say. "Be nice to see you."

"As in sex?"

Okay, so that wasn't the right thing to say. But Claire hadn't posed the question in a nasty way. It was a straightforward question, the generic kind, the kind Thumps dealt with every day. Will the car start? What shall I have for lunch? Should I stay in bed? And Thumps understood this.

"Where are you?" Claire's voice sounded softer now.

"At my place."

"Don't take too long."

Thumps knew better, but he could feel his spirits begin to rise.

"Otherwise, I'll be asleep," said Claire.

DRIVING OUT TO Claire's place was like slipping back in time. Before Europeans and Big Macs. Claire's great-grandfather had built the original cabin on the circle of bottom land that had been carved out and left behind by the Ironstone River as it came out of the mountains and worked its way south. The cabin was no longer standing, had been exchanged for a sky-blue-and-white aluminum prefab rectangle, which was sturdy and functional, though nothing much to look at. Thumps would have described the structure itself as ugly, but not the view. From every window in the house, you could look out at the foothills and the mountains and prairies, and watch the light and the sky turn with the seasons.

In his travels, Thumps had seen only a few truly beautiful places. This was one of them.

Claire was waiting for him at the door as he pulled up.

"Can I park the car in the barn?"

"It's not that cold," said Claire, who was familiar with the Volvo's reputation.

"Just as a precaution."

THE BARN WAS an ancient arrangement of posts and beams, mitred and pinned in place with wood dowels and bracing. The floor was covered with straw, and as the Volvo rolled over the soft carpet, Thumps could feel the car kneading the ground with its tires, as though it were getting ready to snuggle down for the night. Then again, maybe it was.

Thumps had forgotten which of the Merchants had built the barn, but whoever it was had built it to last. Most old barns around Chinook were falling apart, their roofs peeled off by the wind, the siding pulled away by the elements. Claire's barn had simply weathered, and standing inside it felt like standing inside a fortress. Or a mountain.

Thumps wasn't sure if he noticed the rope first or the blood. Some barns were junkyards with tools and tractors and hay and pieces of old furniture tossed in on top of each other. Claire's barn was generally pristine, at least as barns went. Tools were hung up, the hay stacked. So, the rope wrapped around one of the support posts for no good reason was a curiosity. Whoever had done it had wrapped the rope and packed it tight the way you would if you were making a scratching post for a cat. But the arrangement stood at chest level, too high for a cat, and the dried blood on the rope was one of those things that Cooley might have put on his list under Unusual. Next to the post was a set of sawhorses and a small pile of boards that had been snapped in half.

The things you find in a barn.

Claire was waiting for him in the living room. She was sitting on the sofa in her housecoat.

"Car happy?"

The housecoat was terry cloth, a thick dark-green blanket that covered Claire from head to toe. She had had it for as long as he had known her, and from the garment's general condition, Thumps suspected that it was the only housecoat she had ever owned. Frumpy was the kindest word to describe it, but Thumps understood how certain items of clothing could become magic and take on almost mystical qualities, lucky shirts, power suits, shoes that whisked you along. And truth to tell, Thumps liked the robe. There was a sensual quality to its frayed sleeves and threadbare bottom.

"You want some tea?"

No, Thumps thought to himself, I don't want tea.

The other reason Thumps liked the robe was that it generally marked the beginning of foreplay. Most times when Claire was interested in sex, she would begin the complications in the robe. There would be the chatting, the nuzzling, the necking, the hands and lips wandering around, and then, before Thumps could find the belt and undo the knot, the robe would be open, not all the way, but enough so he could slip a hand in and touch warm flesh.

That was the true joy of sex. Not the penetration or the brief but enjoyable thrusting and bucking, but that first moment when you felt someone else's body. For Thumps, being stretched out against Claire, all of his skin touching all of hers, was as good as it gets.

"You find Ridge yet?" Claire pulled the robe to one side and crossed a leg.

Thumps took a deep breath. "No."

"What about his woman?"

There was that phrase again. Thumps could imagine the sheriff or Asah and certainly Morris Dumbo making that mistake. European society, after all, had for hundreds of years cast women as items of property.

"She's not his woman."

"Is she yours?" Claire pulled the robe back over her leg.

"No."

"I didn't mean now."

Thumps shook his head. "Not then either."

"You don't have to tell me."

Thumps eased away from Claire. Why did women say that? He knew it was a gross generalization, that not all women said "You don't have to tell me." Now that he thought about it, he remembered a woman he had met at graduate school, Elizabeth something, who insisted on knowing everything. But more women had told him he didn't have to tell them something than had insisted on being told. Men, in Thumps's experience, didn't want to know all that much. What they needed to know, they could see. Or hear. Or taste. Or smell.

Claire slid across the sofa and leaned up against Thumps. "Don't mind me," she said. "I'm just worried about Stanley."

And there it was. The reason for the invitation. Thumps was getting thick. He had been misled by the tone of Claire's voice on the phone and by the bathrobe. It wasn't sex Claire was interested in. It was her son.

"Stanley's fine."

"What would you do if he were your son?"

Thumps entertained himself for a moment imagining Stick draped over his lap. Thumps was not an advocate of corporal punishment, but he had more than once wanted to give the kid a good spanking.

"Look, when Stick gets home, ask him about the barn."

"What about the barn?" There was just the hint of alarm in Claire's voice.

"Just ask him."

"Is it serious?" Claire put her hand on Thumps's arm and coaxed it toward her.

"No," said Thumps as he felt his hand slide under Claire's robe.

"Can you stay a while?" Claire let the robe fall open. No red thong and push-up bra. It was much better.

"You always entertain with nothing on under your robe?"

Claire swung up and straddled Thumps's lap. She leaned forward and kissed him softly on the mouth, then straightened and let the robe slide off her shoulders.

"What robe?" she said as she eased his head to her breasts.

* * *

THUMPS WOKE CUDDLED UP to a large pillow. At first he thought it was Claire lying next to him, but when he swung a leg over what he thought must be her thigh, he discovered that it wasn't. Claire didn't believe in large beds, and it took Thumps no time at all to find that he was in bed alone. The bathroom was his first guess, but as he lay in bed, waiting for her to return, he slowly came to the realization that not only was he the only person in bed, he was the only person in the house.

If this had been summer, Thumps would have gone looking for Claire on the porch, where she liked to sleep during the hot weather. But not even an Inuit would be on the porch tonight.

Thumps got his clothes on and padded across the living room to the window. There was ice on the glass, but outside the winter sky was ablaze with stars, bright as fire. This was one of the pleasures, Thumps reminded himself, of living close with the land. You couldn't see skies like this in a city, not even a city the size of Chinook.

Thumps didn't really expect to find Claire wrapped in her bathrobe, standing on the prairies enjoying the winter sky, and she wasn't. But there was a light on in the barn. He should have known better, should have mentioned the barn in the morning. Now there was no getting around the problem he had created.

Claire was sitting on a bale of hay next to the beam lashed with rope. When Thumps came into the barn, he had the uncomfortable feeling that Claire had been waiting here all this time for him to show up.

"You need to hear it from Stick."

"I want to hear it from you."

"It's nothing."

"Is that blood on the rope?"

Stubbornness is contagious. If Claire wasn't going to ask the question she wanted to ask, Thumps wasn't going to answer it.

"Ask Stick."

"Stanley isn't here." Claire readjusted the robe so it looked more like chain mail. "You are."

Thumps had read an article that claimed that, after sex, women wanted to cuddle and talk while men wanted to flee. Whoever wrote the piece hadn't talked to Claire. She was passionate enough. And loving, for that matter. But there was also a single-mindedness to the woman that could burn through the afterglow of intercourse with all the grace of an acetylene torch.

"He's training."

Claire looked at the post. "For what?"

"I don't know." It wasn't exactly a lie. Thumps didn't know. Not for sure. Though he was willing to put money on a guess.

"You're sure."

Thumps stepped up to the post and threw a half-hearted punch at the rope wrappings. "It's a homemade makiwara board. Martial artists use it to toughen their hands."

Claire stood up and came to the post. She ran a hand across the blood stains. "He didn't get a black eye from hitting a post."

"That's as much as I know."

Claire eased herself into Thumps's arms. "He's all I have."

The article hadn't mentioned tears. Thumps knew this was a simple matter. He was to put his arms around her and hold her gently but tightly, so she knew she was loved. He was not to say comforting things such as "it'll be all right" or ask questions such as

"what's wrong?" or get frustrated with the contradic-
tions of cause and effect. He was not to try to solve the
problem. He was to keep his mouth shut. Someone,
probably a woman, had told him that many times
women cry not because they're unhappy but because
it relieves stress. Unfortunately, knowing this was not
a great help, and as he stood in the barn with Claire
buried against his chest, Thumps could feel his emotions heading for high ground to escape the flood.

"Can you stay the night?"

"I think the night's over."

"You don't like me crying, do you?"

There were all sorts of trick questions that you had
to deal with in a relationship, and Thumps had never
been able to figure out the right answers. Partly it was
because the answers changed, and partly it was because
there were no right answers. Only wrong ones.

"It's not that," said Thumps, which is what he
always said.

"You always say that," said Claire.

Thumps stroked Claire's hair, but his heart wasn't
in it. His mind had already returned to the matter at
hand. Noah Ridge.

"Well, if you're going," said Claire, pushing away and wiping her eyes, "you should get going."

"Maybe my car won't start."

Claire kissed Thumps on the cheek. "Call me when all of this is done."

The wind had died down, and watching Claire walk back to the house, from the shelter of the barn, almost made the world feel warm. Part of him wanted to go with her, crawl into bed, and stay there. Maybe the car would help. But as he slipped the key into the ignition, he knew the perverse collection of metal and plastic and wires would kick over on the first turn.

And, of course, it did.

TWENTY-FOUR

Thumps arrived at the top of the coulee just as the sky was beginning to soften. Below him on the river bottom was Moses Blood's place. Thumps hadn't seen dawn come up in a very long time, so he waited in the car with the heater running and watched the early-morning colours leave the eastern horizon and climb into the sky. The sun would arrive later. Perhaps it would be a bright day. Maybe even warm.

The track down the side of the coulee was in no better shape than the last time he had taken it, and as the Volvo shuddered and snapped from side to side and plunged in and out of the ruts and potholes, Thumps wondered what he thought he was going to accomplish. Maybe he just needed a place to rest for a while, where neither the sheriff nor Asah, Dakota, or Claire, or Freeway, for that matter, could find him. Someplace safe and quiet. Someplace where people were kind to one another. Someplace where folks didn't kill each other.

Thumps was used to finding the unexpected when he visited Moses, but the green plastic table with its yellow-and-red umbrella, sitting in the snow in the yard, was a startling surprise. Moses was sitting in one of the two lounge chairs. On the table was a large thermos and two cups. Through the windshield, Thumps could have mistaken the scene for a picnic.

"Been expecting you," said Moses as Thumps stepped out of the car.

Thumps had been wrong. Sun or no sun, it wasn't going to be warm.

"Boy," said Moses, "you got to like this weather."

"It's a little cold."

"Sure," said Moses, "but it's supposed to be cold. No point complaining about the cold in winter. Always best to save the complaining for the spring when it's supposed to be warm and it isn't."

Thumps could see the logic of this, but he could also feel his blood beginning to thicken.

"I'll bet you're looking for that famous guy who disappeared."

Thumps was never surprised anymore by what Moses knew. "I figured he was in one of your trailers playing video games."

"Ho," said Moses, "that's what that guy on the university channel would call 'droll.' You got to love English. That language has sure got some great words."

"So, you haven't seen him."

"Nope."

"You know anyone who has?"

"Nope."

Moses wasn't one to hoard information, but like Cooley, if you wanted an answer to a question, you had to ask the right question.

"You hear anything?"

"I hear all sorts of things. Some of it, shouldn't listen to. Especially television. The things those guys say."

"What do they say about Noah Ridge?"

"Some nice television woman said that there was blood in the hotel room." Moses opened the thermos.

"She said there had been a death threat and that a retired FBI agent had already been rubbed out."

That was pretty much it, all right, thought Thumps. There wasn't much more than that. "I should probably be getting back to town."

Moses poured the tea. It came out of the thermos in clouds of steam and rolled into the cups. "You should warm up first. Cold is okay, but you don't want to overdo it."

Thumps eased himself into the chair and gripped the arms to try to stop from shaking. "He could be dead."

"Sure," said Moses, "but who would want to kill him?"

That should have been an easy question, but now that Moses had asked it, had said it out loud, Thumps realized that he hadn't really considered the possible answers as carefully as he had thought. In a perfect world, Mitchell Street would have been at the top of the list, but he was dead. Grover Many Horses would make a good suspect, but only because of a sister he had barely known. That left Dakota Miles and Reuben Justice. Neither of them was a particularly good choice. Dakota had stuck with Noah through good times and bad, and Justice, so far as Thumps could tell, had no particular reason to dislike Noah enough to kill him. And all that before you got to the other question. Why?

The only possibility that made sense was that Noah had staged his own kidnapping and then gone into hiding. And that, when the time was right, he would reappear with a story good enough to send book sales right through the roof. That worked as long as you ignored Street's body lying in Beth's morgue and the blood in Noah's room.

"Here it comes." Moses raised his head and let the first light of the sun strike his face. "Boy, that is one beautiful sight."

Thumps's head was tucked into his jacket, and he wasn't about to move it.

"Sure beats television," said Moses.

"Good tea."

"Most Indians on the run would head back to the reservation or into the mountains," said Moses. "But I don't guess your man is one of those. Maybe he's more like you."

"I suppose."

"So," said Moses, leaning back to enjoy the light, "where would you go?"

"Someplace warm."

"Florida," said Moses. "I hear the Indians in Florida dance with alligators."

"I need some information." Thumps took a pen and a piece of paper out of his pocket. "You think you could ask Stick to check this out on the internet?"

"Sure," said Moses. "We'll talk to the Nephews about it. They're not real smart, but they know a lot of stuff."

Thumps could feel his teeth start to rattle in his head. He wiggled his toes in his shoes to make sure they were still alive.

"Can't beat winter," said Moses. "It's my favourite season. Everything slows way down, and the world gets quiet. If you listen, you can hear mountains talking to each other."

"I prefer summer," said Thumps.

"You ever see otters come down an ice slide? They have a good time in winter 'cause they have a good coat of fur." Moses poured the last of the tea into the cups. "That's the secret. Animals or humans, it doesn't matter. If you're going to enjoy winter, you have to have a good coat."

As THUMPS GOT back to the main road, he reminded himself that he was not Noah. Moses had been wrong about that. For the most part. But he had been right about the rest. Noah wouldn't have headed for the reservation. A stranger, Indian or White, in that world wouldn't stay hidden for long. And he wouldn't go to the mountains either. Certainly not in winter. He would go someplace else. Someplace out of sight. Someplace warm.

Thumps had just turned onto Main Street when he saw the flashing light in his rear-view mirror. Thumps couldn't see who was behind the wheel of the cruiser, but he guessed it was Andy Hooper. He and the deputy were not exactly on speaking terms, and Thumps knew that giving him a ticket was going to make Andy's day.

But the man who lumbered out of the police car and motioned for Thumps to roll his window down was not Hooper. It was the sheriff.

"Went through that stop sign back there." Hockney squatted down so he was on eye level.

"No, I didn't."

"Running a stop sign's a serious offence."

"You're kidding." Thumps tried to think of what he might have done to get the sheriff any angrier than he had been when Thumps had last seen him.

"Where've you been?"

"Out."

"I don't pay you for being out."

"So far, you haven't paid me at all."

"Might have to take the fine out of your salary."

Thumps was much too tired to play this game. "Okay, I quit."

The sheriff rocked back on his heels. "You know, you're getting pretty good at quitting."

"Is there a point?"

"Maybe I won't give you a ticket."

"Duke . . ."

Hockney grabbed the edge of the window and pulled himself to his feet. "Andy just called in. He's found Ridge."

Thumps searched the sheriff's face for the answer to

the question. But all he could find was the weariness that all cops carried with them.

"I was just on my way out there."

"Alive or dead?"

"You got your cameras?"

"Yeah."

"Then you better bring them."

THUMPS FOLLOWED HOCKNEY north out of town. At the Shell station, they turned east and headed out onto the back of the prairies. Here the world was broad and uninspiring, a landscape of space, where the air seemed thin and precious. He had tried creating a series of photographs out by Red Tail Lake, but even with an orange filter to darken the sky and make the clouds appear more dramatic, the final result had been disappointing. Thumps loved water, but not even the lake had been able to save the composition.

But now that seemed to be where they were headed. Red Tail Lake. The sheriff had hinted that they were going to look at a corpse. Thumps had heard the hint but had not followed up on it. Maybe he didn't want to believe that Noah was dead. The more he had thought about it, the more he had liked his theory that the man was just a publicity-seeking egotist who would do anything to get on the evening news. But if Andy had actually found Noah's body, the whole complexion of the case would change, and at that point, Thumps promised himself, he would quit again.

Thumps had been to Red Tail Lake only two or three times. Once for photography and once with Claire, when Sterling Noseworthy, owner of Wild Rose Realty, had thrown a summer party for people with money. Neither Claire nor Thumps qualified, and Thumps wasn't sure why she had got the invitation, though he suspected that it had to do with the con-dominiums at Buffalo Mountain. Wild Rose was the exclusive listing agency for the units, and inviting two Indians to a rich folks' party was probably Sterling's way of saying thanks.

A Radio Shack gift certificate would have been more fun, but it hadn't been a complete waste of an evening. Thumps had been able to sell two of his photographs and had arranged a commission with a banker from Missoula to take a black-and-white picture of the man's house with the lake in evening light. Thumps had spent the better part of two days trying to get the house and the lake to co-operate, but in the end he had had to settle for a sombre portrait in which neither of the participants would smile.

The third time was a fishing trip. Hockney had talked him into his fishing boat, a tiny aluminum shell with a huge motor, which required Thumps to sit at the very front, or the bow, as Duke corrected him, to counterbalance the weight. Thumps suspected that getting the boat trim required a second fisherman, and that if Hockney tried to take it out all by himself, the boat would sink at the back. Or the stern.

They had even caught fish.

Most of Red Tail Lake was wild. The southern end was a state park that nobody used, while the east side dribbled out into a series of capillaries and marshes. The west side contained the tiny town of Red Tail, which consisted of a general store and gas station and a "waterfront" motel.

Dora Manning owned everything in Red Tail: store, station, and motel. Thumps had met her once, on the fishing trip, when Hockney had stopped at the pumps to get gas for his car and his boat.

Hockney pulled into the gas station. Thumps pulled in behind him.

"You need gas?"

"No." Thumps double-checked the gas gauge. It was one of the few things on the car that worked on a regular basis. The needle was on full, which was good, since he knew the car was looking for any excuse to roll over and quit.

Maybe he and the car had more in common than he imagined. Dora was behind the counter stacking cigarettes into the plastic dispensers. Hockney was standing in front of the glass doors looking at the soft drinks.

"You got any root beer?"

"No root beer," said Dora.

Hockney grabbed two lemonades and brought them to the counter. "How's business?"

"Fine," said Dora.

Dora had worked for a big corporation somewhere back east. Not that you would have guessed it to look at her. She was a tall, gangly woman with a long face and thin hair who reminded Thumps of photographs he had seen of sharecroppers from Oklahoma on their way to California.

Hockney laid a five-dollar bill on the counter. "You know where the Connor place is?"

"There trouble out there?" Thumps asked.

"That which is everybody's business is nobody's business," said Dora without blinking.

"Do tell," said the sheriff.

"A man stopped here the other day," said Dora. "Got gas and a couple bags of chips."

Hockney took off his hat and spun the brim around his finger. "That's exciting, all right."

"Asked about the lake." Dora gestured to the community bulletin board at the back of the store. "Talked to Arthur about real estate."

The sheriff nodded. "He use a credit card?"

Dora shook her head. "Cash. Maybe Mr. Dreadful-Water knows him."

"Thumps?" Hockney was looking sour again.

"He was Indian," said Dora. "Don't see too many Indians out here at the lake."

"Yeah," said the sheriff, "I'll bet. Can you draw me a map to the Connor place?"

"Journey over all the universe in a map, without the expense and fatigue of travelling, without suffering

314

the inconveniences of heat, cold, hunger, and thirst."

"Was that a yes?" said the sheriff.

"No," said Dora, "that was Cervantes."

THE CONNOR PLACE was one of the newer houses on the north end of the lake, an area that had come to be known as The Shore. It was a pretentious designation for a strip of lakefront that consisted of rocks and sand and a slight elevation, which gave you the illusion of being on high ground. There was nothing particularly wrong with the view, but neither was there anything to recommend it. The Shore was the water version of Glory, a seasonal shelter for the wealthy.

Archie had told him that The Shore had originally been a series of fishing cabins. It didn't have a name in those days, and that didn't change even after the cabins had been converted into summer cottages. But then money moved in, and the cabins and the cottages were bulldozed to make way for real houses with floor-to-ceiling windows, hot tubs, and wraparound decks.

Mind you, no one lived year-round at The Shore. The houses were winterized, but as soon as the geese

took to the sky, so did the people. Which meant everyone who lived at The Shore had at least two houses.
Thumps suspected that many of them had more.

"Who's Arthur?"

"Dora's husband," said the sheriff.

"I thought she was on her own."

"She is," said Hockney. "Arthur died about two
years back."

"But she said Arthur talked to the man."

"You know," said the sheriff, "nothing much gets
by you, does it?"

THE CONNOR PLACE sat on a promontory of land that
ran out into the lake. It was a split-level affair with
blue-grey hardboard siding and a series of large port-
hole windows at the front. Thumps suspected that all
the real windows were at the back overlooking the
water, and he found himself moderately excited about
seeing the inside of the house.

Andy's cruiser was parked in the driveway, and
Thumps could see right away what had made Andy

suspect that something was amiss. Fresh tracks in the snow.

"You believe it?" said Hockney, climbing out of his car. "They build a house like this in the middle of nowhere, and then they don't live in it."

"They do in the summer."

"Two months," said the sheriff. "Three, tops. You got your cameras?"

"So, Ridge is dead."

Hockney hitched up his pants as he walked through the thin snow to the front door. "Guess that blows your publicity theory."

"Wasn't my theory."

"You got any others?" said the sheriff. "'Cause we're going to need a good one right about now."

TWENTY-FIVE

Thumps had been right about the windows. The entire south side of the house was a wall of glass. He wondered what the panorama looked like in the summer, because right now the view was desolate. That's why no one stayed past early autumn. Sitting on the designer couches and looking out the windows could really get depressing. Not that there was much room on the couches. Andy was stretched out on one, eating his lunch, and stretched out on the other was Noah's body.

"Hey, sheriff." Andy slipped his feet back in his boots. "You believe this place?"

"You call Beth?"

"As soon as I found him." Andy smiled at Thumps.

Noah was curled up on the couch, his face buried in the cushion. If it hadn't been for the large blood stain that covered the back of his shirt, Thumps might have thought he was simply taking a nap. He looked smaller now, as though death had shrunk him. Thumps tried to find the emotions he should be feeling, but all he could think about was Dakota and how she was going to take this. And whether she had anything to do with it.

"Looks like he was shot," said Andy. "Could have been a suicide."

"You mean like Street?"

"Come on, Duke," said Andy. "It was a joke."

"You want me to take the pictures now?"

"Take them later." The sheriff looked out the windows at the deck and the lake. "Right now, you're a deputy and we need to talk."

"A deputy?" Andy swung himself off the couch. "Him?"

"Don't worry," said Thumps, "it's just temporary."

"Duke . . ."

Hockney stopped Andy with a gesture. "Watch the

body until Beth gets here. Eat your lunch, and don't make a mess."

"Shit! He's a fucking civilian!" Andy had a short fuse and it was lit. "I'm the one who found him."

"And you did a good job," said the sheriff, as though each word were cutting his tongue. "Let me know when Beth gets here."

THE DECK WAS the last place Thumps wanted to talk.

"Couldn't we talk inside?"

"Andy's there."

"Have him eat his lunch out here." Thumps stuffed his hands in his pockets. "We can watch the body."

"Get a warmer coat."

There was a mean streak that ran through Hockney, which could have passed for simple stubborn, if you didn't know the man. If Thumps remembered correctly, it was Flannery O'Connor who said that there wasn't any pleasure in life but meanness, or something to that effect, and he supposed that even though she had never known Hockney, she had him in mind.

Thumps began moving from side to side to stay warm. "It wasn't your fault."

"Course it wasn't," said the sheriff. "And I'm not blaming you either."

"Me?"

"He was your friend."

"No, he wasn't."

The sheriff blew a long silvery cloud out of his mouth toward the lake. "How much you think one of these things costs?"

"Half a million minimum."

"You think they'd care if my wife and I moved in for the winter?"

Thumps tried to stop the smile. "Rich people don't like company."

"Yeah," said Hockney. "You think she killed him?"

Thumps had been waiting for the question. "Dakota's life is the movement. Like it or not, the only thing of value that RPM has is Noah."

"Had," said Hockney. "So, you don't think it was a triangle or something like that?"

It was cold as hell outside, but the sheriff was

beginning to warm him up. "You mean me and Dakota and Noah?"

"That would make a triangle."

"Sounds like something Andy would come up with."

"Say what you will," said Hockney, "he did find the body."

"And exactly what was he doing out here?"

The sheriff shrugged. "Doing what all good law enforcement personnel do. Making the rounds. Checking the territory."

"So, he's on his regular patrol. He knows all the houses are closed for the season, and he drives by one that has fresh tracks going to the garage." Thumps waited to see if the sheriff wanted to give it up.

"He found the body, that's all that counts."

"Blind squirrel could have found that acorn."

Hockney turned his head to the sound of scrunching snow. "That'll be the body lady."

"You don't expect me to congratulate Andy, do you?"

"Couldn't hurt," said the sheriff. "You can never have too many friends."

Thumps was sure that Andy had friends, other men

who thought bigotry was simply personal opinion and that sexism was funny as hell. And if he was being honest with himself, Thumps had probably laughed at the same jokes that amused Andy and his buddies.

Beth looked at the house. "Nice place."

Even buried under a couple of layers of fleece, Beth looked good. Thumps knew that she went to the gym at least four times a week and watched what she ate, and he knew he was never going to follow her example. Still, the results were marvellous.

"Inside or out?"

"In," said the sheriff, and he led the parade back to where the air was warm and where Thumps could take his hands out of his pockets and stop shivering.

"You boys have been busy." Beth set her bag on the floor next to the body.

"I found him," said Andy.

Beth slipped on a pair of rubber gloves. "You take any pictures yet?"

"Not yet," said Thumps.

"Then give me a few minutes to get organized."

"Take all the time you want. Me and Thumps are going to look around."

"What about me?" said Andy, who was not keen on being left behind again.

"Tell Beth how you found the body," said the sheriff.

THUMPS WASN'T SURE how many summer homes had three-car garages, and he couldn't remember if he had ever been in one. He would have been happy with a single garage in which to store the Volvo. Three seemed excessive, even ostentatious.

"Well," said the sheriff after he found the light switch, "that's what I call a garage."

"Yeah," said Thumps. "But it doesn't solve your problem."

"You mean our problem," said Hockney.

The garage was empty. There was a set of tracks in the middle bay, tracks left by melting snow. But no car.

The sheriff squatted down by the tracks and felt the concrete. "Shit. Get a shot of this."

Thumps could feel Hockney's frustration. Street's murder was bad enough. And now this.

"All right." Hockney stood up and wiped his hands on his pants. "We have a body that didn't get here by itself. We have fresh tire tracks in the snow that come off the road and into this garage. So, someone beats Noah up, brings him out here, and shoots him, or they shoot him at the hotel and then bring him out here. That the way you read it?"

"Yeah," said Thumps, "but it doesn't make any sense."

"It sure as hell doesn't. If you're going to kill the sonofabitch, why not do it at the hotel and leave the body there? No profit in dragging it all the way out here."

"Maybe our killer is a real-estate agent."

"Hysterical," said Hockney. "You and Andy ought to go on tour."

"Sorry."

"No," said the sheriff, "two murders in less than a week is real funny."

"You figure it's the same guy?"

"Little sexist, isn't it?"

"You know what I mean."

The sheriff walked over to the workbench and ran his hand along all the tools that were neatly organized on pegboard. "Compound cut-off saw," said Hockney.

"I was going to buy one, but I've already got one mortgage on the house."

"At least we don't have to deal with reporters."

"They'll be here soon enough."

Thumps wondered how the Connors would feel about an army of journalists invading their home. Not that they were using it right now. They might even enjoy the notoriety. It would certainly give them something to talk about with their friends and neighbours for the two months they spent at the lake.

"My wife's got this chart that shows the effect that stress has on life expectancy." Hockney strolled to the door that led back to the house. "Wants me to be more optimistic. Wants me to look on the bright side of things."

"How's it going?"

"Great," said the sheriff as he flipped off the lights. "According to the chart, I should have died two years ago."

Beth was waiting for them. "Just in time," she said. "Anybody want to tell me what we have here?"

Andy swaggered over, his hands on his hips. "Sure," he said. "We got a dead guy on a couch."

Beth kept a straight face. "Any of the other children want to answer the question?"

Thumps had learned a long time ago that there were times when it was best to keep your mouth shut, and so far as he could see, this was one of those times. Besides, making Andy look foolish was too easy.

Hockney waited as long as he could. "She's asking about the pillow and the blanket."

Andy looked. "Yeah? What about them?"

"The pillow's under his head," said the sheriff. "The blanket is over his feet."

"You mean it could be suicide?"

Hockney turned around in a slow circle. Thumps wondered if the sheriff was working on seeing the bright side of Andy.

"He was shot in the back," said Beth. "Probably at the hotel. I don't think we have to worry about suicide."

"Okay," said Andy, who was not enjoying being the centre of attention, "so someone shot him."

"And then brought him out to the lake and made him all nice and comfy, so he could enjoy the view?" Hockney took a deep breath and held it for a moment.

"Why don't you ask your new deputy those questions?" Andy had switched from stupid to angry.

"Because," said the sheriff, in the most fatherly tone of voice he could muster, "he knows the answers."

NORMALLY, CRIME SCENES had any number of things to photograph, but besides the tire tracks in the garage, there was only Noah's body. Thumps took it from several angles, while Andy tried to make small talk with Beth.

"So, you work out?"

"That's right," said Beth.

"At Marco's gym?"

"That's the one."

"I work out sometimes," said Andy.

"Good for you."

Thumps couldn't believe it. Andy was trying to hit on Beth. Even the sheriff looked amused.

"You know what I heard?" said Beth. "I hear that you're an avid heterosexual."

"Me?" Andy sounded genuinely alarmed. "Who the hell told you that?"

"You get shots of the front?"

Thumps checked the film in the camera. "Not yet."

"No time like the present," said Beth. "Come on, Andy. You look like a strong man."

Thumps had seen enough bodies loaded onto stretchers and gurneys to last a lifetime, but as Beth and Andy rolled Noah off the couch and into the body bag, he felt a new and unpleasant sensation.

"Shit!" Hockney growled and stepped away. "Fucking great."

Thumps wasn't sure if the sensation was anger or relief or a little of both.

"I'm getting real annoyed," said the sheriff, "and what I'd like right about now is for someone to tell me who in the hell this is."

"Noah Ridge," said Andy, pleased that he had got the answer to the question right.

"What about you," said the sheriff, glaring at Thumps, "you know him?"

"Yeah," said Thumps as he looked at the face of the dead man for the first time. "It's Reuben Justice."

TWENTY-SIX

Thumps could feel the full weight of Hockney's anger descending on him, and he knew it wasn't going to do any good to protest.

"Who?" said Andy, who was trying to catch up.

"Another one of your old friends?" Hockney tried to scorch Thumps with a glance.

Thumps liked to think of Andy as a reasonably complete idiot, but he had to admit that the mistake had been an easy one to make. From the back. Reuben and Noah did resemble one another. Thumps hadn't noticed. Neither had the sheriff.

Hockney pulled up a chair and sat down. "Don't you dare tell me that you all look alike."

"Wouldn't do that."

"Damn it, DreadfulWater."

Outside, it was beginning to snow again. The flakes floated past the bank of windows, and for a moment, the world looked soft and gentle.

"Not guilty," said Thumps.

"You know," said the sheriff, "I'm beginning to take a real interest in our Mr. Ridge."

"Don't let me stop you." If Thumps were the cop working the case, he'd sure as hell want to talk to Noah. "FBI knows more than it's telling."

"Don't I know it."

"You're going to have to tell the bureau about this."

"As far as I'm concerned," said Hockney, "Special Agent Asah can find his own damn bodies." The sheriff put his hat on and walked to the window to watch the snow come down. "Andy and I are going to stick around and do all that crime-scene stuff you see cops do on television. I suppose you still want to quit."

"You bet."

"But you're going to stick around and help, aren't you?"

***

THUMPS FOLLOWED BETH into town. The sheriff hadn't asked, but Thumps knew what Hockney expected him to do. No matter which way you looked at the two murders, everything revolved around Noah Ridge, and the first order of business was to find him as quickly as possible.

The box of articles Moses had given him was still sitting on the coffee table where he had left it. Freeway was sleeping on top of the box.

"This is work." Thumps moved the cat to the couch. Freeway glared at him, meowed once just to let him know that she would make her own decisions, thank you very much, and disappeared down the hall.

The articles that dealt with Reuben Justice and his trial all contained pretty much the same information. If Justice was to be believed, Buckhorn and Scout and Begay arrived at his house late one night. Begay had been shot, and Justice treated him. Buckhorn didn't say anything about Denver, and if Justice was telling the truth, the first time he heard anything was when the police came by the hospital to arrest him. It was a thin arrest, but the FBI was able to parlay minor offences, such as treating a gunshot wound and not reporting it along with providing shelter to suspects in a kidnapping case, into a conspiracy charge.

Thumps had seen this before. A cop was killed. Local or federal, it didn't matter, and someone had to pay. Most of the time, it was the guilty party.

Yet here was Justice in Chinook. Just like Mitchell Street. And the only common denominator in the equation was Noah Ridge.

It took two hours to go through all the articles that Stick had pulled off the internet, and by the time Thumps opened the refrigerator door in the hopes of finding something to eat, something that could be warmed up in the microwave, he was no smarter than when he had begun.

There was half a bottle of apricot juice, a carton of orange juice, a glass container of rice neatly stacked on a glass container of peaches. Thumps settled on the peaches and a bowl of cereal. With soy milk. He looked at his watch. Enough time to eat and grab a long, hot shower before he had to begin everything again. The only question now was where to start.

As he saw it, he had two choices. One was to talk with Dakota to see if she would trust him. That was what Hockney was hoping he would do, and Thumps knew it. The second choice was to stop by the old Land Titles building and check in with Beth and her new corpse. Choice number one was the hands-down favourite, but number two was the right one.

Beth answered on the third ring. "This better be good."

"It's me."

"I'm working."

"I know."

"You pass out, you're on your own."

Thumps wondered if you could desensitize yourself to the smell of morgues. Logic told him that you could. Otherwise, you wouldn't have coroners or morticians. But by the time he reached the bottom of the stairs and headed into what Beth liked to call her "kitchen," Thumps was sorry he had promised anything.

"I wasn't fooling." Beth was standing beside a steel table that held the body of Reuben Justice. And she had already begun the autopsy.

Thumps tried to find something neutral and friendly to focus on. The smell of disinfectant was strong, and the blood in the air tasted damp and bitter. Even in winter, the morgue seemed to be able to create its own environment.

"You're fast."

"Sheriff is anxious."

Thumps could just imagine what Hockney had said. The second murder would have shifted him out of high gear into something considerably quicker.

"He was shot," said Beth as she rolled the body on its side for a moment. "But he didn't die right away."

"Not at the hotel."

"No, not enough blood there."

"And not at the house."

"He was dead by then."

Thumps turned away as she pushed the nose of the tongs into the bullet hole in Justice's back and began rooting around. "Actually, I wanted to look at Street's effects."

"The dead guy in the motel?"

Thumps tried breathing through his mouth.

"All the stuff's in the file cabinet."

The drawer marked *STUV* did not slide out smoothly. Thumps had to rock it from side to side, and it groaned every inch of the way.

"There's nothing here."

"Look under *F*."

"*F*?"

"For *FBI*."

The *DEF* drawer was more co-operative. Thumps took the plastic bag out and laid it on Beth's desk.

"Hey, have a look at this."

Thumps wasn't sure he wanted to look at all.

"Same calibre as the bullet that killed Street." Beth held up the tongs. "Ora Mae's painting the bedroom. After we finish here, you want to come up and help pick colours?"

Beth dropped the bullet into a metal pan. It made a sharp pinging sound, which echoed through the basement. "She wants to use a dark colour like burgundy or navy, so it feels like a cave."

"How about this colour?" Thumps gestured to the dark walls and ceiling.

"I don't think so," said Beth. "It would remind me too much of work."

* * *

THERE WERE TIMES when standing outside in the snow wasn't a bad choice, especially when the alternative was standing indoors in a morgue. There was a clean taste to winter air, and as Thumps came out of the building, he paused, closed his eyes, and breathed it in.

"DreadfulWater!"

Thumps didn't have to open his eyes to see who it was. Special Agent Asah. Stomping down the street in his great parka, but not looking happy.

"You seen the sheriff?"

Thumps tried to decide if his duties as a temporary deputy included telling the FBI about the house on the lake and Reuben Justice.

"Did you lose him?"

"Very funny. I just got off the phone with Denver. They're sending in a team. You can tell them all your jokes."

"They're pulling you out?"

"Of course they're pulling me out." Asah looked angry and embarrassed. "I was supposed to watch Ridge. Did a great job, don't you think?"

"Wasn't your fault."

"Tell that to Denver."

Thumps tried to remember if the sheriff had told him specifically not to tell Asah about Justice. "He's at Red Tail Lake."

"The lake?"

"They found a body at one of the summer houses."

Asah waited for the bad news. "Ridge?"

"Reuben Justice."

Asah stood there for a moment and looked at the snow, trying to place the name. "The guy from Utah," he said finally. "He's in jail."

Thumps wondered if the feds taught lying. If they did, they taught it well. "He's been out for more than a month. I wouldn't run that rabbit by Hockney, if I were you."

Asah traded in his dumb look for an annoyed expression. "Okay, so what shall we do until I'm sent packing?"

"How much time do you have?"

"Two days at the most."

Thumps brought his hands to his mouth and blew on his fingers. "First, let's find someplace warm."

"And after that?"

"We find Noah Ridge."

THE "SOMEPLACE WARM" was the lobby of the Tucker. Thumps was getting used to walking into the place as though he owned it. A part of him regretted that his temporary deputy job didn't come with a badge, which he could take to the front desk and flash. Asah found a corner with two chairs.

Thumps leaned back in the chair. "I'm comfortable," he said. "How about you?"

"You know where Ridge is, don't you?"

"Nope," said Thumps, "but I know when I'm being lied to."

Asah held his hands out, palms up. "You know as much as I do."

"Tell me about Denver."

"I've already told you everything."

"Tell me again."

Asah folded his hands in his lap. "You want the trailer or the feature?"

"I'd like to see the whole movie," said Thumps.

"Not much to it," said Asah. "Early one Saturday morning, Matthew Colburne, CEO of Morgan Energy, wakes up and finds three men in the bedroom of his Denver home. Clinton Buckhorn, Wilson Scout, and Wallace Begay. Colburne's family is away in Florida. He's tied and gagged and driven to corporate headquarters, where Buckhorn makes him open the safe. No great harm so far, but Colburne decides to play hero. He grabs a gun from his desk and opens fire on his kidnappers, wounding Begay. But that's as good as it gets. Buckhorn or Scout, it doesn't matter, shoots Colburne and leaves him for dead. Buckhorn takes the bearer bonds and some cash, and the three of them disappear."

"The Xerox that Street had. A bond from the robbery?"

"Yes."

"How'd they get in and out of Morgan?"

"Parking garage. In through the mailroom and up the freight elevator. Out the same way."

"What about Colburne?"

"A security guard found him later that day. He was badly wounded, but he survived."

"What happened next?"

"We don't know," said Asah. "But on Monday, Buckhorn, Scout, and Begay materialize in Salt Lake City at Reuben Justice's house. From there you know the story."

"Tell me anyway," said Thumps.

"Street gets a tip from his informant, and the FBI raids Justice's house. Buckhorn and his friends are waiting for the agents, and five people are killed."

"What about the cash?"

"Most of it was recovered."

"And the bonds?"

"Never seen again."

"Is that what you're here for? The bonds?"

Asah ran his hand through his hair. "The FBI is not a retrieval service for corporate America."

"So, you have no interest in the bonds."

"None whatsoever." Asah looked around the lobby. It was empty for the most part. One clerk at the desk. A businessman checking in. Or out.

"You think Noah has the bonds."

"That's always been a possibility," said Asah. "Where do we find him?"

Thumps sagged in the chair and imagined that he was sitting in the X-ray trailer at Moses Blood's place, watching Stick rescue bits and pieces of information from the computer. Thumps was reasonably sure that a computer, with Stick at the helm, would be far more forthcoming than Asah had been. And if he could figure out the right questions, it probably wouldn't take any time at all to locate the right answers.

TWENTY-SEVEN

Asah didn't need Thumps to tell him how to find Noah. The FBI trained people to find people. Asah's question was a test to see if Thumps was really going to help or if his allegiances lay elsewhere. With Dakota, for instance. Any way you looked at the situation, Dakota was the key. If Noah was alive, he would come back to Dakota. He would come back, because he had nowhere else to go.

"Watch Dakota."

"That's the right answer," said Asah.

"Sheriff will come up with it too."

"Three pairs of eyes are better than two."

"But that's not what you want me to do?"

"Stakeouts are boring," said Asah. "Sometimes they work, and sometimes they don't."

"You want me to beat the bushes."

"Can't hurt," said Asah. "Never know what might break cover and run."

THUMPS CALLED FROM the lobby. "Can I come up?"

"Who's with you?"

"Just me."

The door to Dakota's room was open. Dakota was sitting in a chair by the window. She reminded Thumps of a painting he had seen at a gallery in San Francisco years ago. It was of a woman waiting on a balcony overlooking the ocean, waiting for her lover's ship to appear on the horizon. Or at least that's what the write-up next to the painting said.

"I don't know where he is."

"Has he called?"

Part of the mystery of the painting was that you couldn't see what the woman was looking at. It could have been street vendors or the bustle of a wharf or another woman sitting on another balcony. The window Dakota was sitting in front of offered no such mysteries. Thumps could see what Dakota could see. Snow and the vague outline of buildings.

"Yes."

"When?"

"A couple of hours ago."

"He knows we're looking for him."

"He knows."

Thumps tried to imagine what Dakota was feeling. Betrayal. Confusion. Anger. Perhaps all three. Noah had brought the house down on his head. But most of the pieces were going to land on Dakota.

"Why can't you believe him?" Dakota turned away from the window. "Why can't you believe that someone is trying to kill him?"

"I believe him." This was the part Thumps didn't like, and once he began, there would be no going back. "We found a body."

Dakota held her face steady.

"It wasn't Noah." Thumps waited to see if he could read anything in Dakota's eyes. "It was Reuben Justice."

"Reuben?" Dakota hadn't seen this coming. "You're lying."

"Shot. Same gun as Street." Thumps was suddenly tired of playing cop. It was time to stop. "The sheriff is going to come by before the day is out."

"Reuben can't be dead."

He had expected Dakota to be angry. But her voice was almost matter of fact, as though she had run out of anger, as though all she had left were echoes. Thumps pulled up a chair and sat down next to Dakota. There were any number of ways to begin, none of them easy. He leaned in and touched Dakota's shoulder. "Tell me about Salt Lake," he said as gently as he could. "Tell me about Lucy Kettle."

BY THE TIME Thumps got back to the lobby, Asah was gone. Not surprising. He was probably on the phone to Denver, explaining why they didn't need to send a team of agents, telling his bosses that he had everything in hand. If Thumps read the man correctly, Asah would not like anyone thinking that he couldn't do his job.

He walked briskly down Main Street toward the

sheriff's office, the snow dancing around his feet. The skiers would be happy. So would the snowboarders. And the cross-country skiers. Thumps didn't harbour any malice toward any of these sports, but they could all go to hell as far as he was concerned.

Hockney's SUV was parked at the curb. Andy and the sheriff were standing around the desk drinking coffee. If Thumps hadn't known better, he would have thought he had walked in on an office party.

"Figured you'd show up soon enough."

Hockney set his cup on the desk. "Tell Deputy Thumps what we found." Andy picked up a plastic bag. Inside was a letter. "Guess what this is?"

"A letter."

"You're a real smartass," said Andy. "You know that?"

Hockney took the bag from Andy and tossed it to Thumps. "Looks like your girlfriend's been busy."

The letter was short and to the point. Thumps read it quickly and handed it back to Hockney. "You found this on Reuben?"

"I found it," said Andy quickly. "It's what real cops do."

Checking the pockets of a dead man hardly constituted brilliant police work, but Thumps let it go. Maybe the sheriff was right. Maybe he should try to make friends with Andy.

"Dakota and Reuben knew each other," said Thumps. "No big secret there."

Andy could hardly contain his excitement. "Sounds to me like she's arranging a hit."

Making friends with Andy was going to be harder than Thumps had imagined. "You must be kidding."

"She tells him where Ridge is going to be and when."

"It's a letter to a friend."

"What I'm curious about," said the sheriff, stepping into the line of fire, "is why Ms. Miles would write Mr. Justice and invite him to our fair city, and why he would come."

"Well, you sure as hell can't ask Justice," said Andy.

"Then," said the sheriff, turning to Thumps, "we should probably ask Ms. Miles. That make good police sense to you?"

Thumps was getting tired of people lying to him. Especially people he cared about. Dakota could have told him that she knew Reuben was in town. She could have told him that she had written him. But if she hadn't been willing to share that information with him, Thumps doubted she was going to share it with Hockney.

Andy picked up the phone on the first ring. "Okay," he said, "that's great. Yeah, we'll let you know."

"That the rental company?" said the sheriff.

"Yeah," said Andy. "South side of the lake. Near the park."

Hockney slipped into his coat. "Justice rented a car in Missoula. Blue Taurus. Had one of the GPS devices in it."

"You think Noah's driving Justice's car?"

"Not for long," said Andy. "Stick around and watch real cops work."

Andy had all the enthusiasm and optimism of a fourteen-year-old, and all the brains of a dinner roll. If Noah had killed Reuben, and if he had driven off in Reuben's car, he would certainly not be sitting in the vehicle waiting to be arrested.

"You tell Special Agent Asah about Justice?"

"Who says I saw him?"

"Now, that," said Hockney, "is what we in law enforcement call 'evasive.'"

"Oh, he told him," said Andy. "Probably used to kiss federal ass all the time back in Oregon."

"California," said Thumps. "Yeah, I told him. That a problem?"

"Nope," said the sheriff. "Saves me the bother."

"Why don't you do something useful," said Andy, "and watch the place while we're gone."

"Not a bad idea," said the sheriff. "Give you time to figure out why this case doesn't make any sense."

ANDY MIGHT BE an idiot, but Hockney wasn't. The case made little sense. Lots of pieces, to be sure, but none of them connecting to anything.

Thumps eased himself into the sheriff's chair. It was an old-fashioned swivel chair, wooden and broad with a high back. It was comfortable enough, especially if you put your feet up. And Thumps might have sat there all day had Cooley not come in through the front door.

"You practising for the sheriff's job?"

Thumps took his feet off the desk. "Just watching the store. You want some coffee?"

"Sheriff make it?"

"Probably."

Cooley looked at the pot for a moment and decided to play it safe. "Heard they found a body out at the Connor place."

"One of your associates?"

"The doctor lady stopped for gas at the Red Tail Lake store. Dora said she had a body bag in the back."

"Dora? Dora Manning is one of your associates?"

"Lot of people think she's antisocial," said Cooley, "but she's not."

Thumps ran through the reasons why he should not tell Cooley about Reuben Justice and couldn't think of any. "Guy by the name of Reuben Justice."

"Justice," said Cooley. "He got something to do with Ridge?"

"Maybe."

Cooley smiled. "That's what the sheriff would have said."

"Is that what you came to ask the sheriff?"

"Nope," said Cooley. "I came to give him some information."

"Okay."

"You're not the sheriff."

"I'm a deputy."

"Yeah," said Cooley, "I know."

There were any number of people who would figure Cooley for a man of average intelligence. They'd make the mistake of thinking that, because he was large, he was slow or stupid. Thumps had made that mistake once, and he had never made it again.

"You know where Noah is?"

"Maybe."

"That's the kind of answer I'd expect from the sheriff." Cooley nodded. "You know how to make coffee?"

THUMPS AND COOLEY sat in the warmth of the sheriff's office and ran through the current pieces of reservation gossip while the water and the coffee grounds bubbled away. Thumps wasn't sure there was any hope for the coffee, fresh or otherwise. The inside of Hockney's pot looked as though it had been coated with black lead. Even Cooley, who tended to be an optimist, wasn't enthusiastic.

"My cousin makes coffee in a pot like that," said Cooley, "but she knows what she's doing."

Thumps was able to get caught up on Elaine Browning's new business, a computer-dating service that matched Native people from around North America, and Cooley filled him in on Marvin Bigcorn's legal battle with Chief Motors.

"Elaine puts everyone into their major cultural groups and languages first," said Cooley, "so they'll have something in common."

"How's it going?"

"Not as well as she hoped," said Cooley. "Lot of Indians are marrying Whites these days. The Irish are real popular."

Chief Motors had sold Marvin a truck that came up lame with a bent crankshaft, and the two of them had been arguing for more than a year about who should pay for the repair.

"Marvin says the truck was like that when he bought it, and Chief Motors is insisting that Marvin bent the shaft."

"They going to go to court?"

"Nope. Both of them are too cheap to hire a lawyer."

By the time the coffee was done, the conversation had slid back to the matter at hand. Cooley poured himself a cup and took a tentative sip.

"It's not real good," he said, "but it probably won't hurt you."

"You know the sheriff is out looking for Noah right now."

Cooley took another sip. "Where's he looking?"

"South end of the lake."

"Won't find him there." Cooley took a notebook out of his jacket.

"Is this one of those things in the Unusual column?"

"Just before the snow really began coming down, Dora says that she thought she saw someone out on the lake."

"It's not frozen yet."

"Not so you could set up a fishing hut."

"She sure about this?"

"Saw him for just a moment." Cooley set the cup on the edge of the desk. "If she saw anyone at all."

"So, she's not sure."

"By the time she got Arthur's binoculars, the lake was empty."

Thumps looked at the pot and decided not to take a chance. "But if she did see someone on the lake in the snow . . ."

Cooley yawned and shifted his weight to one side of the chair. "Then that someone was headed north."

"North?"

"Walking around in a snowstorm like that on Red Tail Lake, you got to figure one of two things." Cooley poured himself a second cup. "Either the guy's lost or he knows where he's going. And if he knows where he's going, then the only reason to be out walking on the lake is to make sure that no one else does."

TWENTY-EIGHT

Thumps seemed to recall the sun coming up big and bold that morning, but if it had, there was little left of it now. As they headed north out of town, all that remained of that bright beginning was the memory and the headlights of Cooley's car reflecting off the snow.

"You don't have to tell me where we're going," said Cooley, "at least not right away."

"Red Tail Lake."

"Snow's been coming down pretty good," said Cooley. "We'll be okay to the store."

"You got snow tires, right?"

"Sure," said Cooley, "but they're not on the car."

The sheriff's SUV would be able to get through this weather. It had four-wheel drive, a bank of halogen spotlights, a winch, and a two-way radio. If Hockney got into trouble, he could pull himself out.

So long as he kept his temper.

Thumps hadn't known the sheriff to be a volatile man, but the two murders had put him on edge. Any other time, Duke would have sent Andy out by himself to find the car and gather any evidence, but now Hockney wasn't about to trust Andy to do the job that needed to be done.

"We should stop and say hello," said Cooley. "Arthur might have made apple pies."

"He's dead."

"Yeah," said Cooley, "but I wouldn't mention that to Dora."

The Red Tail Lake store had its lights on. There was something festive about the store in the snow. The windows glowed in the darkness, and all you would have needed to make it look like Christmas were a few strings of coloured lights and maybe a big star with reflective tape.

"Dora and Arthur used to come out here regular," said Cooley as they got out of the car. "They bought Red Tail just before she retired."

Tourists from the east coming west to find paradise were a common-enough romance. No one called it that, but you could see it in their eyes, hear it in their voices.

Paradise.

Nothing ostentatious. A small acreage on a trout-fishing river with a view of the mountains. Or a property on a lake with a piece of the shoreline. And if they found it, they would build something with logs and glass, so they could feel that they were part of the land, while watching the panorama from the comfort of an open-beamed living room. Then slowly, painfully, they would realize that they had mistaken space and solitude for desire and happiness, and they would sell their dream home to the next dreamer who came through and head back home to Sodom or Gomorrah. Or Los Angeles.

Not everyone, of course. Just most.

"So, is she . . . ?"

"Nope." Cooley knocked the snow off his boots. "She just misses him."

Thumps knew that feeling, losing someone you cared about. "He die out here?"

"He loved the lake," said Cooley. "I think she stays to be close to him."

ANNA HAD BEEN like that. She had loved the coast, had loved the beaches between McKinleyville and Trinidad Head, had loved walking in the surf while the world around her vanished in fog. But after the murders, the coast had taken on a sinister presence, and everywhere Thumps looked, he saw only reminders of her death, not her life. Little by little, he came to resent the very things that had made her happy, until the only thing he could do was to walk away.

THE AIR INSIDE the store was warm and moist and smelled of apple pie. Dora was standing in the kitchen at the back of the store.

"Hey, Dora, what's the news?"

Dora came into the store with a pot of tea and set it down on the counter. "Cups are behind you."

"I told Thumps about what you saw," said Cooley.

Dora brushed her hair back. "You find that Indian you were looking for?"

"Not yet."

"Saw the sheriff's car go by."

"South?" said Thumps. "Toward the park?"

"Hope he wasn't planning on going for a hike," said Dora. "Arthur likes to hike, but he's not fool enough to go out in this weather."

"Hockney stop?"

"Nope." Dora took three plates from the shelf. "You boys want some apple pie? It's Arthur's speciality."

"Sure," said Cooley.

The snow slowed, and by the time Thumps and Cooley had cleaned their plates, it had stopped altogether and the wind had come up. Thumps waited until Dora finished her tea.

"Cooley tells me that you might have seen someone on the lake."

"Movement," said Dora. "At a distance, what you see is movement."

"Maybe an animal?"

"Movement was all wrong. And he was moving fast."

"Running?"

"No," said Dora. "Not running. Jogging. When I saw him, it looked like he was jogging."

Cooley put a huge hand on Dora's shoulder. "Just so Thumps can keep things straight," he said quietly, "we're not talking about Arthur, are we?"

Dora put her hand on top of Cooley's. "Is that what your friend is worried about? That I'm crazy?"

"He doesn't know you well enough yet."

"'There are worse things waiting for men than death.'" Dora waited to see if Thumps recognized the quotation. "You needn't worry, Mr. DreadfulWater," she said at last. "I know that Arthur's dead. And I did see someone on the lake."

SOMEWHERE BETWEEN the snowstorm and Arthur Manning's apple pie, the road had vanished, and Cooley had to guess where it had been. On high ground, the wind had cut across the road, leaving open patches and the line of telephone poles to navigate by, and Cooley made it all the way to the Connor place without finding a ditch.

"Nice lady," Cooley stopped at the driveway. "Swinburne's not a favourite of mine, but Dora likes the aesthetes."

There was no sign of anyone's having come back to the house. Which didn't mean a thing. If Noah was on the run and if he had doubled back, the storm would have covered his tracks.

"You think he's here?"

"Maybe." Thumps tried to sound positive.

"He could have picked any of the houses along the lake."

"He knows this one."

"And the cops have already been here." Cooley eased the car into the driveway. "I always thought that was one of those cliché things."

"What?"

"Returning to the scene of a crime."

"You bring that rifle?"

"We going to need it?"

Thumps went around the west side of the house. Cooley took the east. They met at the back in front of the bank of windows.

"No tracks," said Cooley. "What about you?"

Up to this moment, Thumps had been reasonably certain that he would find Noah inside. Now, standing in the snow with Cooley, watching the moon shine off the frozen lake, he wasn't so sure.

"Any of the windows broken?"

"Didn't see any."

"Doors?"

"All locked." Cooley set the rifle on his shoulder. "How'd he get in the first time?"

Thumps had missed it completely. When he and the sheriff had arrived, Andy was already inside. Andy wouldn't have had a key, so the house must have been open when he got there.

"He had a key." Thumps said it out loud before he had a chance to think it through.

"Noah? Where'd he get a key?"

If Thumps were a betting man, he would bet on the small rock garden near the front door. Leaving keys under doormats or under flowerpots was predictable. Phony electrical outlet boxes and plastic rocks were now the hiding place of choice. The rocks were great. You couldn't tell the fake ones from the real thing. Maybe that's what Noah had done, picked up a rock to break a window and discovered, quite by accident, a more efficient way to get in. Andy had missed that little detail, but so had the sheriff. And so had he.

"What do you want to do?"

Breaking a window was never as easy as it looked in the movies. The glass in the French door was triple glazed, and Thumps had to use Cooley's tire iron to break out one of the panes.

"Shit."

"What's wrong?"

"It's a keyed dead bolt on both sides."

"That's smart." Cooley felt around the door. "But the door's wood. So is the frame. I know a side kick that should take out the jam."

"You got a flashlight?"

"That's good thinking," said Cooley. "Look before you leap."

Thumps was surprised at how little you could see, shining a light in through a window. In place of deep shadows, you got regular shadows. Nothing looked out of place, but as Cooley played the light around the room, Thumps realized that he hadn't really been paying attention to the particulars when he took the photographs of Reuben lying on the couch. A good cop would have made a mental note of everything.

"Anything out of place?"

"Can't tell."

Thumps had seen any number of doors broken down in his years on the force, but he had never seen a door explode.

"Sorry."

Cooley had been modest about his side kick. It took out the door, the frame, and most of the moulding. The door itself slammed back into the wall, burying the knob in the sheet rock. Anyone in the house would have had to be dead not to hear that entrance.

Cooley stepped over the wood and glass. "What do we do now?"

It didn't take a great deal of time to search the house. The second floor was one large bedroom, with a bathroom the size of a small apartment. There were two cedar-lined walk-in closets and a dressing area with another couch. The main floor was completely open so you could see the kitchen, the living room, the dining room, and the foyer all at once.

Cooley was waiting for him. "Expensive house."

"You check the basement?"

"There's a wine cellar down there and a big-screen television and an exercise area. It's pretty impressive."

"But no Noah."

"Maybe he didn't come back. Maybe we should check out the other houses."

No, thought Thumps, if Noah was looking for somewhere to hide, this place was his best bet.

"What about the garage?"

The way to the garage was through a large room that doubled as a mud room and a laundry. Unlike the French door that Cooley had destroyed, the door to the garage was heavy metal with a metal frame.

"How about you flick on the lights," said Cooley, "and I'll jump in with my rifle and yell, 'Freeze, sucker!'"

Thumps tried to imagine the effect that Cooley, leaping into the garage, would have on Noah, and he found that the thought cheered him for a moment.

"Thought you wanted to protect him."

"We got to catch him first."

Thumps knew what he was going to find when he opened the door and turned on the lights. An empty garage. Which meant Noah was still on the loose, and they were no closer to solving two murders than they had been that morning. Worse, he was going to have to explain to the sheriff, and, eventually, to the Connors, just why a perfectly good door had been kicked in.

Thumps opened the door and tried to imagine an excuse that would sound plausible, that would convince Hockney and the home owners that the door had been a casualty of law enforcement. The light switch was to the right, and as he bent forward to find it, he felt something large and hard sail over his shoulder and crash into the frame where his head should have been.

And before he had time to right himself or say something apropos, he heard Cooley shout and felt the large man shove him through the doorway and straight into the arms of whoever it was had just tried to kill him.

TWENTY-NINE

It didn't take all that long to sort things out. First, Cooley turned the lights on. Then he picked Thumps up off the floor with one hand and, with the other, aimed his rifle at Noah Ridge.

"Should I shoot him?"

Thumps's shirt was bunched up around his shoulders. He wondered if Freeway felt the same way about being picked up by the scruff of the neck as he did.

"No." Thumps shoved his shirt back in his pants.

"I thought you and Thumps were friends." Cooley loomed over Noah. "Trying to bash his head in like that wasn't very friendly."

"We are friends," said Noah.

"No, we're not," said Thumps.

"I thought you were coming to kill me." Noah started to get to his feet, but Cooley wasn't ready to shake hands just yet. He pressed the muzzle of the rifle into Noah's chest.

"Let him up."

"You sure?"

"No," said Thumps, "but if we're going to beat the truth out of him, let's find someplace warm to do it."

The living room wasn't exactly warm, especially with the French door lying on the floor. Cooley picked up the pieces and set them back in place as best he could.

Noah stood in front of the fireplace, his back against the stones. "I suppose you want to know what's going on."

Thumps waved him off. "Tell it to the sheriff."

"He won't believe me."

Cooley tucked the rifle under his arm. "That's probably true."

"He thinks I killed Street, doesn't he?"

"Tell me about Reuben."

Noah looked at his hands. "Reuben showed up at the hotel. I hadn't seen him in years."

"What happened?"

"We talked about old times."

Thumps was willing to make allowances. He supposed that living on the edge for all those years had made Noah paranoid and uncooperative. But he wasn't willing to waste time.

"What?" said Thumps. "You talked him to death?"

"I didn't do it." Noah tried to keep his voice level. "I left him in the room. When I got back, I found him on the floor. He had been shot."

"And that's why you brought him here?" Thumps made little attempt to hide his disbelief.

"No," said Noah, "I took him to the hospital."

Thumps turned to Cooley. "Shoot him."

"Sure thing," said Cooley, bringing the rifle up.

Noah flinched. "I was going to take him to the hospital, but by the time I got him to his car, he was dead."

"You could have stayed in the room and called for an ambulance." Thumps could feel his disbelief turning to anger. "What the hell were you thinking?"

"What movie are you watching?" Noah looked as if he had just heard something funny. "What did you want me to do? Stick around and wait for the killer to show up to finish the job?"

"You think whoever killed Reuben was really after you?"

"No," said Noah, "I don't *think* it."

"So, why'd you bring him here?"

"What would you have done?"

Thumps had heard this question any number of times, mostly from people who were sorry that they had done what they had done, who wanted sympathy and understanding, who wanted to make the world a co-defendant, so they wouldn't have to be guilty of something alone. Thumps knew why Noah had brought Reuben out to the lake. To get away. To buy time. To try to figure things out.

"I would have called Hockney."

"No one's trying to kill you."

"This the same person who beat you up?"

The question hung in the air, as though it had been frozen by the drafts coming in around the ruined door.

"That was different."

Thumps wasn't about to let Noah slide away. "You tell the sheriff and me that someone beat you up on your morning jog. You go to the hospital and play the injured Indian."

"I did get beat up."

"Sure," said Cooley. "The Mustang can be one tough place."

"Hard way to drum up publicity."

"What the fuck do you know!"

"Oh," said Cooley, "you'd be surprised what Thumps knows."

"And just who the hell are you?" said Noah, most of his courage having returned.

"I'm the guy who's protecting you," said Cooley.

Noah looked at Cooley, and then he looked at Thumps.

"Cooley Small Elk," said Thumps. "He runs his own security service."

"Small Elk Security," said Cooley.

"I don't know you."

"Yeah," said Cooley, "but now that we've been introduced, I should tell you about my executive-protection program."

Thumps turned to Cooley. "You really want a client who lies to you all the time?"

"It is a problem, all right," said Cooley.

"So, what now?" Noah sounded tired suddenly, as if someone had let the air out of his bluster. "You going to turn me over to the sheriff?"

"Works for me."

"You can't arrest me." Noah was trying to sound like the old Noah. "You're a photographer."

"Good news," said Cooley. "This week he happens to be a deputy."

It had been a while, but Thumps was reasonably sure he could remember most of the speech. It was just a matter of beginning it right. "You have the right," he said, trying not to enjoy the moment too much, "to remain silent."

THE RIDE BACK was more exhilarating than Thumps appreciated. The big trucks had packed the pavement and turned the snow into ice. From the turnoff, the road was a ski slope, and Cooley had to slalom his way down into town.

Noah sat in the back in silence. Thumps might have supposed that he was contemplating the mess he had helped to create, but common sense told him that Noah was working on a story that would fit the facts, a story that would make him the hero, or at the very least a victim, a story that would play sympathetically on the front page of dailies around the world.

Chinook was buried in snow. The main streets hadn't been cleared yet and drivers were trying to dig their cars away from the curbs. Thumps tried to remember how many animals slept right through winter. He had thought of six by the time Cooley was able to plow his way into a parking space in front of the sheriff's office.

Hockney was on the phone. Special Agent Asah was sitting in the chair by the coffee pot. Andy was nowhere to be seen. Whoever the sheriff was talking to was doing most of the talking, and Hockney was doing most of the listening.

"Well, well, well." Asah got out of the chair. "'Home are the hunters, home from the hills.' The sheriff said you'd find him."

"We got lucky."

"And I lose twenty dollars." Asah walked around Noah. "Why isn't he handcuffed?"

"Didn't have any."

"Just as well," said Asah. "Probably not going to need them."

Hockney waved Thumps over while he talked on the phone. "Yes, that's right. Yes, I know how irritating that can be. Yes, I'll call you when we get more information." The sheriff let the phone dangle in his hand for a moment and then put it back in its cradle.

"That was George Connor. He's not happy." Hockney ran his hand through his hair, glared at Noah. "Where'd you find him?"

"The Connor place."

"Again."

Thumps rubbed his hands and blew on his fingers. "There was some damage to one of the doors."

"What?"

"I didn't do that," said Noah. "I don't even know why I'm under arrest."

"Trespass," said Thumps, "and breaking and entering."

"I didn't break anything."

"Well, I guess we should have a talk." Hockney took

the keys to the cells out of his desk. "And if I don't like your answers, you can join your executive assistant."

"Dakota?"

"That's what I was going to tell you," said Asah. "She's confessed."

"To what?"

"The murders," said Hockney. "She says she was the one who shot Street and Justice."

"You're joking."

"Hard to joke with a confession," said the sheriff.

As if winter wasn't bad enough, now Thumps found himself in the middle of a Three Stooges film directed by Federico Fellini.

"Come on, Duke," said Thumps, "you can't possibly believe that Dakota has anything to do with this."

Hockney swivelled around in his chair. "Make me a better offer."

"Let me talk to her," said Thumps. "Alone."

"Sure," said the sheriff. "It'll give Mr. Ridge and Special Agent Asah and me a chance to catch up on old times."

* * *

THERE WERE ONLY two reasons why Dakota would have confessed to the killings. One, she was guilty. Two, she was protecting Noah. Thumps didn't believe the first and couldn't imagine why she would do the second.

"He's not worth it."

Dakota was huddled in a corner of the cell. Thumps remembered the last time he had seen her like this. In a hospital bed in Salt Lake City.

"Neither is the movement." Thumps waited to see if there was any smoulder left in Dakota. "The only thing worth saving is you."

"How's Noah?"

"He called you again, didn't he?"

Dakota sat up, her elbows on her knees, her eyes looking at the floor.

"Did he ask you to confess to the murders?"

"What difference does it make?"

"It matters to me."

Dakota shook her head. "No, it doesn't. You don't like him."

Thumps couldn't argue with that at all. He didn't like the man, and the more he was getting to know him, the more he didn't like what he found. It wasn't just that

Noah was conceited, it was that he expected other people to sacrifice themselves for him, to throw themselves in harm's way so he could slide through unscathed.

"I care about you."

"What makes you think I didn't kill Street?"

"Because you didn't kill Reuben."

Dakota stood up and came to the bars. "Remember what you said when you put me on that train all those years ago?"

How was it that women could remember those moments? Especially at a time like this. Claire could do it too. Once, she had asked him if he remembered what he had said to her on their first date. He hadn't been able to recall that either.

"Probably something encouraging."

Dakota smiled. "You made me promise to eat something."

"I'm not going to let you take the blame for Noah."

"He didn't do it."

"Maybe not," said Thumps, "but he sure as hell is responsible."

* * *

Asah was still encamped by the coffee pot. Duke was relaxing in his swivel chair.

"She say why she did it?" said Hockney.

"She didn't do it."

"Well," said the sheriff, "that makes me feel better." On the edge of Hockney's desk was a blue key and a cellphone. "She tell you who did?"

Thumps suddenly realized he hadn't been paying attention. "Where's Noah?"

"Street's murder makes this a federal case," said Asah, "so that makes Noah mine."

"You let him go?"

Hockney held up the blue key. "Guess what this is."

"The key to the Connor place," said Thumps. "You didn't let him go."

"And this," said the sheriff, picking up the cellphone, "is the Connors' cellphone."

"What the hell is going on?"

"Evidently, Mr. Ridge found the cellphone in one of the drawers in the kitchen and charged the battery. Probably used it to call Ms. Miles." Hockney was enjoying making Thumps wait. "He found the key under the wooden Indian on the porch. That's what you would call ironic. I'm going to have to have a word with the Connors about homeland security."

"Jesus, you did let him go."

"Well," said Hockney, "I'm not about to waste good cell space on him right now."

"What about the breaking and entering?"

"He's not going anywhere," said Asah. "He's under 'town arrest.'"

"Town arrest?" Thumps looked at Hockney. "This is bullshit!"

"Not much I can do about it," said the sheriff. "Even if I wanted to."

"Law and order in action," said Asah.

It was an old game. Let the suspect loose and see what he does. Asah and Hockney were hoping that Noah would slip up somehow and lead them to enough incriminating evidence to hang him.

"You're dreaming."

Asah shrugged. "It's happened before."

Thumps turned to the sheriff. "Am I still your deputy?"

"You're not going to quit on me again, are you?"

"What about it?"

"Sure," said Hockney. "Just don't bother Mr. Ridge, and don't do anything that's going to piss me off."

THE TRICK TO beating winter, Thumps discovered as he stormed out of the sheriff's office, was to stay really angry. Right now he was furious enough to melt a polar cap.

"Hey, wait up." Asah jogged up behind him. "Nobody thinks your girlfriend did the deed."

Thumps swung around ready to set Asah on fire. "Then why is she in jail?"

"She confessed." Asah sighed. "You know what that means."

"Yeah."

"And until we get this straightened out or until she comes to her senses, that's where she stays."

"You check the cellphone?"

"Yes, we did." Asah shoved his hands in his pockets. "Noah called the Tucker."

"And talked Dakota into taking the blame."

"Probably, but we can't prove it. And if we toss Ridge in jail, nothing is going to happen."

"He's too smart. He hasn't survived this long on luck."

"Maybe," said Asah, "but a little luck never hurts."

"So, what do you do now?"

"Well, first of all, I'm going to give you my parka." Asah slipped off the coat and handed it to Thumps.

"I don't want your coat."

"It's a gift. You can't refuse it. Besides, you admired it."

"Is this a bribe?"

"Agents of the federal government don't do that kind of thing," said Asah. "Unless it's a matter of national security. Or in the service of a sensitive case. Or if the bureau's reputation is on the line."

"Or if you just feel like it."

"Take the coat." Asah turned back to the sheriff's office. "I have another. Besides, I'm tired of watching you freeze."

"What about Noah?"

"Oh," said Asah, "don't worry about Mr. Ridge. I'll take care of him."

THIRTY

It was after midnight before Thumps got home. Asah's parka made the walk almost pleasant. Freeway was curled up in the middle of the carpet, next to a lump of yellow vomit. She didn't meow, and she didn't rush over and turn figure eights around his feet. She just glared.

"What do you think?"

If Freeway liked the parka, she wasn't saying. Thumps tore a paper towel off the roll and tried to pick up the puke in one piece. Most of it came away cleanly, but part of it stuck to the pile. Thumps really disliked Freeway's darker side. The cat could at least be considerate and throw up on the stretches of hardwood or on the linoleum in the kitchen. Places that were easier to clean and sanitize.

Thumps flopped on the couch and turned on the television. Enough. He had done what he could. Had done more than he should have. Noah wasn't going to help, and neither was Dakota. Fine. Let the feds arrest everyone and sort things out later.

CSI was on, a show that Thumps vaguely liked. So was a rerun of *Magnum P.I.* He flipped back and forth between the two for a while and then turned the set off.

"What about it?" he said to the cat as he moved the table and put the box of articles in the middle of the floor. "You going to help?"

He had been through all the articles that Stick had given him and hadn't found anything other than the details of the various events. Now he began to put everything in piles by date and subject. There was a pile for Lucy Kettle and a pile for the raid on Reuben Justice's house and a pile for the robbery at Morgan Energy.

But nothing in any of the piles answered the question that Thumps kept coming back to. How was everything connected? He was sure it was. He even imagined that he could almost see the outline of the web. Yet every time he looked hard, it vanished.

Thumps took a pillow off the couch, lay down on the floor next to the Lucy Kettle pile, and looked at the stacks of paper from a new angle. The trouble, he had to admit, was that he had no idea what he was looking for, probably wouldn't recognize it even if he saw it.

The pillow was comfortable. Freeway evidently had decided to forgive him for leaving her alone. She slid over his hips like a warm breeze and curled up against his stomach. Thumps closed his eyes to clear his mind, and for a moment, he could see the answers floating on the horizon, just out of sight.

When Thumps opened his eyes, it was morning, and Freeway was sitting on the kitchen table having breakfast with Moses Blood and Stick Merchant.

"This cat is one good storyteller," said Moses. "Has she told you the one about the ducks?"

For a moment, Thumps thought he was having one of those silly dreams that late-night pizza can induce.

"What time is it?"

"Six-thirty," said Stick. "You always sleep in this late?"

"We found the coffee," said Moses. "Boy, is your kitchen organized."

"He's probably gay," said Stick.

Thumps sat up and rubbed his head. His hair was piled up on one side, his tongue thick and metallic.

"You got those piles organized too," said Moses, pushing his chin at the stacks of articles. "Just like your kitchen."

"You didn't have any bacon." Stick put a forkful of scrambled eggs on a piece of toast.

"I don't eat bacon."

"That's okay," said Moses. "Elk is better."

"Bacon tastes better."

Thumps tried to remember if he had invited Moses and Stick for breakfast. Not that it mattered. They were welcome any time. Well, certainly Moses was.

"We saved a plate for you," said Moses. "Your cat wanted some, but I explained that you had a hard day in front of you."

"I should catch a shower."

"Sure," said Moses, "we'll wait."

* * *

THUMPS TURNED THE TAPS on and let them run until steam filled the bathroom. Hot water always felt better in winter, and if he hadn't had guests, Thumps would have stayed under the spray until he drained the tank. Though he was curious. He didn't see Moses in town all that often, and the old man had never stopped by the house. If he and Stick had driven in from the reservation this early, it must have been for a reason. Whatever else their visit might be, it wasn't a social call.

Stick was loading four pieces of bread into the toaster. "You're out of bread. You got any strawberry jam?"

"Apricot."

"Nobody eats apricot."

Moses had a stack of articles in front of him. "Pretty exciting stuff. It's like that action movie I saw on television the other night."

Thumps would have probably described the week's activities as a melodrama or a soap opera if it hadn't been for the bodies.

"Which pile do you have?"

Moses looked at Thumps over his glasses. "You got names for the piles?"

As Thumps recalled, he had made six distinct stacks on the floor. Moses had one pile in front of him, but there were still six stacks on the floor.

"Which stack is that?"

"It's new," said Moses. "It doesn't have a name yet."

Stick's toast popped up. "That's all new stuff I found. Moses said you might be able to use it."

"Great."

"You got any peanut butter?"

"No."

"You a vegetarian or something?"

"There's cereal."

"Froot Loops?"

Thumps thought about taking out the box of Shredded Wheat just to hear Stick squeal. Instead, he sat down next to Moses, who was running a finger down one of the pages.

"You find anything?"

"You bet," said Moses. "Lots of chickens."

"Chickens?"

"Yeah," said Stick, who had his mouth full of toast, "wait till you hear about the chickens." Moses held up the article. "That's what this story reminds me of," he said. "Chickens."

Thumps looked at the article. At a quick glance, it was no more than a summary of what had happened in Salt Lake City. All the players were there: Clinton Buckhorn, Reuben Justice, Wilson Scout, Wallace Begay, Lucy Kettle, Noah Ridge, Mitchell Street.

"You don't even rate a mention." Stick went looking for more bread.

"I wasn't part of it."

"Sure," said Moses, "but you were there."

"Tell him the cannibal-chicken story, Grandfather."

"That boy likes to eat," said Moses, "and that one likes to hear stories too."

Thumps looked at the clock. He wondered how Dakota had managed the night in jail. How she was going to manage the day. And the days to come.

Thumps settled in the chair. "I'd like to hear the story."

"It's not an old story. I heard this one from Jimmy Frank, before Jimmy married that White lady and went to live in Florida." Moses sipped his coffee. "There was this guy from New York who came out to see us, and he liked what he saw so much he bought a bunch of land and built this big house, and then that one built a bunch of chicken coops."

Moses put his hand up to his face and began laughing. "Old John Samosi came by one day and asked the New York man, 'Why did you build all those chicken coops?' And the New York man tells Old John that raising healthy chickens on the open range and selling them to White people in the east was going to make him rich."

Stick opened the refrigerator. "Hey, Thumps has chicken."

"See," said Moses. "So, that man begins raising chickens, and he begins making money by the bag. But one day a coyote comes along and sees all those chicken coops and all those chickens in those coops, and he tells all his friends. 'Holy,' says all those coyotes, 'this is too good to be true.' But the coyotes know that the White man isn't going to share his good fortune, and that if they eat his chickens, he'll try to rub them out. So, they sit around one night and think, and in the morning, they have a plan."

Moses stopped for a moment and closed his eyes. "Boy," he said, "telling stories can wear you out."

"You want more coffee?" Thumps got the pot from the stove.

"Coffee is always good with stories," said Moses. "Maybe Stick should tell the rest of the story."

"Sure," said Stick, and he flopped himself down in the chair. "What the coyotes figure is that if they disguise themselves as chickens and act like chickens, then if the farmer sees one of them grabbing a chicken, he'll figure that the problem is with the chickens."

"And that's just what happens," said Moses.

"Yeah. One day that farmer comes out, and he sees about five of his chickens grab five other chickens and eat them on the spot. Man, he doesn't know what to do. He figures that his chickens have turned cannibal."

"Pretty scary, eh?" Moses leaned over and patted Thumps's hand.

"He starts calling around, but no one he calls has ever heard of cannibal chickens. And in the meantime, he's losing a lot of chickens."

"This is the exciting part," said Moses.

"Old John Samosi hears about the man and his cannibal chickens, and he stops by and asks him if he can see the cannibal chickens. So, the both of them go out to the coops, and Old John and the man watch as one chicken grabs another and eats it on the spot. And while that one chicken is eating the other chicken, Old John takes out his gun and shoots the cannibal chicken."

"It's a little violent," said Moses, "so I don't tell this one to children unless they ask for it."

"That White guy is really pissed off. 'You crazy Indian,' he shouts at Old John. 'What the hell are you doing, shooting my chickens like that?' Old John doesn't say anything. He just goes over and takes the chicken disguise off the coyote. Well, the farmer is real impressed, and he asks John how he knew that chicken was really a coyote. You know what Old John said?"

Thumps knew better than to guess.

"He said, 'What else could it be?'" Stick sat back with a big grin on his face. "Good story, huh?"

"Stick is getting pretty good with stories," said Moses. "And he's still a young boy."

"So, you think I should be looking for a coyote."

Moses shrugged. "Somebody's killing your chickens."

STICK FINISHED OFF the rest of the bread while Moses caught Thumps up on news from the reservation. Rose Many Bears was getting married for the fifth time.

Buster Gladstone was graduating from law school. The recreation centre needed a new roof. And the council was looking at getting into the cellphone business.

Stick had found a can of peaches and was banging around in the drawers, looking for a can opener.

"You tell your mother you're training with Cooley?"

Stick stopped what he was doing. "Cooley tell you?"

"Nope," said Thumps. "I saw the makiwara board in the barn. The rest was easy."

"You tell my mother?"

"Nope. But she saw the board too."

"It's none of her business."

"Oh, no," said Moses. "Children are every mother's business. That never changes."

"I'll tell her when I feel like it."

"Not knowing makes them nervous," said Moses. "It's never a good idea to make a mother nervous."

"You want some more coffee?"

"No," said Moses. "We have to be going. Stick is going to take me to the mall for lunch at that Chinese place with the spicy chicken and the thick noodles."

Thumps put his hand on the articles Moses had brought with him. "Can I hold on to these?"

"Sure," said Moses. "Maybe they'll help you find that coyote."

IT WAS AFTER NINE before Moses and Stick headed off to the mall. Thumps wondered how Stick was going to tell his mother that he was training with Cooley Small Elk to be a security agent. Thumps didn't suppose Claire would be crazy about the idea, especially since it involved some degree of bodily harm to her only child. Still, part of him wanted to be there in the room when Stick shared the good news, while part of him knew better than to be anywhere near a "nervous" Claire Merchant.

Thumps found the end of a block of cheese and half a tomato that Stick had missed and made himself a toasted-cheese sandwich out of the crusts that Stick had ignored. The can of peaches had survived only because Stick hadn't found the can opener, and Thumps put it back in the refrigerator next to the apricot jam.

The new set of articles was pretty much the same as the old set of articles. There was an in-depth profile on Morgan Energy and its CEO, Matthew Colburne, a series of stories about poverty in the urban reservation, and a brief history of the Red Power Movement. The most interesting item was an interview with Lucy Kettle, in which she talked about the FBI and its attempts to destroy organizations involved in social activism. She didn't mention Massasoit by name, but hinted at a bureau informant within RPM.

By eleven, Thumps had read everything, and all he had to show for the effort was seven piles of articles instead of the six with which he had started. Freeway had selected one of the taller stacks and knocked it over so she could stretch out on top of it. Most cats liked catnip. Freeway liked paper. It didn't matter what kind—a magazine, a newspaper, a flyer, a book, a sheet of Kleenex. Put it out and she would be on it in a flash.

He was reaching for the stack of articles that Moses and Stick had brought that morning when the phone rang. There were only two people who would have any reason to call him. The sheriff and Claire. He didn't want to talk to the sheriff, but he did want to talk to Claire. And if she was calling him, it meant that she wanted to talk to him.

"DreadfulWater?"

It wasn't the sheriff, and it certainly wasn't Claire. It was a deep voice with a reservation accent. At first he couldn't place it.

"You know Al's?"

"Sure . . ."

"Meet me there, now."

"Who is—" but before Thumps could finish the question, the line went dead. Freeway rolled over on her back and did her dead-squirrel routine. It was her way of inviting him to lie down on the floor with her and rub her belly. Most days he would have been happy to do that, but today, he suspected, wasn't going to work out the way he had imagined.

THIRTY-ONE

Thumps walked to Al's, bundled up in his new parka. It was a marvellous thing, light but wondrously warm, the dark fur around the hood soft and luxurious. Thumps suspected that it was Asah's way of saying that he was sorry for how things had gone. Though Dakota hadn't made it easy. Thumps was ready to help her, but first she had to want the help. And as far as he could see, she didn't. Pride or commitment or loyalty, it didn't matter. They could all get in the way of good sense.

He knew the voice on the phone, or at least he had heard it before. As he trudged through the snow, he ran through the people who it might have been and came up empty. Memory was a shy creature, in the open one minute, back in the woods the next.

Wutty Youngbeaver was sitting at the counter when Thumps got to Al's. Wutty and Al had a long on-again, off-again relationship, and from the way Wutty was smiling and bobbing his head, Thumps supposed that they were friends again.

"Hey, Thumps," Wutty swung around on his seat. "You got any of those photographs left?"

Thumps had never thought of Wutty as an art enthusiast. "Any one in particular?"

"My girlfriend said she saw a poster of the Snake River. Black and white with the Tetons in the background. Real nice sky."

"That's probably Ansel Adams."

"You got any like that?" said Wutty. "You know, maybe something with a ding that you're going to throw away anyway."

Al came out of the back with the coffee pot. She filled Wutty's cup and gestured toward the back of the café. "At the back," she said. "You want breakfast?"

* * *

GROVER MANY HORSES was sitting in the last booth, hunched over a cup of coffee. On the seat beside him was a plastic bag. He didn't look particularly happy, but that could have been the weather. Thumps slipped off the parka and carefully hung it on the hook by the side of the booth.

"Is it true about that Justice guy?" said Grover, without the courtesy of a greeting. "They think Ridge did him?"

Thumps sat down across from Grover. "Is that why you called me?"

"I kicked the shit out of him." Grover took a spoonful of sugar and slowly lowered it into the cup. "I guess you know that."

"At the Mustang."

"Wasn't my fault. Stupid shit just kept riding me."

"Did you know it was Ridge?"

"I was pretty sure," said Grover. "He looks a lot older now."

"You knew him before?"

Grover put the bag on the table and opened it. "Lucy used to write me all the time. She'd tell me about Salt Lake City and the Mormons and what she was doing. Sometimes she would send me clippings and stuff about that Red Power thing she was into. There were a couple of articles with pictures of the two of them."

Thumps looked at the letters, neatly tied together in bundles.

"They were lovers."

"Noah and Lucy?"

"No." Grover showed his teeth. "Lucy and Justice. It was supposed to be a secret, but she told me. They were going to get married."

There was one of the missing pieces, dropped into his lap, a minor *deus ex machina*. No brilliant police work, no clever deductions, no intuitive revelations. Just dumb luck. Thumps had supposed Reuben had come for Dakota. But he had come for Lucy.

"I never knew her," said Grover. "But she never forgot me."

"She must have loved you."

"Yeah." Grover closed the bag and pushed it across the table to Thumps. "Old man Blood said you might want to read these. He said maybe you could figure out who killed her."

"It was a long time ago."

"There's other letters too. From that friend of hers."

For a moment, Thumps tried to think of who would have written Grover. "Dakota Miles?"

"Yeah," said Grover. "Nice woman. She liked Lucy a lot. Told me all sorts of great stories."

"They were good friends."

"No one else sees these. Just you." Grover slid out of the booth and put on his coat. "We straight on that?"

"Yeah," said Thumps, "I understand."

Grover started to go and then turned back. "You going to see Ridge any time soon?"

"Maybe."

Grover bent down, his voice soft and delicate. "Tell him if he comes back here, I'll kill him."

AL KEPT HIS CUP filled while Thumps sat in the booth and read the letters one by one. When Grover had given him the letters, a part of Thumps hoped that they would contain answers. But all he found was the Lucy Kettle who liked lemon sorbet and tacos, who had seen *Billy Jack* and *Blazing Saddles* at least four times, who missed her family, especially her baby brother. Grover had been right about Lucy and Reuben. She wrote about him as only a lover could. Grover hadn't given Thumps the letters because he thought they would help. He had given Thumps the letters to show him who his sister really was.

Thumps tied the letters together and put them back in the bag. He would have liked to have known the woman who had written them. Perhaps they could have been friends. Dakota was right. Lucy Kettle wasn't Massasoit. The woman who wrote these letters wouldn't have betrayed something she believed in, something for which she had sacrificed her family, something she had spent her life defending.

"You know, it's not polite to read other people's mail." Al put the pot on the table. "Unless you got a good reason."

"Grover's sister, Lucy."

"I remember that one," said Al. "Headstrong."

"Sheriff been in this morning?"

"Nope. Saw him heading over to the courthouse about fifteen minutes ago. I hear he's in a foul mood."

"Two murders aren't going to make him happy."

Al ran her hand over the parka, stroking the fur around the hood. "I see photography is beginning to pay off."

"It was a gift."

"What's the fur?"

Thumps shrugged. "Rabbit?"

"I know rabbit when I feel it." Al opened the parka. "Sometimes they got a tag, tells you what the thing is made of."

Thumps tied the bag shut. If the roads were good, he'd drive up to Glory tomorrow and give them back to Grover. Maybe he'd call Claire and see if she wanted to go for a ride, see the mountains in snow.

"You know, if this was a Pendleton, it would be worth a pretty penny."

He could take his cameras along and give winter another try. Other photographers had turned winter into spectacular images. Maybe if he could create something beautiful out of the bleakness of the season, he wouldn't resent it so much.

"Well, la-di-da," Al tapped at a small tag sewn into the seam of the coat. "It's mink."

"No kidding."

"Now that's one sneaky son of a buck," said Al. "You ever know Joshua Cotton?"

"Before my time."

"Joshua ran a trapline until he couldn't walk anymore. Always had a story about a mink. Hardly a winter went by that he didn't have one of those varmints in his supplies. Little beggars would tear everything apart. Some of it they would eat, but Joshua figured that, most of the time, they just liked to raise hell."

"Sounds like some people I know."

"Sure as hell wouldn't want one for a friend."

Thumps slid out of the booth. "I need a favour."

"Sure," said Al, "long as you don't need to borrow my car, my gun, or my husband."

"You don't have a husband."

"Then that improves your odds of my saying yes."

Thumps handed Al the bag of letters. "Can you hold these for me? Keep them safe?"

"Not much of a favour."

"If something happens to me, make sure they get back to Grover."

"You planning on getting yourself killed or something?"

"No."

"Can I read them?"

"No."

"You got to read them."

"That's because I'm a deputy."

Al took the bag and wandered behind the counter. "And here I thought you were a photographer."

"I could use a large envelope." Thumps pulled the parka on. "And a couple sections of newspaper."

Al put her hands on her hips and cocked her head. "This another favour?"

THUMPS TRIED STROLLING to the sheriff's office, to see if embracing the season would change his attitude toward it, but after a block of wading through the snow and the cold, he pulled the hood over his head and picked up the pace to a brisk walk. Not that his mind was truly on the winter landscape or the weather.

He hadn't seen it. Even when Moses had told him what to look for, he hadn't seen it.

Not that he could prove anything. In fact, he doubted that any real proof existed. Only one man knew, and Thumps was sure he wasn't going to hang himself. But one thing was sure. Lucy Kettle was dead. A witness-protection program might have kept her away from Dakota, but it wouldn't have separated her from Reuben and most certainly not from her brother. Somehow or other she would have got word to the two men. The woman who wrote those letters would not have given up her life for safety. Someone had taken it.

ANDY WAS SITTING at the sheriff's desk, trying to look as though he belonged in the same area code as Hockney.

"Where's Duke?"

"He's out."

"Where'd he go?"

Andy came out of the chair slowly, in one motion. "Sheriff wants to make you a deputy, that's his business. But I don't work for you."

"All right. Then I'll go find the sheriff."

Andy's face broke into a broad smirk. "Fat chance of finding him. You haven't got a clue where he went."

"That's right," said Thumps, "so when I do finally find him, he's going to be mad as hell."

The smirk melted. "What do you mean?"

"Well," said Thumps, dropping the envelope on the desk, "Duke told me to check on a couple of things, and I did, and now he's going to want to know what I found."

"This about the murders?"

"Can't say."

"That woman confessed," said Andy, trying to think and talk at the same time, "but I always figured Ridge for the killings."

"So, how do I find the sheriff?"

"Is that it?" Andy's eyes were bright with interest now. "You got proof that Ridge shot Street and Justice, don't you? I told Duke not to let him go."

"You're smarter than people give you credit for."

"Tell you what." Andy picked up the envelope and turned it over. "I'll get this to Duke."

"I'm not sure that that's a good idea."

"Yeah, well, you don't get to make those decisions." Andy grabbed his jacket and hat. "You get to stay here and mind the store."

* * *

THUMPS WATCHED ANDY slide his way down the street. Then he pushed Duke's chair into the cellblock. Cellblock was probably too grand a word. The sheriff's office had two cells. One was empty. Dakota was in the other.

Thumps wheeled the chair to the cell and sat down. "Andy went to find the sheriff. We probably have twenty to thirty minutes."

"Are you here to rescue me?" Dakota didn't look as though she needed rescuing. She looked as though she had given up.

"How long have you known that Noah was Massasoit?" Thumps rolled the chair against the bars.

"What are you talking about?"

"How long?" Thumps said quietly.

Dakota sat down on the floor next to the bars. "We were working on the book, and Noah said something."

"What did he say?"

"He said that Mitchell Street killed Lucy."

"Noah didn't like Street."

"It was the way he said it."

"In the book, he says that the FBI put Lucy in a witness protection program."

"You didn't know Lucy," said Dakota. "There's no way she would have run for cover."

"Would Lucy have known?"

"I'm not even sure."

Thumps pressed a little. "Would she have known?"

"No," said Dakota. "If she had, she would have told the world."

"She might have wanted to protect the organization."

"That's something I would do," said Dakota. "Not Lucy. She didn't tolerate lies."

Thumps put his elbows on his thighs and let his head fall into his hands. Noah would have liked the irony of the FBI funding RPM. He could sell them little pieces of information now and then. Nothing important. He would have enjoyed that game, playing spy, playing God.

"Look, it was just a feeling."

"But he would have needed an out, someone to take the blame if things went south. Somebody credible. Somebody who the FBI could believe was Massasoit."

"He wouldn't do that." Dakota leaped to her feet.

"Lucy was second-in-command. Was she trying to push him out?"

Dakota shook her head. "They didn't agree on everything. That's all."

Thumps found himself hoping that the sheriff would arrive and end the interrogation. He wasn't enjoying any of this.

"So, Lucy didn't know about the bonds." It was a cheap trick that cops did. Wait until you had the suspect worked up, and then hit them with a question they weren't expecting. Don't listen to their answer. Watch their face.

"What are you talking about?"

"Next question," said Thumps quickly. "Did Noah ask you to confess to the murders in order to buy him time to find out who's trying to kill him?" He pushed the chair back from the bars. "Is that why you did it? To save his ass?"

"What if it was? Is that such a bad reason?"

No, Thumps thought to himself, protecting someone you cared about was a good reason for a great many actions. Noah wasn't worth it. At least, Thumps didn't think he was. But Dakota did. Or maybe he was all she had left of a life. Not a friend. Not a lover. Something more precious than that.

"Did Noah say who he thought was trying to kill him?"

Dakota walked to the far corner of the cell. "The FBI."

Thumps wasn't sure what the FBI might be willing to do. Certainly the last several decades had not been kind to any of the intelligence agencies. Even before the terrorist attacks in New York and Washington, the FBI and the CIA had been caught in a number of awkward situations that had been both ill advised and illegal. Would the FBI have any qualms about playing fast and loose with a small activist organization? Probably not. Would they kill? Perhaps. Would they then try to cover it up? Absolutely.

"What about you?" Thumps pushed the chair along the bars. "Do you think someone is trying to kill Noah?"

"I don't know." Dakota sat down on the bed and turned toward the wall. "Isn't that what you're supposed to figure out?"

"It is, indeed." Sheriff Hockney was standing in the doorway, the envelope in his hand.

"Hi, Sheriff."

"Andy brought me this new evidence." Hockney patted the envelope against the wall. "Said you got the whole thing figured out."

"Where's Andy?"

"On an errand," said Hockney. "Am I interrupting, or do you have time for a little chat?"

HOCKNEY WAS SITTING on the edge of his desk when Thumps rolled the chair into the office. He had the sections of newspaper in his hand.

"So, you want to tell me what's going on?"

"I'm not sure yet."

"But you needed to get rid of Andy, so you could talk to Ms. Miles again."

"That's about it."

"And?" said the sheriff.

"Where's Noah?"

"In his room. Resting. What about Ms. Miles?"

"She thinks the FBI is behind this."

"Yeah," said Hockney, "that makes sense. They send Special Agent Asah up from Denver to kill Ridge, and while he's waiting for the right moment, he kills

Mitchell Street and Reuben Justice for practice."

"Stranger things have happened."

"Not in my lifetime." Hockney slipped off the desk and lowered himself into his chair. "Let's take a run at the process of elimination. What do Mitchell Street and Reuben Justice and Dakota Miles and Noah Ridge all have in common?"

Thumps had already asked himself this question any number of times.

"They knew each other," said the sheriff. "And since two of them are dead, that leaves two suspects. Which one do you like?"

"What about Grover Many Horses?"

"He was in Glory at the video store when Street was killed. Andy picked up the surveillance tape from the store. It's time-dated." Hockney turned around in his chair. "Of course, there is one other person who knew everybody."

"Yeah," said Thumps. "Me."

"Process of elimination. See how it works?"

Thumps had turned the same set of givens around any number of ways, and he kept coming up with the same answers as the sheriff.

"Unless, of course, we've got ourselves one of those Hollywood hit men running loose."

"What?"

"The movies." Hockney opened the top drawer of his desk and took out a bag of licorice. "You know, where the bad guy comes to town disguised as a priest or a travelling salesman."

Thumps could feel the fur on the hood of the parka against the side of his neck. "We don't have any new priests in town."

Hockney put the licorice down. "You're not serious."

"Where's Asah?"

"Watching Ridge."

Thumps picked up the phone and handed it to Hockney. "Use your contacts. I'll go to the hotel."

"Sure as hell hope you're wrong." Duke slid his revolver across the desk. "But if you're not, for God's sake, don't shoot anyone until I get there."

THIRTY-TWO

The front of the Tucker looked serene. The television trucks were gone, though Thumps was reasonably sure that they were just waiting in the woods for something to happen. News people didn't give up on the smell of blood all that easily.

Inside, the lobby had been magically transformed into a western movie set. There were saddles thrown over bales of hay, branding irons laid out on display tables, and a couple of wagon wheels leaning against the walls. Even the staff had got into the spirit of the moment, with cowboy hats and bright neckerchiefs. From the mezzanine balcony, someone had hung a large banner that read "Western History Conference." The banner was a little on the worn side, and Thumps guessed that this wasn't the first time it had been hung in a hotel lobby.

As he headed for the elevators, he wondered what people did at a western history conference. It was, he assumed, a gathering of academics from various universities around the country who were keen on sharing their research with other academics. He had attended such a conference once. On photography. It had been a mistake, a misunderstanding. Thumps had thought he would meet other photographers, professionals working in the field. Instead, he had met university professors who understood photography, not as art form or even a craft, but as a metaphor, and he had had to sit through a drone of papers that analyzed the "paradigms of imagining" and the "ethnopoetics of photography" and the "repercussions of the postcolonial camera." He did meet one photographer, but he was taking pictures for the local paper. One or two of the papers had been intriguing, but most of them had been brain-numbing things that would have defeated the most dedicated insomniac.

Thumps didn't bother with the house phone or the front desk. He went straight to Noah's room and pounded on the door.

"Noah!"

Cooley had made kicking in a French door look easy. Thumps wondered if a hotel door would be as simple.

"Noah! It's Thumps!"

Thumps leaned against the door to test the give. It felt firmer than he had hoped, but he wasn't interested in wasting time at the front desk, arguing with the staff about the legality of letting him in Noah's room. The trick, he remembered, was to concentrate all the force at the lock itself. As long as the door wasn't sitting in a metal frame, he had a good chance of taking out the jam and the moulding with one kick.

Thumps was balanced on one leg with the other aimed at the door when Hockney stepped off the elevator.

"DreadfulWater!"

Thumps lowered his leg slowly, in a manner that he hoped would suggest that the sheriff had caught him in the middle of his Tai Chi exercises.

"Jesus," said the sheriff, sliding a key card into the slot, "what is it with you and doors."

"What about Asah?"

Hockney opened the door and pushed his way in. "Special Agent Asah is FBI, all right."

"You're sure."

"Absolutely," said the sheriff. "I talked to him myself."

"What?"

"Special Agent Spencer Asah of the Denver office of the FBI is still in Denver."

"So, the feds didn't send anyone to watch Noah?"

"Noah Ridge is nowhere on their radar."

"And they didn't know about Street."

"Nope," said the sheriff.

"Beautiful."

The room was empty. There were no signs of a struggle. No indication of violence. Everything was in its place. Noah's suitcase and all his clothes were in the closet. His toiletry kit was next to the bathroom sink.

"You got any ideas about what the hell is going on?"

"Yeah, but first we have to find Noah." Thumps went to the window and looked out. A police cruiser pulled up to the curb, and Andy Hooper hurried into the Tucker. "You call Andy?"

"Yeah," said Hockney. "The way this thing is heading south, I figure we're going to need all the guns we can get."

By the time Andy got to the room, Thumps and Hockney had gone through the place thoroughly and had come up with nothing. Andy wasn't keen on babysitting an empty room, but the sheriff wasn't much for democratic decision-making.

"Watch some television. Make some coffee. If Ridge comes back, hold him and call me."

"What if he doesn't want to be held?"

"Then arrest him and drag his sorry ass to jail."

"Why don't you make Thumps wait here? The two of them are friends."

"That's why," said the sheriff.

THUMPS AND HOCKNEY rode the elevator in silence. All the way through the lobby and down the steps to the sheriff's car, Thumps had the feeling that Duke was annoyed with him, as though he blamed him for everything that had happened, as though all of this was his fault.

"Okay," said the sheriff as they stepped off the elevator. "Start talking."

"Beth still have Street's effects?"

"No," said Hockney. "Asah picked them up yesterday."

"When Buckhorn, Scout, and Begay hit that corporation in Denver, they got away with five million dollars in bearer bonds."

"Who the hell told you that?"

"Asah."

"So, that Xerox was the real thing?"

"It was just a lure," said Thumps. "To get Street to come to Chinook."

Hockney stopped at the front door of the hotel. "You know who sent it to him?"

"Yeah," said Thumps. "I do. It was Massasoit."

Hockney pushed his way through the doors and stood on the steps huffing and puffing. "Do you know what's going on?"

"Part of it," said Thumps. "Maybe."

The sheriff stomped down the steps to his cruiser, took a black cellphone out of the glovebox, and handed it to Thumps. "This works as a walkie-talkie as well as a phone. I'm going to try to find Mr. Asah or whatever the hell his name is."

"What do you want me to do?"

"Solve the case," said Hockney. "I can hardly afford you as it is."

THE SHERIFF'S OFFICE was as he had left it, warm and bright. The Connors' cellphone was still sitting on the edge of Hockney's desk. Thumps wondered how they were going to like their phone's being used in a felony. Some people found that sort of thing exciting. When Thumps had been a cop, there had been a bank robbery in Arcata, and during the escape, one of the robbers had put a bullet through a corner of the large mirror in the Lumberjack bar. Teddy Maxwell could have had the insurance pay for the damage, but he left the bullet hole there as a conversation piece. Maybe the Connors would feel that way about their phone. Maybe they'd frame the door.

Dakota was standing in the cell by the small window.

"Come on," said Thumps. "I'm breaking you out."

"My hero."

"I'm serious. Noah didn't kill Street or Reuben, and neither did you."

"Then who . . . ?"

"Spencer Asah."

"The FBI agent?"

"Yeah," said Thumps, turning the key in the lock and swinging the door open. "Your tax dollar at work."

"Why are you doing this?"

"Because you're not safe here."

"Where's Noah?"

"I don't know." Thumps was putting the keys back in the sheriff's desk when he noticed the cellphone again. "Shit."

"What's wrong?"

Thumps took the phone the sheriff had given him and pressed the button on the side. "Duke, you hear me?"

There was a moment of silence and then a crackle. "Yeah, I hear you."

"The key to the Connor place, did you leave it on the desk?"

"Yeah, with the cellphone."

"Cellphone is here, but not the key."

"You're kidding."

"You want me to meet you out there?"

"No, I'll take Andy with me," said the sheriff. "He likes to shoot things. You stick around in case either one of our two clowns shows up."

Thumps slipped the phone into his pocket. The sheriff's revolver was still tucked into his belt, and it was beginning to irritate his back, but he was glad he had it. "Grab your coat," he said to Dakota. "We have to get you someplace safe."

"Noah wouldn't hurt me."

"Noah's not the problem right now."

THUMPS WAS ALWAYS amazed how early night came in winter. By the time he and Dakota left the sheriff's office, it was already dark. Thumps paused as they stepped through the door and looked up and down the street. Most of the cars were gone and the ones that were left were covered in snow. Asah wouldn't know that they were on to him just yet, but he might have seen it coming and decided to cut his losses and disappear, though Thumps didn't think the man was the type to be so easily detoured. If Thumps was right, Asah would go after Noah. And he might have already found him.

If Asah had taken the key to the Connor place from the sheriff's office, he must have expected to use it. And why not? Noah had already been to the house twice. If Asah had grabbed Noah and wanted a quiet place for the two of them to talk, Thumps couldn't think of a better choice.

Not that Noah was to survive such a talk. Sounds tended to carry for long distances across water, but at Red Tail Lake in the middle of winter, no one would hear him scream.

"Where are we going?"

"My place."

He had been tempted to leave Dakota in jail and race out to the lake to help Hockney. Asah had already killed two men. Two more wouldn't make a difference. Not that the sheriff would be that easy to kill. He was smart enough not to walk into a trap. And on this kind of a chase, Andy, for all his faults, was the perfect partner. He was a crack shot with a short fuse. Having a chance to shoot a bad guy would be the high point of his career in law enforcement.

"Why your place?"

"I have an attack cat."

Every so often, Thumps would stop and search the street. Asah might well be at the lake, but then again he might be following Dakota to see where she might lead him. If he hadn't found Noah yet, watching Dakota would be the next best thing. But the streets were clear and quiet, and the only people on the move were the two of them.

Dakota leaned into Thumps as they walked. "Do you know what's been happening?"

"Some of it."

"I'll tell you everything I know," said Dakota. "As soon as you get me someplace warm."

COMING HOME IN THE DARK reminded Thumps that he needed to replace the porch light. This was one of the little matters of home ownership that always got left to the last. A busted pipe or a broken window or a toilet that had backed up got fixed right away, but a sticky lock or a doorbell that stopped working for no apparent reason or a burned-out light bulb on the porch might go unattended for a year or more.

Thumps opened the door and stepped inside quickly, dragging a foot to keep Freeway from bolting past him. It was a summer habit, a way to keep the cat from escaping and disappearing into the warm summer evenings for days on end. Not that she was about to run off into this kind of weather. She had tried it one winter, and as soon as her paws hit the snow, she stopped dead in her tracks and meowed until Thumps picked her up and carried her to the safety of the house.

"What's your cat's name?"

"Freeway."

"That's not a name for a cat."

"She likes it."

"So, where is she?"

Normally by now, Freeway would be on the table, doing her cat dance and rebuking him for leaving her alone again. Since she wasn't here scolding him and her dish was half-full, sleeping had to be the correct answer.

"Probably in the living room." Thumps opened the refrigerator. "She likes to throw up on the couch." He bent over and looked at the juices on the shelf. "You want something to drink? I've got apple juice, cranberry-grape, pineapple, and apricot."

Claire liked apricot. Thumps found it a little thick. He had tried cutting it with pineapple, a compromise that turned out to be surprisingly good. The cranberry-grape was generally for guests, and the apple was for baking squash.

"I could mix a couple together." Thumps grabbed the pineapple and apricot and swung the door shut. "What do you think?"

Evidently, Dakota wasn't going to be drawn out of her depression with the promise of fruit drinks. Thumps poured two glasses and carried them to the living room. He wasn't sure what he could say to make things right. The Red Power Movement had been a fragile world at best. Now it had come apart completely.

He expected to find Dakota lying down on the couch, with Freeway curled up behind her legs. He would put the drinks on the floor and sit with her, maybe hold her for a while, and say those encouraging things you say to people who are without hope.

But Dakota wasn't lying on the couch. She was sitting on it ramrod straight, her hands clutched in her lap. Noah Ridge sat across from her, his arms and legs taped to a chair. And standing behind him, with a squat silencer screwed onto the barrel of a .45-calibre automatic, was Spencer Asah.

THIRTY-THREE

There were any number of emotions that Thumps could have felt standing there in his living room with a gun pointed at his chest, holding two glasses of fruit juice, but mostly he felt foolish.

Asah gestured to the glasses. "Orange?"

"Apricot and pineapple." Thumps set the glasses on the coffee table. "The FBI is going to be disappointed."

"They'll get over it."

Noah's lip was cut, the side of his face bruised. But it was his hands that had taken most of the damage. The knuckles had been smashed, several of the fingers dislocated.

"Mr. Ridge and I have been having a chat." Asah ran the barrel of the gun through Dakota's hair. "Perhaps you can persuade him to be a little more forthcoming."

"Leave her alone." Noah was in pain, but he hadn't lost any of his arrogance.

"I assume you have a gun."

Thumps opened the parka slowly, lifted the pistol from his waistband, and placed it on the table next to the drinks.

"You're a lot of help," growled Noah.

Thumps had stopped feeling foolish, but he was in no mood to be sympathetic. "It's your own damn fault."

"I didn't kill anyone."

Asah collected the gun. "Technically, he's correct about that."

"Yeah," said Thumps. "But he put everything in motion."

Dakota's hands were beginning to tremble, not out of fear and not out of rage. Something deeper and more painful. "Do you plan to kill us?"

Asah sighed and tried to look sympathetic. "I'd prefer not to. It's bad for the bureau's image to have its agents running around injuring taxpayers."

"But Morgan Energy probably wouldn't mind," said Thumps. "Would they?"

Noah tried to turn his head to one side. "Morgan Energy?"

"He's not FBI," said Thumps.

"Touché," said Asah. "So, what gave me away?"

"Hockney called Denver."

Asah nodded. "And there is a Special Agent Spencer Asah in the Denver office."

"I know," said Thumps. "The sheriff talked to him."

"Ah, yes, well, he was supposed to be on vacation." Asah shrugged. "Just can't depend on the government anymore. Have you put all the pieces together yet?"

"Not yet."

"Me neither," said Asah. "But I'm curious. You want to compare notes?"

"You first," said Thumps.

Asah closed his eyes for a moment. "Okay. Here's what I know. Twenty-five years ago, Clinton Buckhorn, Wilson Scout, and Wallace Begay kidnapped Matthew Colburne, Morgan Energy's CEO, and forced him to open the safe at corporate headquarters."

"But they weren't looking for cash or bearer bonds."

"No," said Asah. "They weren't. They were looking for documents that would incriminate Morgan Energy in the bribing of state and federal officials. Over the years Morgan had been quite successful in getting drilling and mining contracts on Indian reservations. Problem was, it was a little too successful, and it tended to play fast and loose with environmental regulations."

"That doesn't make any sense." Thumps could feel his courage beginning to return. "To get that kind of evidence, they would have had to go through all of Morgan's files. It would have taken them weeks, maybe months, to find anything of use."

"It would have," said Asah, "if Matthew Colburne hadn't saved them the bother. As a CEO, the man had a great many admirable characteristics, but he wasn't the book of the month. He tended to be a bit on the obsessive side and quite secretive. Over the years, he had taken the time to organize all the pertinent documents into one file. There were probably a great many good reasons why he wanted to keep all the damning evidence close by and in one package, but as it turned out, the decision was exceptionally indiscreet."

"He kept the file in the safe?"

"Right next to the bonds."

"So, the bonds were a bonus."

"Dumb luck," said Asah. "The bonds were part of Morgan's bribery slush fund. Almost impossible to trace."

"But things didn't go as planned."

"Colburne grabbed a gun from his desk and began blasting away. By the time both sides ran out of bullets, Colburne and Wallace Begay had been wounded, and what had started off as an extreme act of social and political activism had turned into a federal offence."

"And a potential public-relations nightmare."

"Buckhorn and the boys fled the scene and wound up in Salt Lake City at Reuben Justice's place."

"They were cousins."

"Buckhorn told Justice that Begay had shot himself by accident. Colorado wouldn't have made the national news yet, so Justice would have no way of knowing what his cousin had been doing in his free time. Neither the local police in Denver nor the FBI got up to full speed until Monday morning, and the feds were still trying to tie their shoes by Wednesday."

"Sounds like you've been reading Street's field notes."

"Street had the file with him." Asah looked pleased with himself. "Most considerate. The man kept very detailed notes."

"What happened to the package? The bonds and the documents."

"No one knows. They were never recovered."

"Mitchell Street." Thumps had the answer at the same time he asked the question. "Street came to you?"

"To Morgan Energy, to be exact. Said he could recover the bonds. For a finder's fee."

"But he didn't know about the documents."

"No. The FBI knew about the bonds, but not about the documents."

"Because the documents were more explosive than the loss of the bonds."

Asah's eyes were bright and alive now. "Oh, yes. Twenty-five years ago, the release of those documents would have been dynamite. Today, it would be nuclear. When Street showed up with his Xerox, it sent shock waves right through upper management. After all this time, Morgan thought that the file had been lost or destroyed. But if Street could find the bonds, he might also be able to find the documents as well."

"So, Morgan sent you."

"It's what I do."

"That was a long time ago."

"True," said Asah, "but a great many of those executives and politicians have gone on to bigger and better things. Morgan Energy is a multinational corporation now. A scandal like that, even if it never went to court, would have brought everyone down."

"Did Street know who had the package?"

Asah nodded. "Someone named Massasoit. From his notes, it would appear that this Massasoit was an FBI informant, highly placed in the Red Power Movement."

Noah sat stone-faced in the chair, his teeth clenched.

"Lucy Kettle." Thumps said the name slowly and without emotion.

"The woman who disappeared right after the raid. In his notes, Street was quite sure that Lucy Kettle was Massasoit." Asah squatted down next to Noah. "But I could tell when he called me at the hotel that he had another name in mind."

"Did he say?"

"He didn't know for sure."

"So, you shot him."

"He was a blowhard," said Asah, running his hand over Noah's shoulder. "Almost as bad as this one. He didn't know where the documents or the bonds were, though it shouldn't have been that difficult to figure out. There weren't many candidates left. Reuben Justice, Dakota Miles, and Noah Ridge. When it was clear that Street wasn't going to be of much use, he became a loose end."

"And Reuben's dead."

"Yeah, that was unfortunate," said Asah. "Wrong place, wrong time. But it did reduce the possibles to two."

"Lucy Kettle could still be alive."

"I don't think so," said Asah. "When I raised that question with him, Street said there was no point wasting any time with ghosts. Personally, I think his money was on Ridge."

"Go to hell!"

"I had hoped that if I could arrange a little quality time with Mr. Ridge, we would be able to come to an agreement," said Asah. "But as you can see, he's proven to be surprisingly difficult."

"Fuck off!"

Asah helped himself to one of the glasses of fruit juice. "Of course, Buckhorn could have stashed the package somewhere between Denver and Salt Lake, and this would have all been a waste of time."

"Buckhorn didn't have the bonds or the documents when he left Denver." Thumps glanced at Noah. "It would have been too risky. If they got caught, all the evidence they had grabbed would have disappeared."

"But you know what they did with it."

"I'm guessing."

Noah glared at him. "Fucking apple!"

Asah put the gun to Dakota's head. "Guess away."

"Buckhorn mailed the bonds and the documents. He and the other two men got into Morgan through the mailroom. On the way out, it would have been an easy matter to put everything into a box and mail it to a friend."

"I like that," said Asah. "Morgan delivers the instrument of its own destruction into the hands of its enemy. It's almost biblical. Certainly Shakespearean."

He walked over to Noah and pressed the barrel of the gun on his hand. Noah didn't scream, but Thumps could see the pain bead up on his face. "Do you know to whom they mailed the package?"

"No."

"But you're good at guessing."

"Lucy Kettle."

"The woman who disappeared. That's rather convenient."

"Buckhorn wouldn't have sent the bonds and the documents to Noah. He didn't trust him. Lucy was Justice's lover and in that sense family, but she was also the only one in RPM with the integrity to follow through with what they had found in Denver."

Asah finished the juice and put the glass back on the table. "So, where is Ms. Lucy?"

Dakota began to pull at the skin around her fingers. Thumps had seen this before. The distress. The desperation. At the train station in Salt Lake.

"Lucy's dead."

"And you don't know where the bonds and the documents are, do you?"

"No," said Thumps. "So, what now?"

"Well," said Asah, "I have a number of intriguing choices. I can kill Mr. Ridge and assume that he's the only person who knows where the package is. But if I do that, then I have to kill the rest of you too because you'd be witnesses to a murder, and that would never do. Or I could cut my losses and disappear."

"I like the last choice."

"Actually," said Asah, "so do I. But I don't think my employers would be too crazy about my coming home empty-handed."

"Do the math," said Thumps, hoping he could make four plus four add up to nine. "Street led the raid on Justice's house, but he didn't find the package. If it had come to Noah, why would he have sat on it all these years? Those documents would have given him an international platform. The bonds alone would have funded every project RPM ever dreamed of starting."

"I wouldn't want him for a friend," said Asah. "I've read Street's files. Ridge would let his mother die to save his skin."

"If the package was mailed to Lucy," said Thumps, trying to complete the problem before Asah saw the flaw, "the bonds and the documents vanished with her."

Asah smiled and looked at his watch. "The sheriff should be heading back from the lake about now. I need a couple of hours."

Thumps nodded. "You have my word."

"By the way," he said, "I'm not Kiowa. I thought you would want to know that." Asah slipped the gun into his pocket. "Oh, and check the refrigerator. You're out of orange juice."

THIRTY-FOUR

Thumps sat in the chair and listened to the front door shut. There was no sound of a car starting, but Asah wouldn't have parked it in front of the house anyway.

"Cut me loose." Noah worked his arms from side to side.

Thumps looked at his watch. "I gave him my word."

"Are you crazy? The man's a fucking murderer!"

Dakota sat on the couch and quietly tore at her fingers.

"You okay?"

"Yeah," she said.

"Damn it! Cut me loose!"

With his handkerchief, Thumps picked up the glass that Asah had used and took it to the kitchen. It would have prints on it, though he was reasonably sure that Asah would not pop up on any of the databases. The man was too careful for that.

He slipped the phone in his pocket, took a knife from the drawer, and opened the refrigerator. Asah hadn't looked closely enough. There was a carton of orange juice on the top shelf. Right next to it, tied together with string, was a thick folder. There was dried blood on one corner. This is what had been on the desk in Street's motel room. Even before he opened it, Thumps knew what it was. Street's field notes. A goodbye present from a killer.

When Thumps got back to the living room, Noah was still raging in the chair.

"It's about fucking time!"

Thumps put the phone and the knife on the coffee table and held up the glasses. "Anybody want juice?"

* * *

NOAH, NOT SURPRISINGLY, was not in the mood for juice, and by the time Thumps cut him loose, he was sorry that Asah hadn't shot the man.

"Sheriff'll hear about this." Noah rubbed his wrists and tried to work his fingers back in place.

Maybe it was all the tension, but Thumps found himself thinking about a nap.

"You listening to me!"

"Not really," said Thumps. "But while we're all here, why don't we get a small matter cleared up."

"What the hell is there to clear up?"

"Massasoit."

Noah stopped rubbing his wrists. "That's old news," he said. "Lucy's gone. Leave it be."

"Sure," said Thumps. "But Lucy wasn't Massasoit."

Noah tried to lift himself out of the chair. "I don't have time for this bullshit."

"I just saved your life," said Thumps. "Make time."

Noah sank back into the chair, more out of pain than agreement.

"I'm going to tell you a story, and when I wander off course, you let me know. Okay?"

"I need a doctor."

"RPM comes to Salt Lake and sets up shop. Almost immediately the FBI takes an interest and assigns Mitchell Street to watch the organization. Street takes an instant dislike to one Noah Ridge and makes it his life's work to bring you down. How am I doing so far?"

"How about calling an ambulance?"

"That's just the opening. So, for the next number of years, Street tries to find something with which to hang you. But you're too smart. In the meantime, the organization isn't doing so well financially, and one day you get this bright idea. It's brilliant, actually. You take on a persona, in this case the name of the Indian who helped the English at Plymouth, and you sell information to the bureau. Nothing large, nothing critical. No one is hurt. The FBI thinks it has an informant in RPM, and the money you make from the feds goes to help fund the organization's social programs."

"That's a great story." Most of the blood on Noah's hands and face had dried. "I wish I were that smart."

"Oh," said Thumps, "you are. There was only one little problem. The more information you gave the feds, the closer they were to finding out who the informant was. You couldn't have that. If they had known it was you, they might have exposed you, which would have destroyed RPM from within and kept the bureau from looking like the heavies. So, you had to keep them busy looking in other directions."

Dakota slowly put her hands to her mouth. "Is that true?"

"Of course not. It's bullshit."

"No, it's not. And here you could take care of two problems at the same time. Lucy didn't like the way you managed the organization. She thought you were an egotist, more interested in your own image than the work that needed to be done. Given enough time, she might have pushed you out. She was smart, and she was committed. So, you used Lucy to take the heat off yourself. You pointed Street at Lucy. Street wouldn't have said anything, because he wanted the flow of information to continue. Everything was just fine until Clinton Buckhorn and Wilson Scout and Wallace Begay arrived in Salt Lake with the FBI hard on their heels."

Noah lurched out of the chair. "I'll call the damn ambulance myself."

"Sit down," said Thumps, taking the phone out of his pocket. "I'll call for one."

"How much of what he's said is true?"

"Jesus, Dakota, you really think I would do something like that?"

"Ambulance is on its way." Thumps put the phone on the table. "But we don't want to miss the good part. When Buckhorn, Scout, and Begay came to town, they headed for Reuben Justice's house. Begay was wounded and couldn't be moved. Now, the cops don't know that they're in town. The FBI has only just figured out who hit Morgan. They're at least two days behind. Yet somehow or other, they raid Justice's house the next morning."

"What the hell is your point?"

"The only person who knew where Buckhorn, Scout, and Begay were was Reuben Justice, and the only person he would have told was Lucy Kettle. But Lucy would never have turned them in. She cared too much for Reuben to do that, and she had too much integrity. So, how did you find out?"

"About what?"

"About Buckhorn and his buddies. The only way

the cops could have found out where they were staying that quickly was if someone told them, and the only person who would have had any reason to tell them was Massasoit." Thumps took a deep breath. "Lucy told you, didn't she? And you told the feds."

"You're wrong," said Dakota. "Noah would never have done something like that."

"It's the only thing he could do." Thumps tried to conjure up some sympathy for Noah. "If Buckhorn, Scout, and Begay were caught in Salt Lake, it would only be a matter of time before the FBI would be able to link them to Lucy and then to RPM. The only way to avoid such a disaster was to get the three men out of town before the cops found them."

"Listen to yourself," said Noah. "You sound like a cheap television show."

"It gets worse. I'm betting that Massasoit called Buckhorn to warn him that the FBI knew where they were and to get out of town immediately. And here's where you made your mistake. You waited to allow the men enough time to disappear before you called Street. How am I doing?"

"It's your story."

"No harm done. Massasoit makes a little money, and the FBI arrives just a little late. But what Massasoit doesn't know is that Begay is too badly wounded to be moved and that neither Buckhorn nor Scout is willing to leave Begay behind. When the feds did arrive early that morning, they expected to take the fugitives with little difficulty."

"And instead, they walked into an ambush." Dakota was on her feet now. "Street led that raid."

"Yeah, and he wouldn't have been happy. He would have wanted to know why Massasoit had sent them into a firefight."

"And if he thought Lucy was Massasoit . . ."

"He would have gone after her."

Through the window, Thumps could see the ambulance pull up to the curb, its lights flashing.

"That's a great story, DreadfulWater." Noah sat in the chair and waited. One of his hands had begun to bleed again. "It's crap, but it's a great story."

"It was the Xeroxed bond that brought Street to Chinook. You knew he couldn't pass up the chance to catch the person who had made a fool out of him and ruined his career. You were counting on that, weren't you? What were you hoping? That Street would make a scene? Turn the reading into a circus?" Thumps wasn't sure if he was feeling angry or numb. "How much would that have been worth in terms of publicity?"

The attendants settled Noah onto a gurney and wheeled him to the ambulance. Dakota climbed into the back.

"You don't have to go with him."

"What if you're wrong?"

"What if I'm not?"

The ambulance sped away down the block, its lights breaking the silence of the night. Thumps stood outside in his shirtsleeves and watched the street long after it disappeared, until he could no longer hear the siren or feel the cold.

THIRTY-FIVE

He had promised one hour, but by the time Thumps caught up with the sheriff, Asah had more than two hours on any pursuit. Not that anyone was going to catch him.

"You kept your word to a murderer?"

Street's field notes were amazingly detailed. The man had collected every fact, every notion, every guess, every fiction about RPM. There was a separate folder for Massasoit with dates and payments. Thumps wasn't sure he would have liked Street the man, but like Asah, he certainly admired Street the bookkeeper.

"He didn't shoot me."

"Shit."

"What about Noah?"

The sheriff made a face. "He'll live."

"You going to arrest him?"

"For what? Being annoying?"

Thumps ran through the offences that Noah had committed since he arrived in town. Breaking and entering, moving a body, hindering an investigation, public mischief, lying to the police. Breaking and entering a second time.

"Everybody lies to the police," said Hockney. "And he's written a cheque to cover the damage at the Connor place."

Thumps knew that Hockney could make Noah's life uncomfortable for at least a week if he set his mind to it, but he could see that the sheriff wasn't going to do that. All Duke wanted was to be rid of the man.

"Besides," said Hockney, "he gave me an auto-graphed copy of his book."

Thumps knew that Hockney had little time for the kind of nonsense that Noah could pull out of a hat, but he hadn't expected that the sheriff might be subcon-sciously pleased at having a celebrity in town.

"Those Street's case files?"

"That they are." Thumps dropped the package on Hockney's desk.

The sheriff looked at the folder. "How about I read them later. How about you tell me what's in them now."

"You know most of it."

"You know what I like?" Hockney screwed his lips up as if he had just sucked on something sour. "Even if we catch Special Agent Ass-hole, we've got nothing. That's what I like. You like that?"

"Nope."

"But you can't think of a thing to do about it, can you?"

Thumps had run out of negatives. More than that, he was tired of being reminded of what he could not do, what he could not change.

"So, this thing is over."

No, Thumps thought to himself, surprised that he still had a negative left, it wasn't over quite yet.

THE CHINOOK GENERAL HOSPITAL was a mixed marriage gone bad. The older part of the facility was a stately four-storey brick colonial, while the newer part was a series of squat cinderblock buildings lined up in rows that reminded him of a graveyard.

Thumps found Dakota sitting in the coffee shop, alone.

"How is he?"

"Resting."

"How are you?"

"You're wrong about him, you know." Dakota sat up straight and put her hands on the table as though she were going to push it away.

Thumps checked the cream and poured a little into his coffee. "Massasoit used a keyword so that the FBI knew the information was authentic. That word was 'kemo-sabe.' It's in Street's notes."

Dakota shook her head. "Lucy said that all the time. Anyone could have used it."

"Sure," said Thumps, "but who might have had a reason to frame Lucy? Who had access to the kind of information that the FBI was getting? Who could have known that Buckhorn, Scout, and Begay were in town?"

"Lucy could have been Massasoit."

Thumps knew he was bringing Dakota nothing but pain. She didn't believe Lucy was Massasoit, but if she had to save someone, she was determined to save the living.

"It's possible," he said, trying to soften the blow. "She might have decided that selling information to the FBI was a means to an end, but why would she want to incriminate herself by using a catchword everyone knew she used? And if she and Reuben were lovers, why would she tip off Street and put Reuben in harm's way?"

Dakota cradled the coffee cup in her hands. She looked stronger now, determined. Thumps didn't know where the strength had come from, but there it was.

"You don't like Noah."

"Doesn't change the matter," said Thumps.

Dakota rubbed the back of her neck. "They're going to release him in the morning."

"You heading back to Salt Lake?"

"No," said Dakota, "we have to fly to Los Angeles for a reading and media. Noah's doing the Jay Leno show at the end of the week."

Thumps almost smiled. The very thing that Noah

had worked so hard to get. A four-minute spot on a national late-night talk show.

"No such thing as bad press, right?"

"The publishers are bringing out a second printing." Dakota pushed the cup away and stood up. "But I don't suppose you see that as justice."

Thumps had been wrong. It wasn't strength, it was resignation, a kind of calm that he had noticed in people who had just been told that their child had been killed or that they were dying of a terminal illness. There was no power to it, just enough brute determination to continue.

"Good luck." It was all Thumps could think to say.

Dakota extended her hand. "It was nice to see you again."

THUMPS SAT AT THE TABLE by himself and moved the salt and pepper shakers around.

There were only two people who could answer the questions that were left. Of course, there was the chance that Buckhorn hadn't mailed the package to anyone, that it was in a safe-deposit box somewhere or rotting in a bus depot locker or buried by the side of the road. But that wouldn't explain the Xerox that someone had sent Street.

Noah was in a private room. Thumps had expected that he would be asleep, but he was sitting up in bed as though he had been waiting for someone to arrive.

"You just missed Dakota."

"How you feeling?" said Thumps.

"Like shit," said Noah. "Sonofabitch broke my finger."

"He could have shot you."

"You sound disappointed." Noah tried to grin. "You still a cop?"

"Another day," said Thumps. "No more."

"But you didn't come to wish me well."

"Nope."

"You came to harass me."

"It's what I live for."

Noah adjusted the bed so that he was more upright. "You want to know if I feel responsible for what's happened."

"No," said Thumps, "I want to know who killed Lucy Kettle."

Noah's face darkened for a moment. "It's probably time you go back to your photography."

Thumps pulled the chair closer to the bed. "Here's the deal. You talk to me, and I won't talk to the press."

"And just what would you talk to them about?"

"Massasoit."

"Old news."

"I'll make it new."

"Why do you care?" Noah looked more amused than concerned. "You sure as hell didn't care back in Salt Lake. When it counted."

"It must have been fun," said Thumps, waving the insult away, "screwing with the FBI, selling it worthless information, controlling the game."

"What about you? You feel responsible for doing nothing?"

"And then Denver comes along, and the game gets deadly." Thumps willed his body to relax. "You killed Lucy. You know that, don't you?"

The fury was back in Noah's eyes. "You know shit!"

Thumps rolled the chair back a little so he could see Noah and the heart-rate monitor on the wall above the bed. "Street must have been furious about being blindsided like that. I'm guessing he thought he had been set up, so he went after Massasoit. Or at least the person he thought was Massasoit. Maybe he meant to kill her. Maybe it was an accident."

Noah pulled an arm onto his chest. "It's a great story."

"But what I don't know is how you knew that Street killed Lucy." As Thumps watched the monitor, Noah's heart rate took a jump.

Noah leaned back into the pillow and closed his eyes. "You know, I'm really tired. Why don't you get the fuck out of here."

"And I don't understand why Street would hide the body. He would have left it where it was. Moving it would have been too great a risk. Where Lucy's body was found wouldn't have mattered to him."

"I'm going to be on Leno." Noah kept his eyes closed. "Did Dakota tell you that?"

"Yeah, she did."

"I'm going to talk about casinos and how they're destroying Native communities. What are you going to do with your life?"

Thumps walked through the main doors of the hospital just in time to see the sun light up the ice crystals in the air. This was the second dawn he had had to endure in as many days, and while the cold glow of the sun off the snow was interesting, he hoped that these early-morning affairs were not going to become a habit. They certainly hadn't made him any happier. They certainly hadn't made him any smarter.

THIRTY-SIX

Al's was crowded. Archie was sitting at the counter, and as soon as he saw Thumps come through the door, he began herding people up and down the stools until he had freed a seat next to him.

"Boy," said Archie, "have you been keeping up on all the excitement?"

"Sorry about your reading."

"Did you see me on television?" said Archie. "Now everyone in the world is going to want to come to Chinook."

It was nice to hear a positive spin put on the events of the last few days. Thumps would never have imagined felonies and mayhem as tourist attractions, but that was one of the things he liked about Archie. The man could find a fresh peach in a barrel of old motor oil.

"How are our friends in the media?"

"Gone," said Archie. "They all left last night. On their way to Los Angeles."

So, Noah had his media parade, and if Thumps knew the man, Noah would be able to milk the coverage for weeks, maybe months.

"What are you going to do now?"

"What do you mean?"

"The FBI guy," said Archie. "Aren't you going to track him down and throw him in jail?"

News in Chinook travelled at the speed of sound. If Archie knew, everyone in town knew. Not that there was any reason to keep it a secret. Except maybe Hockney's pride.

Thumps tried to catch Al's eye. "I'm going to eat breakfast, and then I'm going home."

"That's it?"

"That's it."

Al slid the coffee pot along the counter, filling cups

as she came. When she got to Thumps, she stopped. "You going to catch that FBI guy?"

"No."

"You want breakfast?"

"I guess."

"You want to send me a postcard when you make up your mind?"

"Hey, Al," said Archie. "Tell Thumps your good news. That'll cheer him up."

Thumps wasn't sure he was in the mood to be cheered.

Al wiped her hands on her apron. "Got my cheque."

"Great."

"Ten days for a letter to come from San Francisco," said Archie. "You believe that? Tell Thumps what they said."

"Stella at the post office said that wasn't unusual." Al put her hands on her hips. "She said if it had been a parcel, it would have taken longer."

"If this was Greece," said Archie, "that letter would have been here the next day."

"I guess if it took me nine days to make your break-fast," said Al, "I could get a job at the post office."

Thumps could feel a smile lurking somewhere in his face. "Yeah," he said, "I'd like breakfast."

Al wandered back to attend to her grill, and Archie settled into a marathon of local news, items, and events that Thumps might have missed while he was chasing bad guys around the countryside. There were days Thumps found great comfort in simple things. Casual conversation, good food, a warm place to sit. This was one of those days.

Before it was done, Noah would be on his way to Los Angeles and fame and fortune. Thumps didn't think any better of the man now than he had in Salt Lake. In fact, he had seen a side of Noah that was more sinister and callous than he had remembered. But maybe that was how you had to be to do the work that Noah did. Or maybe that was what the work did to you.

"First thing this spring," said Archie, "we should go up to the Pipestone Range and look around."

"Sure."

"You never know," said Archie. "This could be the year we get rich."

"Maybe the snow will melt early."

"That's the spirit." Archie cut one of Thumps's sausages in half and ate it in one bite. "Always plan ahead. That way, if something goes wrong, at least you have a plan."

Thumps wasn't sure if it had come to him in pieces, and he just hadn't noticed until everything had worked its way into place, or if the answer he had been looking for had just arrived, suddenly and complete.

"Jesus."

"You okay?" Archie put the toast back on Thumps's plate.

"You know when Noah plans on leaving?"

Archie shrugged. "Only one plane to Missoula. Doesn't leave until this afternoon."

"Call the sheriff." Thumps slid off the stool. "Tell him to meet me at the Tucker."

CHECKOUT AT MOST HOTELS was eleven. The Tucker would probably let you stay longer, especially if you were a celebrity. Thumps went straight for the house phones. There was no answer in Noah's room. Or Dakota's.

"Hey, Thumps."

If ever Thumps was happy to see Cooley Small Elk, it was now. "You still working security?"

"Just signed on with the hotel for another six months."

"I need your help."

Cooley's eyes sparkled. "Do I need my gun?"

"Yes," said Thumps.

"Outstanding," said Cooley.

On the elevator, Thumps considered explaining the situation to Cooley, but it would have taken too long, and he wasn't sure he could explain it to himself without getting lost.

Dakota's room was the first stop. Thumps slid Cooley's card key into the lock while Cooley stood to one side, his gun at the ready.

"Doesn't look like she's here. You want me to call downstairs? Maybe they checked out."

Thumps waited while Cooley called the front desk. He should have seen the problem in the timeline long before now. He couldn't imagine that Asah had missed it. Buckhorn had mailed the bonds and the documents from Denver. Thumps was sure of that now. It was the only explanation that fit the facts. And he was reasonably positive that Buckhorn had sent the package to Lucy. But the package wouldn't have left Morgan's mail room until Monday morning at the earliest. There was no chance that it had arrived before Buckhorn was killed and Lucy disappeared. So, what had happened to it?

That was why Asah hadn't killed them all when he had the chance. He didn't have to. Somewhere in the process of torturing Noah and chatting to Thumps, he had figured out who had the bonds and the documents.

"They're still here."

The kettle on the stove was hot. Thumps picked the coffee cup up off the floor. She had been here not too long ago, and she had left in a hurry.

"Come on."

Noah's room was two floors up. Cooley didn't even bother knocking.

Noah was lying down, reading a newspaper. Thumps ignored him, checked the rooms, and came back to the couch on the fly. Cooley stood in the doorway, the gun cradled against his stomach. "Why didn't you answer your phone?"

"What?"

"Why didn't you answer your phone?"

"Because I didn't feel like it."

"Where's Dakota?"

"In her room. Don't you get tired of harassing me?"

"No, she's not," Thumps grabbed Noah by the shirt and jerked him up. "Asah has her."

"Take your hands off me!"

"You don't care, do you?"

"Bullshit," said Noah. "That sonofabitch is long gone."

"Dakota has the bonds and the documents. She's had them all these years."

"I wouldn't know."

"No, you wouldn't. If you had known where they were, you would have used them by now. You would have spent the money, maybe turned the documents over to the press. But you wouldn't have sat on them."

"If you say so."

Thumps turned to Cooley. "Give me your gun."

"You going to shoot him?"

"Yes."

"Okay."

Thumps took the pistol, broke the cylinder, and took out the bullets. He held one up so Noah could see it and slid it back into the chamber.

"You're not going to kill me." Noah started to lean back just as Thumps stepped forward and pressed the gun against his kneecap.

"Yes, I will," said Thumps. "Just not all at once."

Noah looked over his shoulder at Cooley. "Aren't you supposed to protect me?"

"You fired me, remember?"

Thumps pulled the hammer back. "Who killed Lucy Kettle?"

"Fuck you!"

The hammer made a sharp crack as it hit the empty cylinder.

"Jesus!"

"Let's try this again." Thumps cocked the pistol.

Noah jerked his knee away. "Mitchell Street. The bastard beat her to death."

"And you moved the body."

"You don't get it, do you? They find Lucy's body, the cops don't come looking for an FBI agent. They come looking for me."

Thumps eased the hammer forward.

"That evening, after the raid, I went to Lucy's house. I saw Street go out the back. Lucy was in the living room,

dead. I cleaned the place up and took her into the mountains and buried her. Is that what you wanted to know?"

"Yes."

"Well, enjoy it, because it's the only time I'm going
to tell it."

"You could have gone to the police."

"Oh," said Noah, "is this where you give me the
speech on the integrity of law enforcement, where you
promise me a fair trial? Why don't you give Leonard
Peltier a call and share those thoughts with him."

"You set Lucy up. Street didn't go to her house by
mistake. You pointed him at her."

"I didn't kill her."

"No, you just arranged for it to happen. The same
way you set up Mitchell Street."

"I didn't send the bond to Street. Okay?"

"So, you knew it had to be Dakota."

"Only person it could be. But I don't know how she
got them. And I don't know where they are."

"But you didn't want to share that piece of information, did you?"

"So what."

"Sounds like he wanted the money for himself," said

Cooley. "Always easier to get something if you know where to find it."

Thumps reloaded the gun and handed it back to Cooley. Noah sat up and shoved his feet into his shoes. "You're one crazy sonofabitch."

Thumps stopped in the doorway. "You better hope I find her alive."

Noah was on his feet now. "Or what? Massasoit? Massasoit's dead. He died when Lucy died. Whether you like it or not. You want the world to have sharp colours and clean edges. Well, it doesn't. You think I'm the bad guy. You ever see what a coal-mining company can do to the land, you sanctimonious shit? You complain about what's wrong with the world, but you don't do a damn thing to change it. You leave that dirty job for someone like me."

Thumps let the platitudes blow past him in a rush. "Save the speech for Leno."

THE RIDE TO the lobby was slow. Someone had pressed the button for every floor.

"He's right, you know," said Cooley. "There are lots

of people who want to see the world change but who don't do anything about it. I'm like that sometimes."

"He's no hero."

"Sure," said Cooley, "but good ideas don't always come from good people."

THUMPS SAT IN the lobby and waited for Hockney. Not that the sheriff was going to be able to help. A professional such as Asah couldn't have left empty-handed. He had doubled back. Thumps should have seen that coming.

Dakota had sent the copy of the bond to Street. Thumps guessed she had sent the postcard too. Only Massasoit knew that the authenticating phrase for any communication with Street was "kemo-sabe." But Dakota wasn't Massasoit. Of that, Thumps was sure. But she had wanted Street and Noah to know who was coming at them, and the messages she sent to both men were exactly what Lucy would have said.

Thumps was pretty sure he knew the why and he was working on the how when Hockney came puffing into the lobby.

"This better be good," said Hockney, "because, as a deputy, you're getting to be more trouble than you're worth."

"Asah has Dakota."

"You know," said the sheriff, "I kind of liked the sonofabitch."

"Dakota has the bonds and the documents."

"Documents?"

"The documents are what Buckhorn was really after when he and the others hit Morgan Energy. Proof that Morgan was bribing state and federal officials in order to get energy contracts on Indian land."

"That's what all this is about? A bunch of twenty-five-year-old office memos?"

"Stick ran off some articles for me. One of them was a profile of Morgan Energy. It listed the board of directors." Thumps took a pen out of his pocket and wrote three names on his hand. "Any of these catch your fancy?"

"You're kidding." Hockney tried to frown and smile all at the same time.

"Nope."

"That's one big bucket," said the sheriff. "No wonder

they sent Asah. If that shit ever hit the fan, Morgan wouldn't be able to buy enough mops."

"Once he has what he came for, he'll kill her. He won't even think about it."

"How'd he know she had them?"

"I told him." Thumps stood up and brushed himself off.

Asah would need to find someplace private. But he didn't know the town that well, so it would have to be a place he knew. "You got any ideas?"

"No."

"You think Dakota has the bonds and the papers with her?"

"No," said Thumps.

"Maybe she left them with a friend."

And there it was. The answer to the question. Hockney had it all along. Thumps had no doubt that Asah had already figured it out. Or maybe he had got Dakota to tell him. It didn't matter. What mattered now was how fast Hockney's SUV could get them to Glory.

THIRTY-SEVEN

It had been a long time since Thumps had been in a
police car that was racing to the scene of a possible
crime with its lights flashing. The road was snow-
packed and slick, and even with four-wheel drive, the
SUV had no more traction than a pig on grease. But
this didn't seem to bother Hockney, who was able to
drive at speeds well above the posted limit and talk
at the same time.

"Hope to hell you're right about this."

"So do I."

"You were going to tell me about these documents,
weren't you?"

"Absolutely."

As Thumps tried to put all the parts in order, he realized that the problem was people. There were far too many, and they all wanted different things. Asah had come looking for the missing documents. Street had come looking for Massasoit. Noah had come looking for a way to get back on top. Reuben had come looking for Lucy. And Dakota had come looking for justice. Not for herself. Maybe not even for Lucy. But just a fair reckoning for the grief and tragedy that Noah had caused. The postcard she had sent to him, the Xerox she had sent to Street, and the letter she had written to Reuben were reminders of the past—a past of confusions, of betrayals, of unfinished business. Dakota had discovered that Noah was Massasoit, but try as she might, she couldn't believe it. Yet she knew it was true. And if Noah was Massasoit, then it meant that Lucy was dead, and it meant that Noah was responsible. Not guilty, perhaps, but responsible nonetheless. Chinook was to be the place of judgment, the place where the guilty and the innocent, the living and the dead, were to come together one last time.

Old Testament. Not New.

But Dakota hadn't imagined how deep Street's hatred for Massasoit ran, hadn't understood his greed or his desire for vengeance. A Jewish friend had told Thumps of a monster that could be made out of mud and prayer, a creature that would exact revenge on one's enemies. Very scary. Impossible to stop. And the only problem was that once set loose in the world, no one could control it.

As HOCKNEY TURNED onto the dirt road, he shut off the lights. "See they haven't settled up on the road yet."

Thumps wasn't sure he had all the facts right, though in the end, it wouldn't matter. Some of the facts had already been lost. Others had proved to be worthless. Of those remaining, only a handful had made any difference.

Lucy was dead. Street was dead. Reuben was dead. Thumps wasn't sure that solving any of the mysteries, past or present, was going to be worth the cost.

But then again, he hadn't lost anything of value. Not this time.

Hockney eased the cruiser into the Coast to Coast

parking lot and turned off the engine. "Now what?"

"We find the bad guy and arrest him."

"Hell of an idea," said Duke. "Why didn't I think of that. You still got the gun I gave you?"

"Lost it."

"Wonderful." The sheriff opened the glovebox and took out an older Smith & Wesson. "I'm reasonably fond of this gun," he said. "Try not to lose this one."

The lights were on in the Glory Video Emporium, but there was a Closed sign in the window. Thumps and Hockney stood in the archway of the Glory Antique Mall and watched the store.

"How you want to do this?" said Hockney. "Front door, back door? Break out the bullhorn and pretend we've got him surrounded? Wait until he comes out the front door and gun him down?"

"He wants the bonds and the documents." Thumps handed the pistol back to Hockney.

"Jesus," said the sheriff. "We're not going to go in and try to reason with him."

"Not we," said Thumps. "Me."

Hockney took his gun from his holster. "You see this? This is a Glock 9mm. It's a reliable firearm, and in the hands of a good marksman, it has an effective range of about sixty feet. After that, you're hitting golf balls."

"You the marksman?"

"No," said Hockney, "I'm the golfer."

Thumps shook his head. "I don't need you to back me up."

"That's a relief."

"I need you to make a phone call."

"Now that," said the sheriff, patting Thumps's shoulder, "I can do."

The main street of Glory was deserted. Thumps knew that there had to be people around. Even in seasonal communities, there was always a percentage of folks who stayed on and looked after the place, who cleared the roads, worked the hotels, rented videos. Maybe during the off-season they got to sleep in late.

The front door of the Glory Video Emporium was locked. Thumps rattled it so he wouldn't startle anyone inside. The sign in the window said the store opened at eleven. It was now twelve-thirty. Thumps knocked on the glass and waited. There was the chance that he was wrong, that Dakota had not left the package with Grover for safekeeping. But it was the only place that made any sense. Half of the letters that Grover had given him were from Dakota. It was as if she had stepped in to take Lucy's place, to be a sister to Grover for the sister he had lost.

Thumps knocked again, hard this time, insistent. He didn't want another door on his conscience, but he wasn't about to stand around in the cold all day, waiting for a killer to kill again.

"Grover! It's Thumps!"

Thumps put a knee against the door and leaned into it. Kicking it down was not going to be an easy task. It might be more effective to shoot the lock off the way they did it in the movies, and he was wondering if that method would actually work when he saw the lights in the store go out and heard the deadbolt snap open.

As he opened the door, Thumps looked for the reflection of the Glory Antique Mall in the glass. There was no sign of Hockney, which was good, but for a moment, as he stepped into the shadows, Thumps had the disturbing feeling that he was suddenly vulnerable and completely alone.

"Hello." Thumps stood just inside the doorway and

allowed his eyes to adjust. Grover was standing at the back of the store. He didn't say anything. He simply turned and disappeared into the backroom. Thumps took a deep breath, let it out, and followed him.

The backroom of the video store was set up like an apartment, and from the posters on the wall, the clothes draped over the couch, and the unmade bed, Thumps deduced that this was where Grover lived. Men who lived on their own tended to have reputations for being slovenly. It was a cliché, to be sure. Thumps knew that somewhere in the world, there were hundreds of neat single men. Maybe more.

Dakota had found an open spot on the couch between the jeans and the T-shirts. Grover was on an old beanbag chair in one corner. Asah was sitting at a desk, a cardboard box in front of him. Asah didn't look happy to see Thumps, but then again he didn't look surprised either.

"Anybody ever tell you that you'd make a good cop?" Asah took a bundle of bearer bonds out of the box, set them on the desk, and put his gun on top of them.

"The documents too?"

Asah nodded. "All safe and sound."

"And nobody else is dead."

Asah pushed the box to one side. "Did you get another gun?"

Thumps nodded. "In my belt. The sheriff asked me not to lose it. Says it has sentimental value."

Asah glanced around the room. "Right. And where is our good friend Sheriff Duke Hockney?"

The phone made everyone jump. Asah stood up and came around the desk. "You expecting a call?"

"It's the sheriff," said Thumps. "I asked him to let me come in and try to talk you into giving yourself up. He wants to know how I'm doing."

Asah's face hardened. "And you'd like me to believe that he's not out there alone."

"What do you think?"

"I think I have three hostages."

"That might impress the sheriff. But he's not really in charge." Thumps slowly reached over and picked up the phone.

"You're bluffing," said Asah. "They don't move that fast."

"I know you never called the bureau about Street," said Thumps. "But Hockney did. Four agents drove over from Missoula this morning." Thumps held up the phone. "I need to tell him something."

"Tell him if he tries to come in, I'll shoot everyone." Asah cocked his head. "But I'm guessing he knows that."

Thumps held the phone to his face. "If you try to come in," he said, "he'll kill all of us." Thumps looked at the phone and smiled.

"What'd he say?"

"He said I wasn't much of a deputy anyway."

"Now," said Asah, returning to the desk and the chair, "hang up the phone."

FOR THE NEXT twenty minutes, Asah sat behind the desk and read through the documents that Matthew Colburne had so carefully organized. Dakota kept her head down, ignoring everyone in the room. Thumps couldn't tell if she was angry or frightened or exhausted, not that it mattered. Grover was angry, was ready to pounce on Asah at the first opportunity. Thumps didn't know which was the more dangerous: Grover looking to play the hero; Asah looking for a way out; or Duke

Hockney looking down the barrel of his Glock, trying to keep the good guys and the bad guys in focus. In the end, Thumps decided that it was a three-way tie.

"You ought to read this shit," said Asah. "Morgan was really screwing the tribes."

"They're not going to go away."

"How many sharpshooters?"

"Two."

"They must be really pissed off."

"Somebody killed an FBI agent," said Thumps. "They think it's you."

"But you're going to convince them that they're wrong?"

"Nope," said Thumps. "But they can't prove they're right. My guess is they'd rather shoot you than go to trial."

"And Justice?"

"Same deal as before. Knowing is one thing, proving is another."

"You sound like a defence lawyer," said Asah. "Maybe today is a good day to die."

"No, thanks," said Thumps. "I'd rather die in the summer."

"And all of this?" Asah ran his hands over the bonds.

"Either way," said Thumps, "you can't take it with you."

Asah dropped the folder back into the box and laid his car keys on the table next to his gun. "Sorry," he said, turning to Dakota. "Looks as though you're going to have to manage on your own."

HOCKNEY HANDCUFFED ASAH and put him in the back of the sheriff's SUV. If Asah was angry about the bluff, he didn't show it. The sheriff was not so sanguine. "Just how the hell did you do that?"

"Like you said," said Thumps, "we got nothing."

"The feds are on their way. I'll turn him over, give them everything I've got, and Bob's your uncle." Hockney glanced at the video store. "Anything else I need to know about?"

"Nope," said Thumps.

"Your girlfriend okay?"

"Yeah," said Thumps. "I guess."

Hockney turned and walked back to his car. "Tell her she's got lousy taste in men."

* * *

GROVER WAS WAITING for him when Thumps came into the store. "So, what happens now?"

"I drive Dakota back to Chinook," said Thumps.

Grover glanced over his shoulder. "Is Lucy dead?" he asked quietly.

"Yeah."

"Ridge kill her?"

"No," said Thumps, wondering if the truth set anything free, "but he knows where she's buried."

"You think he'll tell me?" said Grover. "I'd like to bring her home."

"I'll talk to him," said Thumps. "I don't think there'll be a problem."

"You shouldn't have come," said Grover. "Everything was going to work out."

Dakota appeared in the doorway of the backroom, the cardboard box in her arms. She stood there quietly, as though she were waiting for someone to tell her what to do. But Thumps knew that she wasn't waiting for anyone anymore.

THIRTY-EIGHT

Asah had rented a Honda. A silver Accord. A colour that reminded Thumps of icebergs. Why anyone would choose a car the colour of the weather was beyond him, especially when there were all sorts of vibrant greens and yellows and reds in neons and metallics, colours that could cut through the gloom and lift the spirits.

Thumps put the box on the back seat, started the engine, and waited for the windows to clear.

"I wanted him to pay for what he did."

"I know."

The car had decent legroom and a six-way adjustable

seat. Thumps wasn't sure he liked the sunroof. It made the interior feel low and cramped. And the car was an automatic. He understood the convenience of not having to shift gears or worry about a clutch, but it was like shaving with an electric razor or baking a potato in the microwave. The Volvo was temperamental and heavy, but when you closed the door, you felt as though you were sitting in a vault. The Honda made Thumps feel as though he were trapped in a roll of tinfoil.

"After I came back to Salt Lake, Mrs. Tomioka called me."

"Lucy's neighbour?"

"She was always worried about Lucy. Worried she didn't eat enough. Worried that she would never get married and have children. Worried that she lived alone. Worried about her job. You name it, Mrs. Tomioka worried about it."

"Sounds like everyone's mother."

"When Lucy didn't come home, Mrs. Tomioka began going by the house and picking up all the flyers and the newspapers that had been collecting on the porch. And the mail. She had everything arranged in neat piles on her living-room table."

The defroster was slow and inefficient. Clear glass was just barely showing above the dashboard. Thumps turned the fan up to high.

"I didn't open any of the mail at first. I just took it home. Every week I would stop by and pick up whatever Mrs. Tomioka had collected, and we would talk about Lucy. She was sure Lucy had gone off to find herself and that any day she would return with wonderful stories about her adventures."

"But you knew she was dead."

"I suppose I did." Dakota braced herself against the door. "Lucy had the movement, and she had Reuben. She had already found everything she wanted."

"How long before you opened the box?"

Dakota ran a hand through her hair. "I don't know. Maybe a year. Maybe more."

Thumps glanced at the back seat. The return label was still intact. Morgan Energy. Denver, Colorado. "But when you opened it, you knew what it was."

"Yeah," said Dakota. "I knew what it was."

"But you didn't tell Noah."

"That box was dangerous," said Dakota.

More than dangerous. Thumps would have said

fatal. Clinton Buckhorn was dead, Wilson Scout was dead, Wallace Begay was dead. Two FBI agents had lost their lives in the raid.

Lucy Kettle.

But the killing hadn't stopped there, and the years hadn't softened the danger. Mitchell Street. Reuben Justice. Lives lost. Lives destroyed.

The window was almost clear now, and Thumps could see the sky through the windshield. The sun was breaking through the bank of clouds in streaming shafts of white light, and the world looked bright and clean. He pulled the car into gear and felt his way to the road.

"Are you going to arrest me?"

"For what?"

"I sent that Xerox to Street," said Dakota. "I knew he'd come after Noah."

"What about Reuben?"

"I wanted him to be here when it happened." Dakota took in a deep breath and held it. "He didn't do anything, you know. And I got him killed."

Thumps wished he could tell Dakota that none of this was her fault, that it had been Noah who had set this drama on stage all those years ago when he had decided to play God. It was Noah who had created Massasoit. Noah who set Street on Lucy. And once in motion, once the killing began, there was no stopping it until everyone was dead. Or famous.

In the end, the only player left standing was Noah.

"At your house, Asah figured out that I had the bonds." There was no emotion in Dakota's voice. "He called me at the hotel."

"I don't need to know."

"But you're curious." Dakota's eyes were moist and glazed, as though she had just come away from a long cry. "You're wondering if I made a deal with Asah. You're wondering if I told him I'd give him the bonds if he killed Noah."

"Did you?"

"What if I did? What the hell is the law going to do to him?"

"Nothing."

"Noah always wanted to be famous. He'd be a lot more famous dead." Dakota looked out the window. "You know, you could ride off with me into the sunset. We could keep the bonds and go someplace warm. You interested?"

"Sure."

"Liar." Dakota smiled sadly. "What's going to happen to me now?"

"Whatever you want."

"You're not going to turn me in?"

"I'm not a cop." Thumps kept his eyes on the road. "I'm a photographer."

"I can't walk away from things the way you can."

Thumps pulled the car to the side of the road and skidded to a stop on the hard snow. "You have to be kidding!"

"What do you care?"

"You're going to Los Angeles with Noah?" Thumps could feel the anger burn through him. "He would have given you up. If it had come down to you or him, he wouldn't have even thought about it."

"What about you?" Dakota's eyes were clear now. And hard. "If I had asked you, would you have done it?"

Thumps looked at the box on the back seat and remembered the moment he had walked into the backroom of the Glory Video Emporium. Asah had been behind the desk, the bonds and documents in front of him. Dakota had been waiting on the couch.

Thumps had imagined that she had been waiting for him to come to the rescue. But maybe she had just been waiting for an answer.

"For the bonds? For Lucy?" Dakota touched the side of Thumps's face. "For me? Would you have killed him for me?"

Thumps let Dakota's hand stay on his face. "There's nothing for you in Los Angeles."

"It would have been ironic." Dakota closed her eyes and took a slow breath. "Don't you think Noah would have found it ironic?"

CHINOOK HAD DUG itself out from the storm by the time Thumps pulled up in front of the Tucker. The main streets had been cleared, the downtown side-walks had been shovelled, and everywhere everyone was going about their business, as though winter had never arrived. In his life, Thumps had seen too many tragedies to be bothered by the weather. Yet he was. Maybe it was that tragedies had causes and effects, that they could be softened or avoided or prevented, while the weather came and went as it pleased, without regard for anyone or anything.

Like Noah Ridge.

"You going to give the box back to Morgan Energy?"

"Not my box."

"Then what?"

Thumps opened the car door. "Buckhorn sent the bonds and the documents to Lucy because he knew she would do the right thing. Do what Lucy would have done."

"I don't know what she would have done." Dakota reached over to take Thumps's hand. "I don't know anymore."

"Then," said Thumps as he pulled his hand away and stepped out into the cold, "why don't you keep the box until you do."

The steps up to the Tucker had been swept clean. Thumps wondered if the Mother Lode had a lunch special that he could afford. A soft drink and a sandwich. As he got to the entrance, a young man dressed in a red-and-black uniform opened the door for him, and Thumps walked into the hotel without looking back.

THIRTY-NINE

Thumps didn't watch the Leno show. He had seen too much, heard too much, and knew too much to be able to manage the spectacle of Noah's playing the embattled hero on national television. For the next week, he stayed in his darkroom. Freeway sat outside the door and howled, insisting that it wasn't healthy to hide away like that and that what he needed was company. When he finally let her in, she didn't crawl in behind the studs under the sink, but rather sat quietly on his lap while he worked his way through a set of negatives that he had taken years ago, along the California coast, in the days when he had understood the difference between goodness and evil.

For the first few days, the phone didn't stop ringing. Over the hum of the enlarger, he could hear the answering machine take the calls, Hockney, Archie, the Denver office of the FBI, which wanted to send an agent around to talk with him. Claire called several times, but not even her quiet, patient voice could coax him out of the safety of the basement.

The last message had been from Grover Many Horses to say that he was going down to Salt Lake and that he'd call when he got back.

THERE WERE RHYTHMS to the seasons, and winters in Chinook were no exception. When Thumps finally came out of hiding, put on Asah's parka, and walked to Al's, he discovered that the warm winds had come through and melted most of the snow.

Al was at the grill, working the piles of hash browns with a spatula. "About time you showed up," she said. "Archie was going to file a missing person's report."

"He around?"

"Back booth," said Al. "With your other friend. You going to eat breakfast or you going to sit around and mope?"

"Breakfast, please."

"I'll call Milo. He'll want pictures."

"Thumps!"

Thumps didn't have to look to see who it was. Archie. In a booth with the sheriff.

"Where have you been?" Archie was cutting one of the sheriff's sausages into bite-sized pieces. "You've missed all the excitement."

"You look like shit," said Hockney.

"Did you see the Leno show? They mentioned Chinook twice. Even showed a picture of the Tucker." Archie squirted some ketchup on Hockney's plate next to the hash browns. "And the FBI came by the store."

"They buy a book?"

"A book?" said Archie. "Why would the FBI buy a book?"

"Speaking of books," said Hockney, "your buddy is on the best-seller list."

"That's right," said Archie. "Number five on the *New York Times*."

"Fiction?"

"Sheriff's famous too," said Archie. "He was on television. What did they call it?"

"Never mind," said Hockney.

"'Standoff in Glory.'" Archie took a forkful of hash browns and slid them through the ketchup. "Had a picture and everything. Said the sheriff was a hero."

Thumps didn't want to be reminded of Glory. He had gone there to save Dakota and, in the end, might have saved Noah instead.

"Stop by the office," said the sheriff. "I've got your cheque ready."

"What do you figure?" said Archie. "You think he's going to write another book?"

Breakfast arrived, and Archie alternated between helping Thumps eat it and providing a running commentary on the events of the day.

"He ever stop talking?" said the sheriff as Archie retold, for the fourth time, the story about how Noah had disappeared the night of the reading.

"Nope."

"Article in the *Washington Post*," said the sheriff, keeping his voice low so he wouldn't disturb Archie.

"Justice Department is looking into allegations of bribery at Morgan Energy."

"No kidding."

"You ever wonder what happened to the bonds and the rest of that stuff?"

"Nope."

"Guess it doesn't matter," said Hockney. "I checked with the bank. Bearer bonds are pretty much like cash, so they're probably long gone by now. Nobody's going to sit on that kind of money for twenty-five years."

Thumps pushed some egg on a piece of toast. He had been hungry when he sat down, but now he was just tired.

"That the way you got it figured?"

"More or less."

"You know what we should do?" said Archie, who realized that he had lost his audience. "We should write a book."

It was Della's day at the Salvation Army. "Can you believe this weather?" she sang out as Thumps came through the door. "This keeps up, I won't have any summer stuff left."

"You get any winter coats in?"

"You bet," said Della, "but what's wrong with the one you got? That's a nice coat you got."

Thumps slipped the parka off and laid it on the counter. "Doesn't fit," he said. "Maybe you know someone who can use it."

"Sure," said Della. "Come on, I got something at the back I think you'll like."

THE WEATHER WOULDN'T LAST, of course. A new arctic storm was already on its way out of Canada. But for now, the Volvo wouldn't have any excuses, and as Thumps came out of the Salvation Army with his new coat, he considered driving to Moses's place to see if the old man knew why people expected so much of each other, why they expected so much of themselves, and how it was a person could wind up with so little.

Moses would probably make a pot of tea and tell him a story. And maybe that was it, maybe in the end a good story was the best anyone could do.

THOMAS KING is an award-winning writer whose fiction includes *Green Grass, Running Water*; *Truth and Bright Water*; and *The Back of the Turtle*, which won the Governor General's Award for Fiction. His non-fiction work includes *The Truth About Stories*, winner of the Trillium Book Award, and *The Inconvenient Indian*, winner of the British Columbia National Award for Canadian Non-Fiction and the RBC Taylor Prize. A Member of the Order of Canada and the recipient of an award from the National Aboriginal Achievement Foundation, Thomas King taught at the University of Lethbridge and was chair of American Indian Studies at the University of Minnesota before moving to the University of Guelph, where he taught until he retired. He lives in Guelph, Ontario, with his partner, Helen Hoy. *The Red Power Murders* is the second novel in Thomas King's DreadfulWater mystery series.